Other Titles by Keisha Ervin:

Me & My Boyfriend

Chyna Black

Mina's Joint

Hold *U* Down

by Keisha Ervin

Compilation and Introduction copyright © 2006 by Triple Crown Publications
PO Box 6888
Columbus, OH 43205
www.TripleCrownPublications.com

Library of Congress Control Number: 2006906563
ISBN: 0-9778804-2-7
ISBN 13: 978-0-9778804-2-3

Cover Design/Graphics: Triple Crown Publications
Author: Keisha Ervin
Typsetting: Holscher Type and Design
Editor: Cynthia Parker
Editor-in-Chief: Mia McPherson
Consulting: Vickie M. Stringer

First Trade Paperback Edition Printing
10 9 8 7

Printed in the United States of America

Acknowledgements

First and foremost I have to thank God for blessing me with creative ideas and words for a fourth book. Lord, you have blessed me with so much that sometimes I get overwhelmed but I thank you for it all. I can't wait to see where this journey takes me. I'm a little nervous but trust and believe that I'm gonna buckle my seat belt and hold on for the ride.

Vickie, we're on our fourth book together. Who would have thought? I just want to say thank you from the bottom of my heart for everything you've done for me. Without you acknowledging my work, I wouldn't be in the position I'm in now so thank you.

To the entire TCP staff, thank you for working so hard and diligently on my projects. Without your hard work, my novels wouldn't be what they are.

To my momma Patricia and father Carl, thank you for raising such a smart, classy, determined, fly chick like myself. Nah, for real I love you both and thank you both for being the best parents a girl could ask for.

To my brother Keon, I love you more than words can say.

To the entire Poe, Ervin, Blackshear and my Aunt Hattie's family, thank you all for your continued support and love.

To the five chicks who hold me down on a regular basis, Locia, Tu-Shonda, Monique, Miesha and Janea, ya'll are my dearest and truest friends. Thank you for putting up with my goofy and conceited ways. Thank you for listening to me read my manuscripts over and over again until I get it right. And thank you for being the fly, stand up chicks you are.

To Mrs. Robertson, Mrs. Whitaker, Miss Pascal and Mrs. Snipes, thank you for raising such beautiful, intelligent, caring and giving daughters.

Thank you Danielle Santiago, Caroline McGill, Ashley Jaquavis, Tracy Brown, Deja King, Mary Wilson, Brenda Hampton and Cynthia Parker, for acknowledging and supporting my work.

Wahida Clark, I just wanna say that the day I opened your book and saw my name in it was like one of the best days of my life. You are one of my favorite authors and I wish you continued success.

To all the people on the message boards who love and support my work, thank you!! Ms. Monalisa, Sunshine716, Miss Millie, Mskiki425, Reydee, Chocolate Girl, Andrea Denise, Rosepetals, Virgo, Xtina316, Lady Scorpio, Shalonda 5050, Day Dee 2005, Simply Stephanie, and Lovely E4U, thank you all!!

Last but not least, to all the readers and fans of my work, I thank you all from the pit of my soul. You all have held me down to the fullest and I thank each and every one of you. If you want to get at me, hit me up at keisha_(underscore) ervin2002@yahoo.com with any questions or comments.

Love,
Keisha

Dedication

I dedicate this book to two people - my son Kyrese Ervin and one of my closest friends, Monsieur Pascal. Kyrese, you are my shining light when things get dark in my life. You inspire me to do better for the both of us. You are growing up to be a handsome, funny and smart young man. Know that all of this was done for you and that I love you with all of my heart.

Monique, your strength and courage after all you've been through in the past couple of years shows that no matter what, you can come through and still be a God fearing, giving person. I don't know how you do it, but continue to be everything that you are.

Keisha Ervin

Simply 1 Unique

"*I got, no time for fake niggas … Just sip some Cristal with these real niggas… From East to West Coast we spread love niggas … And while you niggas talk shit we count bank figures,*" Unique sang with her eyes behind shades, strolling down the streets of LA. Fresh to death with Moschino bags, Unique and Tha Get Money Crew strutted down Robertson Boulevard, looking as if they could have been young socialites or "*Sex and the City*" knockoffs. Unique a.k.a. Nique, Kiara, Kay Kay and Zoë had the best of everything — great looks, cars with chrome spinners, designer outfits and money.

None of them needed a man for anything but most of the niggas they fucked wit' were tricks. It was nothing for a man to pay all of their bills. The girls always stayed fly. They all lived life by their own rules. Falling in love was a no-no. To them, men were looked upon as pawns; mere playthings. Catching feelings was forbidden and looked at as a sign of disloyalty. Only rough sex and getting money was allowed. And their motto, *Niggas Ain't Nothing but Hoes and Tricks,* was tattooed on each of their lower backs.

Keisha Ervin

Kiara, a single mother of one, was the loudmouth of the crew. Tall and caramel with full lips and an attitude to match, Kiara butted heads with Unique often. Kay Kay, her identical twin, was the peacemaker, silent type. She kept it gully and always kept her feelings close to her heart. Zoë, the feisty, petite, mahogany-colored mamacita held it down, for real. She was down for whatever even if it meant putting her own life in danger.

Unique, the leader of the clique, had one thing and one thing only on her mind at all times — money. It kept her alive and on the grind, thirsting for more. Hustling was the song she sang and getting money was all she knew. The only men she ever loved were dead ones — Benjamin Franklin and Andrew Jackson.

With smooth peanut butter skin, big brown eyes, Egyptian cheekbones, plump lips, red hair with blonde highlights and a pretty smile to match, she captured the male species' heart. Reaching about five foot five in height, Unique wasn't a slim chick. Her hips rounded out to be size ten and her full breasts filled out a C cup bra. On her left shoulder she had a set of praying hands tattooed with the words "Lord Forgive Me" underneath. To most, she was considered a lethal weapon. She was often compared to the singer Keyshia Cole but to her crew, she was just their girl and the one who called all the shots.

"Niggas ain't shiiiit!" Unique stomped her foot, slamming her Nextel shut.

"What did Tone do now?" Kiara asked.

"That was Patience. She told me she saw Tone riding down Lucas and Hunt with Robin! Then she said that her friend Chantell's sister seen him at Toxic later on that night Big Willyin' it up."

"Ain't she the same chick that blew his cell phone up last

week?" Zoë questioned.

"Yeah, that's her. I swear to God I hate that black mutha-fucka. He thinks just because he pays all of my bills that he can cheat and do whatever he wants."

"I don't know why men think they can cheat, like we won't find out." Zoë shook her head and laughed.

"Because they stupid, that's why! They think with their penises and not their brains, stupid bastards!"

"Just hit them pockets up when you get home."

"That's what's up but have you seen that bitch? She ugly than a muthafucka," Kay Kay added.

"The bitch is wack! She's a broke, bummy, Reebok broad! I mean come on, look at me! How the fuck he gon' cheat on me with a project chick!" Unique stated, looking over her physique.

"OK bitch, you can quit feeling yourself 'cause remember pussy don't have no face." Zoë grinned.

"I don't know why you getting mad. It ain't like you gon' leave him." Kiara rolled her eyes and sucked her teeth.

"That's not the point! It's the principle of the whole thing! As long as that nigga continue to provide for me then I'm good to go! But it pisses me off because the nigga be trying to act like it's all about me when he's out fuckin' other hoes! But you know what, it's all good because I'm getting mine in the end. Love should never be in the equation when it comes to a relationship anyway 'cause once you allow yourself to love that muthafucka, everything in your life becomes about him and eventually you lose yourself!" Staring off into space, Unique knew that her speech was more about her mother than herself.

"Look, when it all boils down to it, you getting paid, so fuck all that other bullshit and continue to get money," Zoë assured.

"Right, so calm down. You should be used to the shit by now. Ya'll been fuckin' around forever and he has cheated the whole time. Ain't none of this shit new to you," Kiara continued.

"Yeah, just keep on tagging them pockets every time he fuck up," Kay Kay chimed in.

"Fuck all this bullshit. We gotta hurry and get back to the hotel so we can do this shit," Unique said, shaking the whole situation off.

"So, what's the deal wit' your boy, Nique?" Kiara asked.

"I set it up for him to meet me at The Ivy at 8 o'clock. Eric's gonna have this valet guy named Thomas to park the Murcielago around the back in the far right corner of the parking lot."

"So, basically all I have to do is get the keys from Eric."

"Yeah, but I told him that you would give him the other three hundred when you got the keys."

"Shit, this crackin' up to be one of our easiest licks ever." Zoë grinned.

"Don't get it twisted — you never know what could happen," Unique cautioned as she eyed a green Foley dress in the Lisa Kline store window.

"Yo', chill Nique. Don't nobody want to hear that shit before a lick," Kiara said, annoyed.

"This real talk. If you don't like it then don't listen. Ya'll hoes need to realize that we could get knocked at any moment for this shit. Don't let this money go to yo' head." Unique checked her as the wind blew through her hair.

"Yeah, I am feeling myself too much, ain't I?"

"As usual."

"Yo', Nique, I just got a text from that nigga Bub up in VA," Zoë declared, going through her two-way.

"Hit that nigga back and see what's up," Unique replied,

still entranced by the dress.

"Yeah, that nigga had a bad-ass Mercedes Benz." Kay Kay nodded her head.

"Right, we can make at least a fifty g's off that," Kiara added.

"I know right, let me hit this nigga up right now," Zoë said, getting excited.

After hitting a couple more stores, Unique and the girls headed back to the hotel to prepare for the heist. Looking at her reflection in the mirror, Unique wondered just how long she could continue stealing cars for a living. She and her cousins had been in the game for three years but recently the life had begun to take a toll on her soul. Unique's pockets stayed on swole but her conscience was eating her up every day.

She constantly wondered if old victims were out to get her; the shit had her paranoid. Something inside told her that something was about to jump off but she just couldn't pinpoint it. Money kept on coming in and her clientele continued to grow but being the leader of a banging organization didn't satisfy her anymore. Yeah, Unique had the fringe benefits of clothes, jewelry and cars but Cezar, the guy she worked for, was the one who really saw the most dough. He was the real balla.

Two years after meeting Tone, her boyfriend of five years, Unique linked up with Cezar. He was a good looking get-money nigga from the South Side of St. Louis. Even though he was fine, Unique didn't look at him like that. She saw something more in Cezar than just being his girlfriend or chick on the side. Unique needed a side hustle and Cezar was the perfect nigga to help her get on the grind. Refusing to hit the block Unique decided to do what she did best — steal.

After a little research, she learned that Cezar already had a small ring of car thieves on his payroll. The little crew of nig-gas he had working for him wasn't really pulling in dough so Unique, being the chick she was, offered her services. At first, Cezar was a little apprehensive because to him, a chick would-n't know anything about stealing cars. Underestimating her talents because of her gender, Cezar slept on Unique's skills.

After recruiting her cousins to be a part of her crew, Unique hit the ground running. As a test, Cezar gave Unique and the girls the task of stealing an '03 Cadillac STS worth sixty grand. He just knew that Unique would be calling him from jail begging him to bail her out. But he was wrong. Unique and the girls not only copped the STS but for show they copped a Mercedes Benz as well. Cezar was dumfounded to say the least. In a matter of months Unique and Tha Get Money Crew stole over a half a million dollars worth of cars. Stepping out of the bathroom, she asked, "How do I look?"

"You look fly as hell, ma," Zoë replied.

"Yeah, even with that ugly-ass wig you got on, you look good," Kiara joked.

"Fuck you." Unique smirked, putting her middle finger up.

"That dress is bad. You gon' have to let me borrow that when we go out."

"That's cool, but look, I'm running late so give me hug." Standing in a circle, they all wrapped their arms around one another and hugged. "Ya'll know that we gotta be safe and dis-crete. I love you and I'll meet you at the airport."

"A'ight we love you too," Kay Kay replied.

"A'ight then I'm up," Unique said as she left out the door with her bags in tow.

Pulling up to The Ivy, Unique searched for Rico's car but she didn't spot him. She then looked for Eric. He was right in place. After she smoothed her dress down she stepped out of her rented Lexus SC 430 and handed him the keys. Unique turned her attention to the busy intersection as she heard a loud engine soaring up the street.

Spotting Rico, she smiled. His yellow Lamborghini stood out among the sea of conservative vehicles. Waving at him, she caught his attention. As he got out Unique couldn't help but be attracted to him. Tall, handsome and muscular were the only words to describe him.

"You take this one, I'm tired," Eric said to Thomas, baiting him.

"You look beautiful." Rico kissed Unique's left check.

"Thank you. You look nice as well."

"Can I take your keys, sir?" Thomas, the anxious valet driver, asked.

"I'm not sure if I want to do the valet thing tonight."

"I promise that your car will be returned to you in tip-top shape, sir. I'm the best valet driver here," Thomas boasted. Looking at him, Unique saw that Eric was right — Thomas was a suck up.

"Sweetie, this is a very nice restaurant. Your car will be safe," Unique added as she put her hand on his shoulder for reassurance.

"I don't think you understand, Lisa. This is a Murcielago. This car is worth ten of their yearly salaries," Rico said, calling Unique by one of her many aliases and not even knowing it. Wanting to smack the holy shit out of him for being so rude but holding her tongue, Unique tried to reason with him.

"Baby, trust me. Everything will be fine," she spoke seductively into his ear.

"I don't know, Lisa, I'd rather park it myself," he said, confused and turned on at the same time.

"If you let them park the car for you, I promise I will give you a very special treat tonight," Unique purred, massaging his dick.

"Um, sir, have you made up your mind because we have other people waiting," Thomas asked, eying Unique's hand moving in a circular motion.

"All right, but make sure you keep a close eye on my baby," Rico instructed, throwing Thomas the keys.

"Yes sir. I will."

Forty-five minutes later, Unique and Rico sat gazing into each other's eyes as they ate lobster and steak. Slow, tranquil music played in the background as Rico became lost in her eyes while he thought about the promise she made to him earlier. Already bored, Unique stared off into space ignoring his every word.

"Lisa, did you hear me? I said dessert just arrived."

"I'm sorry, baby, my mind was somewhere else." Checking her watch, Unique excused herself from the table and went into the restroom. Pulling out her cell she called Zoë.

"Ya'll there yet?" she asked.

"Yeah, we just pulled up."

"A'ight."

"A'ight then, one," Zoë said, hanging up. Flipping her phone closed, Unique took one last look in the mirror and walked back into the restaurant. Rico smiled when he saw her walking toward him. Once she got near the table, he got up and pulled her seat out for her, wanting to be a gentleman.

"How about after dinner we head over to this nice little jazz club that I know about around the corner?" Rico suggested.

"That sounds nice," Unique said, giving her best fake smile. Sensing that he was a little on edge, she asked, "What's wrong?"

"You know I'm kinda worried about leaving my keys with the valet. There have been a lot of auto thefts in this area the

Keisha Ervin

last couple of months."

"Rico, stop worrying about that car and let's just enjoy the evening," she said, rubbing his hand and trying to ease his worries.

"Nah, I think I need to go out and check on my baby." He eased up out of his chair.

"NO!" Unique blurted louder than she should have. Giving her a suspicious look, Rico stopped dead in his tracks.

"I'm sorry for yelling, it's just that I came to enjoy myself not babysit your car. The car is insured, right?"

"Yeah."

"OK then, there's no reason to worry," she assured, walking behind him and pushing his seat back up to the table so that he wouldn't go anywhere.

Sitting back down, Unique took his hand, gazed into his eyes and whispered, "I promise if you be a good little boy you'll have a night that you will never forget." She smiled as she played footsies with his dick under the table.

"Girl you gon' be the death of me." He smiled back gullibly.

"You just don't know," she whispered underneath her breath while checking her watch once more.

$ $ $

"You got the keys?" Kiara asked outside of the restaurant to Eric in a low voice.

"Right here. You got my money?"

"Yeah I got yo' money, nigga, here," she said, placing three new crisp hundred-dollar bills in his hand.

"You know that I could get fired for this."

"Nigga, quit whining and give me the keys so I can bounce," Kiara said, surveying her surroundings and making

Keisha Ervin

sure no one was looking.

Quietly passing the keys to her, Eric went back to work as usual. Dressed like she was out having a good time, Kiara headed around back to the parking area. Cool, calm and collected, she played the role perfectly while putting on a pair of black gloves. Knowing that the restaurant didn't have any security cameras in the parking lot, she deactivated the alarm and got in without leaving a trace behind. The valet driver, Thomas, never even saw her pull off the lot.

Skipping dessert, Unique informed Rico that she was ready to leave so that they could get the festivities started.

"Baby, while you pay the check I'm gonna go freshen up." She kissed his cheek.

"A'ight baby, I'm gon' be outside waiting," Rico said while eyeing her ass. Once in the bathroom, Unique dialed Kay Kay's cell phone number.

"It's here," Kay Kay replied without saying hello.

"A'ight, I'll meet you at LAX in about an hour."

"One," Kay Kay said, hanging up.

Checking her reflection in the mirror, Unique saw that her eyes were red. Going through her purse she found a tiny bottle of Visine. The blue contacts in her eyes were irritating the hell out of her. After dropping a few drops in each eye she fingered through her black wig and touched up her makeup. The contacts and wig were all a part of her disguise. None of Unique's victims really knew how she looked. Meeting Rico back outside, Unique saw him in a heated argument with the valet driver, Thomas.

"I swear sir, I don't know what happened," Thomas tried to explain.

"I trusted you with my car, man! Where the fuck is it?!" Rico yelled.

"What's wrong, sweetie?" Unique asked, pretending to be

concerned.

"My car is gone! I told you we couldn't trust these mutha-fuckas! You betta hope yo' shit is still here!" Giving Eric her valet ticket, Unique listened to Rico's whining until her car pulled around the corner.

"My car is here," she replied.

"What am I gon' do without my baby?" Rico cried.

"I'm so sorry. This is all my fault. I shouldn't have sug-gested that you leave your car with them," Unique said, con-juring up some fake tears.

"Baby, don't cry. This is not your fault." Rico hugged her. "It's this idiot's fault," he said, pointing to Thomas. "Not yours."

"So what do you want to do?" Unique questioned, dabbing tears from her eyes.

"I'm gonna stay here and fill out a police report. You go on back to the hotel. I'll call you later."

"OK," she said, kissing and hugging him goodbye.

Securely in the rental car, Unique gave Rico another wave while thinking, *Good riddance, you stupid fuck*. Whipping the car out into the busy intersection, she never looked back. A couple of blocks away, parked and relieved that the job was almost over, she pulled the wig off and exhaled a sigh of relief. Changing into a wife beater and jeans, she placed another wig on her head and drove to the rental place. Since everything was cool with the car it only took her a total of fifteen minutes to drop it off. After taking a shuttle bus to the airport she checked her luggage in and headed for Gate 16. Once she reached the gate she saw all three girls laughing and talking as if they hadn't just committed a crime.

"Ya'll hoes sure do look cool, calm and collected."

"What up, dawg?" Kay Kay smiled. Taking a seat next to Zoë, Unique placed her carry-on luggage down beside her and began telling the story.

Keisha Ervin

"Girl, that nigga was so paranoid about leaving his car with the valet, it wasn't even funny."

"He was?"

"Yeah, I kept on having to reassure him that the damn car would be all right. He even kept calling it his *baby*."

"Damn, straight up? So how did he react when he found out the car was stolen?" Kay Kay questioned.

"Girl, he went ballistic," Unique laughed.

"It's always funny to see the reaction on their faces. Where is he at now?"

"As far as I know he's still at the restaurant wondering where his car is. Oops, I mean, his *baby*."

"He's probably all like, Dude! Where's my car!" Kay Kay laughed.

"Girl, you silly. Ya'll FedExed the money to Patience, right?"

"Yeah, Nique, Zoë and I went before we came here."

"Ya'll wrapped it up in newspaper and bubble wrap, right?"

"Yeah they did. Damn, quit trippin'," Kiara said annoyed, slumped down in the seat with her arms folded across her chest.

"What the fuck is yo' problem?"

"Why is it every time we do a job you ask us the same stupid-ass questions over and over again? Ain't nobody gon' fuck up!"

"Yo', who the fuck you think you talkin' to? Last time I checked, I ran this shit! Don't ever question me 'cause I'm the one who has to answer to Cezar, not you!"

"You still need to calm down! I get sick of you badgering us all the time!"

"I badger you 'cause this shit will give us ten to life if we fuck up!"

"Ten to life? You buggin'." Kiara waved her off, rolling her eyes.

"First of all, you need to shut the fuck up and play your position! I'm that bitch and what I say goes! If you don't like it, step the fuck off! Kick rocks! The road is that way." Unique stood up pointing her finger in Kiara's face.

"Yo', chill! We don't need this shit right now. We're cousins. Remember that," Kay Kay said, pulling Unique back.

Looking around at the other girls, Kiara tried to see if they agreed with her but neither one of them said anything. To her, Zoë and Kay Kay were nothing but punks; they never stood up to Unique. Whatever she said, they went along with, but Kiara was sick of following Unique's rule.

"I'm sick of this! When we get home, give me my cut and don't say shit to me! I'm done fuckin' wit' you!"

"Bye, bitch. You can take your money and step," Unique replied, heated.

"Everyone boarding Flight 16 from Los Angles to St. Louis please line up to board the plane," the flight attendant said over the loud speaker. Grabbing her bag, Kiara pushed past the girls and got in line alone.

"She be on some dumb shit," Zoë said, shaking her head.

"Yeah, you better get yo' sister before I hurt her, Kay Kay," Unique added.

"I don't know what her problem is. She been trippin' lately," Kay Kay said, supporting Unique.

"All I know is she better come to me correct before I kill her ass," Unique snapped as they boarded the plane.

Got Me 2 Trippin'

The weather in St. Louis was hot and muggy as Unique and the girls stood outside the airport awaiting their rides. Kiara and Unique were still not talking and neither were willing to apologize. Catching each other's glances from time to time, they would roll their eyes at one another. The two had been bumping heads ever since they were little. Unique didn't know if Kiara called herself being jealous or what the problem was.

Either it was a snide remark coming out of her mouth or she wanted to run the clique's business her way. Unique felt that if she could trust her with handling their affairs, she would. But Kiara was way too flashy and often ran her mouth too much to the wrong people. Kiara was too much of a loose cannon to run the business.

Any time they had beef, it was because of something Kiara said or did. As far back as she could remember, Unique always had to fight Kiara's battles, and frankly, she was getting tired of it.

As a matter of fact, she was getting tired of the whole

thing. If they weren't cousins she would have gotten rid of Kiara a long time ago. Hugging Zoë goodbye, Unique watched as she climbed into her tender, Vito's '04 Chrysler 300C Hemi. Hailing down an airport cab, Unique hugged Kay Kay and told her that she would have her cut of the money by the following Monday. Not even acknowledging Kiara's presence, she jumped into the cab and headed home.

Riding past her old neighborhood on the North Side of St. Louis, Unique asked the cab driver to make a quick detour. Pulling up, they parked in front of her old house on Beacon Avenue. Just seeing the house brought back so many memories for Unique. Some good, some bad, some she wished never happened and some she wished she could experience again.

Unique reminisced about the times she spent with her mother, Syleena. Her mother was diagnosed with chronic schizophrenia when Unique was five. No matter how much medication she was given, she could never break loose of the brain disease. Unique tried to help her mother but nothing she did seemed to make the situation better.

Syleena was in and out of mental clinics Unique's entire life. She saw her mother locked up and put in restraints too many times to remember. Unique and her little sister, Patience, were often sent to live with their Aunt Teresa, Kiara and Kay Kay's mom, when Syleena was sent away.

To make matters worse, Syleena blamed Unique for her mental state. As a teenager, Syleena was raped on her way home from school by an unidentified man and became pregnant. The police never caught him.

Being brought up in a heavily religious home, Syleena's parents refused to allow her to get an abortion. Syleena was distraught to say the least. She hated the idea of having a rapist's baby. She tried everything to get rid of the fetus. Everything from not eating to hitting herself in the stomach, but nothing worked.

By the time she was in her third trimester, Syleena came to the realization that no matter how much she wished and prayed the baby away, she was gonna have it. Still, she didn't like the idea. She detested the child inside of her. When Unique was born, she refused to hold or feed her. Syleena's mother had to do all the work. As Unique got older, the hatred her mother held toward her seemed to only manifest. Syleena seriously thought that God was trying to punish her by having Unique, and she constantly reminded Unique of this. The words, *You're a curse from God*, replayed over and over in Unique's head.

Trying her best to make life easier for her mother, Unique began working at different fast food restaurants to support them, but the money wasn't enough. Bills were stacked up to the ceiling, the rent was past due, and every time she looked up she had a 42-year-old and a 12-year-old mouth to feed. Stealing was her only other option, so at the age of 18, Unique began helping herself to a five finger discount wherever she went, but that didn't work either. They were so far behind on the bills that one time when Syleena was sent away, Unique and Patience got evicted from their house.

With nowhere to go and only two hundred dollars saved up, Unique and Patience slept on the streets and ate fast food for meals. They could've gone over to their Aunt Teresa's house but living on the streets was a far better choice. Teresa's house was like living in a death trap with a street name. But once Patience became sick, Unique saw that she had no other choice.

As she got off the bus, she saw that everything was still the same in the Walnut Park section of St. Louis. Same old run down houses, dirty-ass kids running around, crack fiends begging for a hit and nickel and dime dealers on the streets.

Shaking her head, Unique knew that she could only live this way for so much longer. She was tired of giving her all and still having nothing. Walking three blocks she found her Aunt Teresa's house and knocked on the door.

"Who is it?!"

"It's me," Unique mumbled, unsure of what to say.

"Me who, goddamnit!" her aunt yelled from the other side of the door.

"It's me, Unique, Aunt Teresa." Cracking the door open, her aunt peeked her head through.

"What you doing here? Ain't you supposed to be in a group home or something?"

"Nah, Auntie. Me and Patience were evicted from the house and Momma gone to the clinic again and Patience is getting sick," she spoke, holding back the tears.

"Humph, well what you want from me?"

"I wanted to know if we could stay here for a little while, you know, until I get on my feet."

"You got some money? I know you got some ends."

"Yeah, but all I got is fifty dollars," Unique lied, rolling her eyes. Her aunt couldn't care less about them. At the end of the day she was all about the bucks.

"Well give it to me and I want another two in a month so you gon' have to get a job," she said, finally opening the door. "Kiara and Kay Kay, yo' cousins here!"

"What's up?" Kiara spoke, coming out of her room and looking Unique up and down.

"Hey, Nique. Hey Patience." Kay Kay greeted them both with a hug.

"Hi," Patience spoke softly.

"What's up," Unique spoke, too.

"Sista, I'm hungry." Patience tugged on her arm.

"Now look! Ya'll ain't gon' be coming over here eating up

all my goddamn food. And it's only two bedrooms in here so ya'll gon' have to sleep on the floor," Aunt Teresa yelled.

"No problem." *I've slept in worse places*, Unique thought to herself. "I'll get you something to eat, Patience, don't worry."

"It's getting late and I'm getting ready to go out, so make yourselves at home," Aunt Teresa said, grabbing her purse. With a fifty-dollar bill in hand, Harrah's Casino began to call her name.

Placing her bag on the floor, Unique sat down on the couch and surveyed the room. The once white walls were now crème, the carpet was dingy, the couch was worn out and Unique could have sworn that she had seen more than twenty roaches since she entered the home.

"You got a boyfriend?" Kiara questioned from out of nowhere.

"Nah."

"Peep this." She whispered so that her mother wouldn't hear. "When my momma leave, we leaving too."

"Where we going?"

"It's Saturday. We going downtown on the Riverfront. All the ballas be down there."

"I can't go. My sista sick."

"She'll be a'ight. You can leave her next door with Miss Mae. She'll take care of her."

"I don't know." Unique shrugged.

"Come on girl, you only live once," Kay Kay added.

"Patience, do you want go next door with Miss Mae?"

"Yeah, I like going over her house. She always has food and her house is clean plus she be nice to me."

"A'ight then, I guess I'ma go." Unique sprang up from the couch preparing to leave.

"Ah, uh, you ain't going nowhere with me looking and

Keisha Ervin

smelling like that." Kiara scrunched up her nose.

Unique knew she looked a hot mess and smelled an even hotter mess. Her red, green and orange sleeveless top show-cased her dirty bra and brown crumpled deodorant. The orange Guess jeans were two sizes too small and the Reebok Princesses she wore were so run down that the sole flapped when she walked.

"Well, I don't have anything else to wear, so I guess I can't go." She plopped back down, embarrassed.

"You can borrow something of mine," Kay Kay said, shak-ing her head at Kiara. After giving herself and Patience a bath, Unique was fully dressed and ready to go. Dressed in a pink fit-ted tee, tight jeans and a pair of clean white K-Swiss, Unique looked hip and more up-to-date. Kay Kay even styled her hair in a weave ponytail to spice up her look. After dropping Patience off at Miss Mae's, they headed downtown on the bus. The girls weren't even down on the Landing ten minutes before they started getting hollas.

Guys approached Unique left and right but she turned all of them down because none of them appealed to her. One guy in particular caught her eye, though. He wasn't your best looking brotha but his position in the dope game and the money that he brought in every week made him attractive to her. His name was Tone. He sold heroin and embalming fluid also known on the streets as Water.

Unique saw Tone as her opportunity to make it out of the hood so she gave him her aunt's number. Tone was a sucka for love and she fed off that shit. All she had to do was rub his dick and purr in his ear the words, "I love you," and she got what-ever her heart desired. In a matter of weeks Unique and Patience moved in with Tone, and she had gotten him to place her mother in one of the best psychiatric hospitals in Missouri. Now don't get it twisted, Tone wasn't a pushover.

Unique respected his gangsta.

A year into their relationship, she got Tone to rent her a loft in downtown St. Louis which cost twenty-five hundred dollars a month. Unique also got him to furnish her brand new home with furniture from Bang & Olufsen. After getting her GED she even got Tone to pay her way through school while she took classes at the University of Missouri – St. Louis. Trips to Paris and Milan with twenty-five thousand dollar shopping sprees were what came next.

Unique thought she hit the jackpot but slowly she saw that nothing in life comes cheap. Everything was cool between the two until Tone got possessive. He expected Unique to cater to his every need while he continued to lie and cheat. After being together for five years, Unique was slowly becoming tired of Tone and their whole situation. Tired of reminiscing, Unique let the cab driver know that she was ready go.

$ $ $

"Hey Jeffery," Unique spoke to the doorman as she got out of the cab.

"Good evening, Unique."

"Has Patience arrived home yet?"

"Yes ma'am, she arrived about an hour ago. Mr. Robertson is also waiting for you upstairs."

"Thank you." Pressing 10 on the elevator, Unique couldn't wait to get in her bed and go to sleep, but first she had to deal with Tone. She hadn't forgotten about what she had heard earlier from Patience. Getting off on her floor, she pulled out her keys and opened the door to her place.

"What the fuck took you so long?" Tone asked while sitting on the couch flicking the remote control.

There he was, the nigga she had been playing for the past

five years, sitting on her couch with his pants unbuttoned, watching television. Looking at him Unique wondered why she stayed with him so long. Yes, Tone was attractive in his own way. He was dark- skinned with smooth waves in his hair and a muscular build, but his ways made him uglier and uglier every day. He constantly lied to her but Unique, being the chick she was, continued to stay with him. She didn't care if he lied and cheated. He took care of her and that was all that mattered. Rolling her eyes at him, she stomped her feet and entered her spacious living room which was decorated with Parisian art.

"Who the fuck are you talkin' to and button up your pants!"

"Just answer the fuckin' question."

Pausing for a second, Unique tried to pull herself together before she went off. "I stopped by my old hood. Where is my sister?"

"She's upstairs doing her homework. Why you go by there?"

"Because, I wanted to see if it still looked the same. Why you all up in my business?"

"How much of my money did you spend while you were in LA?" Tone yawned as he buttoned up his pants.

"I didn't spend any of your money," Unique snapped while taking off her shoes.

"You need to quit that shit. When you get locked up, don't come crying to me. I don't understand why you feel the need to steal anyway. It ain't like I don't provide for you."

"You will never be able to give me as much as I can steal," Unique shot, getting up.

"Whatever."

"Yeah, whatever." She paused for a second and continued. "So I heard you were at Toxic last night acting a fool. Popping

Keisha Ervin

bottles, buying drinks for everybody, smoking weed, fuckin' with hoes. You did your thing, huh?"

"Don't start."

"Nah, nigga, don't you start! I know you were with Robin last night!"

"You don't even know what you're talkin' about!"

"Yes, I do. Patience told me!" Unique shouted as he followed her up the spiral staircase.

"Man, Patience don't know what she talkin' about."

Ignoring him, Unique poked her head into her sister's room and said, "Hey baby sis."

"Hi!" Patience jumped. She sat on the edge of her white canopy bed with nothing but a towel on. Unique figured she'd just gotten out of the shower so she told her she'd talk to her later. Tone still had to be dealt with.

"Why don't you just tell the truth for once in your life? It's not like this the first time I've found out about you and another bitch!" Unique snapped as she walked into her bedroom. Not ashamed of her body she stood in the middle of her room during broad daylight and took off her clothes.

"Come on, ma, don't start. You know I love you. You're the only one who has my heart." Tone eyed her body hungrily.

Unique's body was the shit. It had more dips and curves than a roller coaster. Her breasts sat up like two plump pillows while her stomach was as flat as the late R&B singer Aaliyah's. Her hips were perfectly round, only slimming down to define her well-toned calves, but the best part of all was her ass. Unique had the perfect stripper's butt. It wasn't big enough to place a drink on it but it was fat enough to catch the male species' attention.

"Are you done? 'Cause I ain't tryin' to hear that shit," she said as she turned on the shower. Tone stood at the bathroom door, watching her. She didn't even close the semi-frosted shower door. She wanted him to see what he had been missing. Tone could feel his dick getting harder by the second as he stood and watched her bend over to lather her legs, only to stand up again and lather her breasts. By the time Unique got under the flow of water and the soap disappeared from her body, his dick was at full attention. She noticed it after she turned the shower off and stepped out. He handed her a towel and she wrapped it around herself as she tried to move past him. "Move boy," Unique said as she bumped into him and made her way to the bed. She got underneath the sheets with nothing on.

"So, you not gon' let me explain?"

"Look, I'm about to go to sleep. Call me later." Unique pulled the covers over her head.

"I ain't through talkin' to you!" Tone snatched the covers from her body.

"What are you doing?!" she asked, annoyed.

"You gon' listen to what the fuck I got to say."

Being a typical man, Tone thought that sex would solve everything. With both of her thighs in his hands, he slid Unique's body toward the edge of the bed. It had been two days since he tasted her pussy. Just the sight of her perfect pink clit made his dick hard. Tone had to hit it. Playing right along with him, Unique massaged her breasts as he placed himself in between her legs.

"Ahh!" Unique squealed as Tone feasted on her kitty cat.

One good thing about Tone was that he gave some mean head. No matter how mad she was at him, whenever he went down on her, Unique always forgave him. The way he licked, probed and sucked her clit all at once satisfied her to the fullest. Inserting three of his fingers into her pussy, Tone finger fucked Unique into convulsions. She came so hard that her juices were not only in his mouth but around it as well.

"Where your rubbers at?" he asked out of breath, still holding her thighs in place.

"Why?"

"'Cause, we getting ready to fuck."

"Noooo we're not." Unique smirked, getting up.

"Why not?"

"You think I'm gon' let you hit this after you fucked that bitch Robin? Nigga, please. You got me fucked up."

"Oh, it's like that?"

"What? You ain't know?"

"I'm up. I ain't got time for this shit. I'ma call you later." Tone wiped his mouth and left.

"Please don't!" she yelled after him.

Happy that she busted a nut, Unique turned over onto her side and slid off into a deep sleep. Five minutes later the phone rang.

"Hellooo?" Unique answered the phone aggravated.

"Damn, ma, what's with the attitude?" Cezar asked.

"It's nothing, what's good wit' you?"

"Handling a little business. You still coming to my man Bigg's coming home party tonight?"

"Yeah, what time does it start?"

"The club opens up at 9 o'clock but we won't be there until 11."

"A'ight, me and the girls will swing through," Unique assured before hanging up. She grabbed her alarm clock from off the nightstand, set the alarm and pulled the covers over her head until it was time to get up.

$ $ $

Even though it was Bigg's coming home party, you would have thought it was Unique's the way everybody showered her with attention. The girl couldn't help it — she got love everywhere she went. Standing in the middle of the club she and Zoë grooved to the beat of the Lloyd Banks' *"On Fire."* Kiara was there, too. The two had made up. As soon as she realized what a mistake she was making, Kiara called and apologized. With the music pumping, neon lights dancing across the room, balloons and champagne flowing, Unique did her thing.

She was backing it up on some dude that she didn't even know. His hands were all on her ass but she didn't care. All eyes were on her and she gave the crowd just what they wanted — a show. Without hesitation Unique took it down to the floor and popped her coochie like she was starring in a Luke video. Easing her way back up dressed in a lemon yellow, plunging V-Neck Versace dress, Unique turned around and busted into the Mono. If Unique could do one thing it was dance and she knew it.

Hot and perspiring, she headed to the restroom to freshen up once the DJ switched from *"On Fire"* to The Ying Yang Twins' *"Salt Shaker."* Back to the VIP section, with a smile on her face, Unique took her place beside Cezar and the girls. Sipping on a glass of bubbly, she bobbed her head to the sound of the beat but Unique couldn't have been more miserable. She had a big dick nigga who gave her any and everything that she wanted but still she wasn't happy. That was, until Bigg walked through the door.

It was like something straight out of a music video. He came into the club and took over the spot. Every chick in the place had her eyes glued to him, even Unique. Sexy, confident and cocky were not the words to describe him. Bigg was the pretty type — you know the kind, sexy than a muthafucka. His presence alone demanded your attention. Once you saw Bigg everything about him would forever be embedded in your mind. Plain and simple, he was that nigga.

"Yo', who is shorty over there sittin' next to your boy?" Bigg's partna NaSheed pointed out.

"I don't know but mommy lookin' kind right," Bigg replied, massaging his chin as he eyed Unique.

"Yeah, homegirl is the truth."

With both of them in full view of one another, sparks began to go off. He was in Timbs; she was in Manolos. He rocked his clothes like a prince from Harlem; she rocked her gear the fly way — a little Paris runway mixed with a little street chic flava. Bigg was rose gold out and Unique was draped in diamonds. They were perfect for one another. Anybody with eyes could see that.

Donned in an all-black Billionaire Boys Club T-shirt and baggy Evisu jeans, the man turned heads. With an all-black STL hat on his head and a pair of black leather Timbs on his feet, Bigg bopped over to the VIP section. For him to have just gotten out of jail, the boy looked good — damn good. Unique tried her hardest not to stare but her eyes just wouldn't focus on anything else.

Bigg's outfit complimented his mocha-colored skin, thick eyebrows, brown eyes, connecting beard and mustache, kissable lips and braids. He stood about six feet two and weighed one hundred and eighty pounds. His body was built like an Adonis. He even had his name tattooed on the side of his neck. The man looked like he'd fuck a nigga up.

"What's really hood?" he yelled as he bopped toward Unique and Cezar.

"Look at this nigga," Cezar said, getting up to give Bigg a hug. "What took you so long to get here?"

"You know a nigga had to cut something first." Bigg grinned while stroking his chin.

"I feel you but let me introduce you to the team. That big head muthafucka right there in the throwback is Yayo."

Keisha Ervin

"What up homey?" Yayo spoke, taking a pull from a freshly lit blunt.

"What up?" Bigg said with a head nod.

"I think Bice and that nigga Stu out on the dance floor tryin' to mack."

"Oh yeah," Bigg mumbled, transfixed on the caramel honey sitting in front of him.

"Yeah, but fuck them, this the star playa on the team right here." Cezar pointed to Unique. "Unique this is Bigg, Bigg this is Unique."

"Nice to meet you." She extended her hand and smiled.

"What's up, ma?" Bigg smiled too, showing off a mouth full of platinum teeth. He had four on the top row of his mouth. Feeling the heat radiating off of the two, Cezar broke up their little show immediately.

"Ay, Cez, this my man NaSheed. You remember him, don't you?" Bigg continued. Looking over at Kiara, Unique saw that she was already on NaSheed. Checking him out from head to toe, Unique agreed that NaSheed was a tender.

"Yeah, I remember dude."

"What's up?" NaSheed said, giving Cezar a pound.

"Shit, another day, different dollar."

"Ahh, uhmm!" Kiara cleared her throat.

"What's the problem, ma? You got something caught in your throat?" NaSheed asked.

"Nah, baby, I'm just tryin' to get your attention."

"Oh, you got my attention a'ight." He took a seat next to her.

"So, what's the deal, homeboy? You ready to get this shit crackin' or what?!" Cezar handed Bigg a bottle of Patrón Tequila.

"Nigga you ain't said nothing but a word."

"Excuse me, but I'm getting ready to get another drink.

Ya'll want anything?" Unique asked both of them. Cezar shook his head no.

"Nah, shorty, I'm straight," Bigg replied.

"A'ight, I'll be right back."

"Damn, the game done changed that much since I've been gone?" Bigg asked as he watched Unique's ass bounce as she walked away.

"What you talkin' about, Bigg?"

"You got chicks working for you now?"

"Ay dog, don't sleep, lil' momma doing her thing. I trained her up right. Ya'll might be working together, so be cool."

"Yeah, a'ight, if you say so."

Bigg tried his damnest to hold a conversation with Cezar but was unable to get his mind off of Unique. To him she was the ultimate chick. Not only was she sexy as hell but she was on the grind just like he was. There weren't too many females that he could say that about.

"Nigga, is you listening to me?" Cezar asked Bigg, trying to get his attention.

"My bad. What you say?"

Peeping the situation, Cezar wrapped his arm around Bigg's shoulder and said, "Hang it up. You can't pull her."

"What?"

"Nigga, you know what the fuck I'm talkin' about. Unique is priceless. I taught her everything she knows. You my boy and all but ain't no way in hell she gon' fall for a nigga like you."

"How you gon' try and play me like that?"

"Hey, I'm just stating the facts. We both know that back in the day you was the biggest hoe in St. Louis. So, whatever game you was planning on kickin' to her you can hang it up 'cause Unique ain't fallin' for it."

"I'm glad I know now that you ain't got no faith in yo' boy.

I'm straight up feelin' shorty. Mommy got a nice swagger about her."

"It's whatever if you gon' holla at her, but don't say I ain't warn you."

"Are you done?" Bigg asked, ready to handle his B.I.

"A'ight, don't say I didn't warn you!" Cezar yelled after him as he went to find Unique.

It didn't take much to find her. She stood out amongst the slew of chicken heads and skeezers. Unique was standing at the bar when she noticed Bigg approaching her. Seeing him coming near she blushed on the inside. She had hoped that he would follow her. The chemistry between the two was just too strong for either of them to deny.

"Yo' man gon' get to trippin' you keep on staring at me like that," he whispered in her ear as he wrapped his arms around her waist.

"Boy, please." She laughed feeling his dick in between her ass cheeks and the burner that lie on his waist in her back. "And why are your hands on me?"

"Correction, my arms are wrapped around you." He grinned. Releasing his arms from her waist, Bigg stood back giving her space.

"What you drinkin'?"

"A blue muthafucka, why?"

"Let me get a blue muthafucka and a Hennessy and coke," he told the bartender. Unique tried not to but she couldn't help but stare at him. The man was amazing.

"See, there you go again. Why you keep staring at me like that?"

"Ain't nobody lookin' at you." She smirked, turning her head.

"Yes you were. I saw you."

"How was I staring at you?" She turned back and looked

Keisha Ervin

him dead in the eyes.

"You lookin' at me like you a want a nigga." Not able to lie, Unique said nothing, knowing he was telling the truth. Being that close to him and catching a glimpse into his brown eyes, she saw a man full of promise and pain. With one look, he made her want to forget about stealing cars and playing men. From that moment on, all she would want was him.

"Oh, so I'm right?" Bigg handed her the drink.

"Thank you. And even if you were right, it doesn't mean anything. You just got home from doing a seven year bid and you're trying to fuck anything with a pulse. So let me tell you something *Mr. Bigg*, if you haven't noticed already, I'm not like most chicks. A couple lines out ya mouth and a shiny chain is not gonna do it for me so try again."

"Are you serious?"

"Damn right, I'm serious."

"Do you know how fuckin' ridiculous you sound? You don't even know me," he snapped, getting heated.

"I don't have to know you. All ya'll niggas is alike." Unique stood her ground. She didn't know it but she was fuckin' with the wrong one. She couldn't talk that slick shit with Bigg and get away with it like she did with Tone. He was about to set her ass straight.

"Get the fuck outta here with that bullshit! You know you played yourself, ma, 'cause for a minute there I actually thought I saw something in you but I guess I was wrong! You just like all of these other hoes in here who only want a nigga for what they got!"

"Excuse me?"

"You heard me! Kick rocks, ma! Beat it!"

"Nigga, please! Fuck you! Wit' yo' broke ass." Unique rolled her eyes and walked away.

"Who was that you was over there arguing wit'?" Zoë ques-

Keisha Ervin

tioned.

"That was Cezar's punk-ass friend Bigg that just came home from jail."

"Girl, you trippin. He fine as hell, lookin' like Young Buck. You better fuck him before I do."

"Trust me, you can have him! He's a lame!" Unique yelled while looking over her shoulder, hoping that Bigg could hear her. He did because he was staring right at her.

"Yeah, a'ight, don't be mad when you call me and I say I can't talk 'cause he got his dick in my mouth," Zoë joked.

"Girl shut up, let's go dance."

Two hours later the club was letting out and the party was over. Standing outside in front of the club, everyone was busy trying to think of where to go next. Unique hadn't been out clubbing in months, so kicking it until 6 in the morning was the only thing on her mind. Running, Unique caught up with Cezar before he got into his truck to see where he was going. Unbeknownst to her, one of her diamond earrings fell out of her ear.

"Where ya'll getting ready to go?"

"We're heading over to the Pink Slip, why?" Cezar replied.

"I thought we were going to hit up another club."

"Nah, you know my man just coming home. We tryin' to see some ass and titties tonight."

"Eww, whatever, I'ma holla at you later then." Unique scrunched up her face giving him a hug goodbye.

Disappointed with the change of events, Unique poked her bottom lip out and got into the car with Zoë and Kiara. Fifteen minutes later they were pulling up to her building.

"A'ight, I'ma holla at ya'll later," Unique said, getting out of the car. Both Zoë and Kiara said goodbye.

Riding up the elevator, she reflected back on Bigg and how fine he was. Deep down she was disappointed at how things

Keisha Ervin

turned out. Closing the door a little harder than usual, Unique startled her sister.

"Unique, is that you?" Patience asked as she entered the house.

"Yeah, did anybody call me?"

"Yeah," Patience replied coming down the steps. Staring at her lil' sister, Unique could only smile. She was the spitting image of their mother. Pretty, with caramel-colored skin, chinky eyes and a bad shape, Patience had it going on. "How was the party?"

"It was cool," Unique sighed, plopping down on the couch. She hated to admit it but the girl was beat. "Did the money get here yet?"

"Yeah, it came while you were sleep earlier. Tone called you about ten times, too."

"Fuck that nigga. He can keep calling but enough about him. What's going on with you?"

"Nothing. I've just been having a lot of stuff on my mind lately."

"Well, whatever is you know you can talk to me about it, right?"

"Yeah ... it's just complicated that's all."

"I'm not going to pressure you but whenever you're ready to talk, I'm here."

"OK. Are we going to see Mommy this weekend?"

"Yep."

"I can't wait, I miss her." Patience got up from the couch.

"Me too. Are you going to bed?"

"Yeah, I'm going to church tomorrow with Miss Mae."

"That woman know she love you."

"You're not going to bed?"

"Nah, not yet."

"Well, all right, love you."

"Love you too."

Looking around the room, Unique examined her spacious loft. The first time she saw it, she knew she had to have it. She had never seen anything like it. The ceiling and floors were wooden and the walls were painted a deep orange color, which gave off a sensual vibe. The crème sectional, brown throw pillows, glass table, wooden ottoman, plants and art set the entire living room off.

In front of the oversized windows, Unique stood and gazed over the city of St. Louis. Every night she thanked God for allowing them to live in a place as beautiful as their home, but she would trade it all in a second if she could have her mother back. Nobody knew how unhappy Unique was, except for Patience. Unique didn't confide in anyone about her true feelings, not even her cousins.

To them she had a perfect life, if you could call stealing cars and playing men for their money a perfect life. Unique had men that provided her and her sister with whatever they wanted without question. Women were dying to be in her position and she would gladly give it up if she didn't have to support her little sister.

Checking her watch, Unique saw that it was going on 3 o'clock in the morning so she decided to head upstairs for bed. Too tired to put on any pajamas, Unique peeled off her clothes and climbed into bed naked.

Over on the East Side of St. Louis, Bigg sat with a drink in his hand and a stripper on his lap but couldn't get the thought of Unique out of his mind. He couldn't quite put his finger on it but something about her was very intriguing.

With her in mind he pulled out the earring that fell from her ear back at the club. Bigg couldn't help but grin. Looking at it brought back their entire conversation. Unique's mouth was a little out of control but he knew that with a little thug love he could fix that problem.

She was the flyest chick he had ever seen. Even though her looks resembled that of your typical girl-next-door, there was a roughness about her that intrigued the hell out of him. He wanted to get to know her, see what was in her head. Tired of the club scene, Bigg decided he was ready to go home so he tossed the broad on his lap a twenty and told her to get up.

"Where you going?" Cezar questioned.

"I'm getting ready to burn out but, ah, where shorty live at?"

"Who?"

"Unique, nigga, that's who."

"You just won't give up, will you?"

"It ain't even nothing like that. She dropped something back at the club and I want to give it to her."

"Yeah, right. She stay downtown on Washington in the Merchandise Mart building."

Less than five minutes later, Bigg was on the highway headed back downtown. Knocked out, dreaming of fucking Bigg, Unique was awakened by the sound of someone beating on her front door. Pissed off because she was in a good sleep, Unique jumped out of bed, grabbed her robe and headed for the stairs.

"Who is it?!" she asked, sounding a little hoarse.

"Bigg."

Startled, she stood shocked for a second.

"How you know where I stay? You some kinda stalker or something?"

"Never that, sweetheart. Cezar told me where you stayed. Your earring fell out while we were standing outside the club so I figured I'd bring it to you."

Reaching up, Unique felt her ear; her earring was gone. Quickly she unlocked the door and came face to face with

Bigg. She couldn't get over how fine he was. Bigg was the kind of nigga that you wanted to go half on a baby with.

"You know you got a smart-ass mouth." He eyed her up and down lustfully.

"Take it or leave it. That's just how I am." She snatched her earring from his hand.

"You're welcome," he said sarcastically while staring at her body.

Bigg had never seen a body like Unique's. She was perfectly proportioned in all the right places. Her robe was short so he had a perfect view of her thighs and legs. For a minute he allowed himself to wonder how they would feel wrapped around him. Just when he thought it couldn't get any better, the top of her robe slightly opened revealing one of her honey-colored breasts. Her brown, round areola was staring him smack dab in the face and was begging him to come suck it. It took everything in Bigg for him to control himself. His dick was hard than a muthafucka.

"Thank you." Noticing his eyes on her chest she realized that her robe was open. Embarrassed, she pulled it together again.

"If you're done staring at my breasts, I was asleep," Unique stressed, standing back on one of her legs with her hand on her hip.

"What breasts? I know you ain't talkin' about those little bitty muthafuckas," he joked.

"What you say?"

"Nothing. I'ma check you later, shorty." Bigg laughed some.

"Yeah, whatever!" Unique slammed the door in his face.

Back upstairs in her bedroom writhing in embarrassment over Bigg seeing her breast, Unique sat on the edge of the bed with her face in her hands. She couldn't get Bigg's eyes out of

Keisha Ervin

her mind. His eyes had shown more intensity and desire in just a split second then any another man she had ever known. Unique knew that she had to stay away from him before she ended up doing something she had no business doing.

$ $ $

A couple of weeks had passed since Bigg's party and things in Unique's life had gotten back to normal. Business was booming and she and the girls were in and out of town at least twice a month. Sitting on Cezar's couch, Unique flipped through the latest issue of *Us Weekly* magazine while chewing a piece of spearmint gum. Over the years she and Cezar built a very close friendship. Unique proved herself to be a ride or die chick. Cezar respected her gangsta. He respected her so much that he gave her the keys to his house. Only she and his mother had a set. Looking around his crib, Unique had to admit Cezar was doing the damn thing.

His five hundred, sixty-five thousand dollar home in Chesterfield held a spacious living room, gourmet kitchen, three bathrooms, four bedrooms, a game room and an outdoor pool. Sitting down on his Mesa leather sectional, Unique ran her hands across the butter-soft material. The Sanibel coffee table that she picked out years before sat in the middle of the floor. On top of it was an exotic, apple-green vase filled with white calla lilies.

Irritated, she checked her watch and wondered what was taking him so long. Cezar had asked her to meet him at his house at 2 o'clock for a meeting. Looking at her watch it was now going on 3 o'clock. If Unique had one pet peeve it was when people were late and didn't bother to call and say anything. Hearing footsteps nearing the door, Unique continued to read the magazine, pissed off.

Keisha Ervin

"Took you long enough!" she yelled over her shoulder without looking up.

"My bad, me and Bigg lost track of time." Hearing his name caused Unique's heart to drop out of her chest. She didn't know what it was about him but the nigga had her going. Playing it cool, she continued to act mad.

"Next time call. You know I hate to wait."

Taking a seat across from her, Bigg scoped out Unique's physique while she pretended to ignore him. She looked fly as hell. Her all-black Gucci glasses shielded her eyes but everything else on her was exposed for all to see. Her reddish blonde hair was flat ironed bone-straight to the back and MAC clear lip glass adorned her lips.

She wore an all-black wife beater which exposed her full breasts and read "Rich Bitch," a pair of black 7 For all Mankind booty shorts that showcased her thick butterscotch thighs and legs and on her feet were a pair of black patent leather Yves Saint Laurent stilettos. Bigg had to admit, the chick was bad.

"You can't speak?" he asked.

"Hi," she spoke dryly. Bigg could only shake his head and laugh. Sitting in his favorite spot on the couch, Cezar leaned forward and began to speak.

"I got a job for you two."

"What is it?" Unique asked perplexed, taking off her glasses. She never did a job without the girls.

"I'm switching my supplier."

"Why? What's wrong with Jose?"

"Jose be on some bullshit. All of sudden this nigga going up on his prices. Ain't no way in hell I'm gon' pay twenty five g's a brick when I can get 'em for fifteen from my man Jackson down in Louisiana."

"So, what you need me and Unique to do?"

"I need for ya'll to go down there and set everything up. I have the car and hotel already set up for you. You'll be leaving Thursday night and I expect you back by Sunday afternoon."

"Why can't we be in and out? I ain't trying to be down there the entire weekend with this nigga." Unique scrunched up her face, agitated.

"Yo', ma, what's the deal? You gotta problem with me or something?" Bigg asked, heated. He had enough of her and her smart mouth.

"Yeah, I got a problem wit' you. I got my own lil' thing going on! I don't want to be bothered wit' yo' crazy lookin' ass!"

"Check it, ma. I've been making moves since you was in a training bra! You and your lil' gang of car thieving friends ain't seen half the dough I've seen! So don't get it twisted! You will show me some respect!"

Appalled, Unique sat quietly. She couldn't think of anything else to say. The only thing she could come up with to do was suck her teeth, roll her eyes and say, "Whatever."

"Both of ya'll need to calm down." Cezar laughed. "Whatever animosity you two got against each other needs to be put aside. I need your full cooperation." He looked at them both.

"I still don't think this is going to work," Unique mumbled, picking at her finger nail.

"Did I mention that both of ya'll will be paid twenty g's?"

"You should've said that at first." Unique hopped up grabbing her Bottega Veneta purse, preparing to leave. Placing her shades back on she gave Bigg one last look and left. Even though he tried not to notice it, Bigg couldn't keep his eyes off of Unique's big ass.

"I guess everything is set then." Cezar got up, too.

Keisha Ervin

Pulling up to the parking lot of the clinic in which her mother lived, Unique looked in the rearview mirror and sighed. It was Family and Friends Friday. Every other week she and Patience would try to attend. Unique dreaded her visits with her mother. Every time she saw her something bad would happen.

It never failed. After ten minutes of being in the same room with Unique, Syleena would have a fit. She never had one when it was just Patience. Syleena could sit for hours in complete silence and never utter a word but when Unique entered the room all hell would break loose. Unique didn't know what it was that triggered those negative emotions in her mother. Maybe it was her father.

When Unique was younger, Syleena often told Unique that she was the spitting image of him. Whenever Syleena looked at Unique, she remembered the rape. As a child, Unique didn't know how to handle hearing things like that. It made her feel dirty and unwanted.

"Come on, let's go get this over with," she said as she unlocked her door.

"Don't be like that, Nique. Maybe this time things will be better," Patience reassured.

"Yeah, we'll see," Unique mumbled underneath her breath.

As she walked down the cold, beige-colored corridor to her mother's room, Unique could feel the air in her lungs begin to fade. Seeing her mother had this effect on her and she didn't like it one bit. Her main purpose in life was to always keep it together and to never let her real feelings show. But when Unique was around her mother it was like she was instantly zapped back to being a little girl, unable to defend herself from her mother's hurtful words and violent tirades.

"There go my girls," Nurse Sandy spoke.

"Hey Sandy." Unique smiled half-heartedly. "How you been?"

"Good. How you doing, Miss Honor Roll Student?" Nurse Sandy said, referring to Patience.

"I'm doing good."

"Well look, your mother's been waiting on you. She's been talking about seeing you all day. Why don't you go see her while I talk to your sister for a bit."

"OK," Patience replied as she turned and walked into her mother's room.

"Did she say anything about wanting to see me?" Unique asked, already knowing the answer.

"No ... not this time, Unique. She'll come around, though."

"Uh huh, but what is it you need to talk to me about? Tone paid the bill, right?"

"Yes. Tone paid the bill but we'll talk about him later. Come sit down with me." Nurse Sandy ushered Unique over to a nearby couch.

"It must be something bad, what happened?"

"We did an exam on your mother the other day and—"

"And, what?" Unique asked, becoming impatient.

"The doctors think your mother might have brain cancer."

"What?"

"We didn't want to alarm you until we had all the facts but for the past two weeks your mother has been having hallucinations. At first we thought it was just her acting out because of her schizophrenia but then the seizures began. She's had two in the past week. The doctors did a CAT scan on her and found a tumor on her occipital lobe."

"I can't believe this." Unique sat with a stunned look on her face.

"Now we're going to do all we can to help her, but with

your mother's mental health it's going to be hard."

"How am I going to tell Patience this?"

"I don't know, but you're going to have to be strong for her, Unique. She's really gonna need you now," Nurse Sandy said, wrapping her arm around Unique's shoulder.

"This is just too much for me to handle right now." Unique let out a loud sigh.

"Just pray, Unique. Everything's gonna be all right."

"Thanks, Sandy."

"You're welcome, sweetie. Now go on in there and see about ya momma."

It took everything in Unique not to buckle over and fall as she stood up. She was so hurt by the news of her mother's illness that she didn't know which way was left or right. Standing on the outside of her mother's door, Unique glanced in and watched as Patience and Syleena laughed and talked like two old friends. Unique and Syleena never had conversations like that.

She hated to feel jealousy toward her sister but Unique often found herself envying Patience. She wondered what it felt like to have their mother look upon her adoringly or to laugh at the things she said. Syleena was always so happy to see Patience. When she saw Unique the only thing she saw were the eyes of her rapist. Now Syleena was sick and Unique knew that she may never get to have the healthy relationship with her mother that she prayed for as a child.

"Hey Momma," Unique spoke as she entered the room.

Each time she visited her mother, Unique was amazed at how beautiful she was and how much Patience took after her. Anyone that looked at her mother could tell that she was a knock out in her day. She had the prettiest caramel kissed-by-the-sun skin, long thick head of hair and the most alluring brown eyes that anyone had ever seen. But as the years went by and her illness became worse, Syleena's looks seemed to diminish.

"Patty Cake, will you get me a glass of water?" Syleena said, ignoring Unique's presence.

"Sure thing, Momma."

"So, Momma, how you been?" Unique asked once again, trying to spark up a conversation.

"Here you go, Ma." Patience handed Syleena her cup.

"Thanks, Patty Cake. You so good to ya Momma."

"Momma, I know you hear me!" Unique snapped.

"Is that man with you?" Syleena asked calmly.

"What man, Momma?!"

"That damn daddy of yours."

"How many times do I have to tell you that I don't even know who my father is!"

"Come on, Ma, you were doing good. Try to be nice today," Patience pleaded.

"Yeah, Momma, I missed you. I even brought you a present." Unique opened up her purse and pulled out a small jewelry box. Opening it up she revealed a white gold necklace with a small heart pendant attached. "See, here, it's a locket. It has a picture of me and Patience in it."

"Get that damn thing away from me!" Syleena screamed, slapping the jewelry box away. "Patty Cake, help me?! She's trying to hurt me again!"

"No she's not, Momma. Unique's trying to be nice. Please calm down."

"Don't you see she's the devil?! She's just like her father, a Satanist!"

"Momma, no I'm not! I wish you would quit saying that!" Unique yelled, aggravated and hurt by her mother's words. "I love you! Why can't you see that?!"

"YOU'RE A LIAAAAR! You don't love me! You're out to finish what your father started! I'm not stupid! Patty Cake, help me! She's out to get me! Please?" Syleena begged while holding onto Patience's arm.

"You know what?! Fuck this! I ain't got time for this shit! I'm sick of you always treating me like this! I AM NOT MY FATHER!" Unique snapped. She grabbed the jewelry box from off the floor and left the room.

"Unique, don't leave!" Patience pleaded, following after her.

"Nah, fuck that! I hate her!"

"You don't mean that, Nique. Calm down."

"Yes I do. I'm tired of this shit. I got other things to deal with besides having to deal with her crazy ass. Now go and finish your visit. I'll be in the car." And with that said, Unique headed back to the car and cried for what seemed like hours.

I Wanna Get 2 Know Ya

It was 2 o'clock Thursday morning. Unique sat patiently in her living room awaiting Bigg's arrival. He was late. Tapping her foot, she sat mad as hell. They were supposed to be on the road by now. Unique tried calling his cell phone but each time his voicemail would pick up. This was the very reason she didn't work outside her circle. At least with the girls she had complete and utter control.

The past week for Unique could be described as hell to say the least. After the disastrous meeting at the clinic with her mother, more bad news came in. The doctors called and confirmed that Syleena indeed had brain cancer. The only thing Unique could do was break down and cry upon hearing the news.

Everything she'd said that day she regretted. She was just so frustrated by the news of her mother possibly having cancer and her mother's behavior that it all just became too much for her. But Unique, being the chick she was, managed

Keisha Ervin

to somehow bring it all back together. She and Bigg had a job to do and she couldn't let her mother's illness get in the way and fuck up her head.

Speaking of Bigg, after doing some background digging, Unique learned that before he got locked up he was doing it real big. He grew up on the South Side of St. Louis with Cezar. They both attended the same high school — Roosevelt. Bigg was a good guy. He played basketball his entire time in school but his dreams of making it to the NBA were dashed when he busted his knee during a game. Bigg was crushed. Playing ball was supposed to be his ticket out the hood.

Since his dreams of playing ball were no longer in reach, he turned to the streets. Cezar was already in the game, so it was only natural that Bigg linked up with him. He introduced Bigg to the drug game. They both sold girl and boy but as time passed, Bigg gained more territory than Cezar. Cezar wasn't the jealous type but no matter how hard he tried he could never bring in a fourth of Bigg's cheese.

Bigg had everything that Cezar wanted. Real estate all over St. Louis, two barber shops, liquor stores, a beauty salon, five luxury cars, celebrity friends and around that time, he had even ventured into the music industry. Business was booming for Bigg. He was living the high life of a young, rich, black bachelor. That was until he was pulled over with ten kilos of cocaine in the trunk of his car. Bigg was 17 years old and sentenced to ten years in prison but only ended up serving seven. With Bigg gone, Cezar took over and began running the streets of St. Louis.

Now fresh out of prison, Bigg was ready to reclaim his spot. He got out of bed, sat on the edge and looked out into the night sky. The room was pitch black except for the slight glimmer of light shining from the moon up above. It had been seven years since he saw the stars. Running his hands down his face, Bigg thanked God once more for bringing him home. This time he was going to do things right. No more jail for him. He would die before he went back.

Since he had been out, Bigg had been making moves left and right. His one and only desire was to regain his crown on the streets. Bigg couldn't stand playing second fiddle to Cezar or any other man. He was grateful that Cezar put him on, but Bigg was used to being his own boss. As he slipped on his pants and zipped them up he checked his watch and noticed that he was over an hour late picking Unique up. Bigg knew that he was going to catch hell once he caught up with Unique.

"Baby, where you going?" a young redbone by the name of Brittany purred, half asleep. Poor thing, Bigg had worn the child out. She could barely move after he was done putting it on her.

"A nigga gotta make moves, ma. I'ma holla at you when I get back," he said, pulling his T-shirt on over his head.

"You can't stay a little while longer?" she whined, exposing her honey-colored double D breasts.

"I wish I could but I'm late. I gotta be somewhere."

"OK." Brittany continued to pout.

"I promise when I get back it's me and you." Bigg kissed her forehead.

"Call me!" she shouted after him.

An hour later, just as Unique was about to pick up the phone and call Bigg again, she heard a faint knock on the door. Pissed, she snatched the door open. She shook her head and rolled her eyes. Just the sight of him made her sick.

"Yo' my bad, I got caught up," he tried to explain.

"Yeah, whatever. Let's just go and get this shit over with," Unique said as she pushed past him. *His nasty ass was probably out fuckin' some hoe*, she thought.

Keisha Ervin

"You're forgetting your bags."

"You can't get 'em for me?"

"Say please."

"Nigga, you got me fucked up. I'll get my own damn bags," she huffed, walking back into her loft. Unique grabbed her heavy luggage which was filled to the brim with designer clothes, shoes and accessories, and lugged it onto the elevator with her.

"You a'ight?"

"I'm fine!" Unique rolled her eyes as she tried to steady her breathing. *I need to get to the gym*, she thought.

"You sure? Those bags look a little heavy." He grinned.

"I said I'm fine!"

Unique couldn't wait to be away from him. Bigg was a self-absorbed, arrogant asshole. Standing side by side, she tried not to notice how good he looked. It was a little chilly out so he sported a gray Enyce jacket, white T-shirt, jeans and on his feet were a pair of white and gray BAPE tennis shoes. *This is gonna be one long weekend*, she thought.

Once they reached the main floor, Unique hoped and prayed that Jeffrey was working the night shift. Stepping off the elevator, she spotted him by the door.

"Jeffrey, can you load these bags in the trunk for me?"

"Sure, ma'am."

Once everything was settled, Unique got into the rented white Denali truck. She had no intentions of talking to Bigg so she placed her seat belt on, slid her pink Juicy flip-flops off, folded her arms, closed her eyes and drifted off to sleep. Hating her attitude but loving the way she looked, Bigg smiled, put the key in the ignition and began their road trip to Louisiana.

Four and half hours into their trip, Bigg turned the volume up on the radio, pulled out a blunt and sparked it up.

Eightball and MJG's *"Don't Flex"* was on. He had no choice but to turn it up; it was his jam. Unique was still asleep. Looking over at her, Bigg couldn't help but laugh. Her head was turned to the left facing him. The girl was snoring and on top of that her mouth was hanging wide open. Bigg even spotted a little trickle of drool sliding down the corner of her lower lip.

"Don't flex baby ... I wanna see you touch your toes in that dress baby ... Bounce it up and down like we having sex baby ... Give me the head and you can give them tricks the rest baby... ain't nothing less baby," he sang in between taking pulls off the blunt.

Stretching her arms and legs out, Unique yawned. The smell of Purple Haze in the air and Eightball and MJG on the radio had her fully awake. Feeling that her face was wet she quickly wiped the side of her mouth. *God I hope he didn't see that*, she thought.

"Where are we?"

"We're in Memphis," he said, passing her the blunt.

"Thanks," she replied, inhaling the smoke into her lungs.

"Yo' you was over there knocked the fuck out, snoring and shit."

"I was not. I do not snore."

"Somebody lied to you 'cause you was over there snoring like a muthafucka."

"Fuck you." She grinned as her stomach began to growl. "Are you hungry 'cause I am."

"Yeah, we can stop." A Denny's was only two miles up the road so they decided to stop there. She put her flip-flops back on, grabbed her purse and hopped out of the truck. Bigg was already at the door holding it open for her.

"Thank you."

"You're welcome," he replied, admiring her ass.

Keisha Ervin

"Hi, can we have a table for two?" Bigg asked the waitress once inside.

"Sure, smoking or non-smoking?"

"Non-smoking, please."

"Follow me."

As they walked over to their table, Bigg continued to eye Unique's thick thighs and plump ass as she walked. The jeans she had on were so tight he swore he caught a glimpse of her pussy print. After guiding them over to a booth by the window, the waitress, Tracy, gave them both a menu and a complimentary glass of water. After ordering, they sat in silence for a minute.

"So, Bigg, what's your real name?" Unique asked, breaking the ice.

"How you know my real name ain't Bigg?"

"I know your momma did not name you Bigg." She laughed.

"It's Kaylin, sweetheart."

Hearing Bigg call her sweetheart caused Unique to blush. She couldn't believe that she graduated to sweetheart level so fast.

"Kay ... lin. I like that."

"So, what's up wit' you and Cezar?" he asked out of nowhere.

"Nothing. Why you ask that?"

"I mean, you got keys to the nigga crib and shit. I figured ya'll was more than just friends."

"Well, you figured wrong. Cezar and I are *just friends,*" Unique stressed, hoping she was making herself clear.

"OK, so what's up with the attitude then, Miss Unique?"

"What you mean by that?"

"You're so cold and defensive all the time. What nigga hurt you?"

Keisha Ervin

"Ain't no man hurt me. Life hurt me."

"What happened in your life that was so fucked up?"

"Basically, I've been an adult since as far back as I can remember. My mother's been in and out of my life since I was little."

"What, she a blockhead?"

"Nah, my momma ain't on crack! She's schizophrenic. She's in a mental institution out in Jefferson City. I've been raising my lil' sister for the past five years by myself. It's hard but I love my lil' sister. She's really the only family I have besides my cousins, Kiara, Kay Kay and Zoë. We try to go visit her at least twice a month."

Out of nowhere Unique's eyes began to well up with tears as she spoke. She hadn't talked about her mother in years and all the frustration seemed to start spilling out of her all at once. Looking out the restaurant window, she folded her arms across her chest and willed herself not to cry.

"It's hard you know ... because ... me and moms don't really get along," she continued.

"And why is that?"

"Because every time she looks at me she sees the man who raped her." Unique turned and looked Bigg square in the eyes. He didn't know what to say. All he could do was sit and looked stunned.

"Yeah, that's right, I'm a product of rape. I don't know who my ole dude is and don't wanna know for that matter. My mother hates me and I'll use anybody or anything to get what I want, so now you see there ain't shit a man can do to me that life hasn't already done." Unique's lower lip began to tremble.

"It's cool, ma. You can cry. Let that shit out." Bigg reached his hand underneath the table and placed it on her thigh.

"I'm cool." Unique wiped her eyes and slid her leg away. She couldn't believe that she allowed herself to have a weak moment in front of Bigg. Unique thrived off of keeping everything together and bottled in.

"Well, if you ever need to talk, I'm here."

"I won't," she sniffed.

"Here you go," the waitress said, placing their meals in front of them and interrupting their conversation.

"Thank you. Can I have some ketchup with this?" Bigg asked, ready to tear into his food.

"Sure." The waitress handed him a bottle. "Anything else?"

"No, that's all."

"Ma'am, do you need anything?"

"No, I'm fine," Unique answered without looking up. She didn't want the waitress to know she had been crying.

Taking a bite of his omelet, Bigg wondered if he should continue to pick Unique's brain or not. He didn't want to dredge up any more horrible memories from her past so he decided to switch the subject to relationships.

"So, tell me, Unique. You got a man?"

"Yeah, why?" She looked him square in the eyes.

"'Cause, I wanted to know."

"We've been together for five years." Taking a bite of her T-bone steak, Unique checked for his reaction.

"Five years?" Bigg was surprised. "Damn, that's a long time. You must love that nigga."

"Actually, I don't." Unique laughed a little bit.

"What? How you gon' be wit' a man for five years and not love him?" Bigg grabbed the salt and shook some onto his omelet.

"Easy." She shrugged her shoulders. "And you shouldn't put salt on your food. You're going to have high blood pressure by the time you're 30."

"It's cool." He waved her off. "But, what you mean, easy? You gotta have some kind of feelings for the dude."

"I mean, he's cool. He gives me whatever I want and that's all I need from him."

"So, you are one of those chicks who only want a nigga for his ends."

"Look." Unique placed her fork down. "I don't believe in fairy tales and happily-ever-afters. Love will never be in the equation for me."

"And why is that?" Bigg listened closely, dying to hear her answer.

"Think about it. What is love? Love is nothing but an imaginary feeling that people trick themselves into believing."

"You really believe that?"

"You damn right I do. Fuck love."

"Wow. That's harsh."

"That's life. Like I said, fuck love 'cause love ain't never gave a damn about me."

Not able to argue with that, Bigg finished the rest of his meal in silence. Once they finished eating he paid the check. Unique was already at the car. The rest of the trip was cool. After the incident at Denny's, Unique kind of withdrew and put her guard up once again. Bigg could understand the way she felt so he didn't pry.

Finally, after a ten hour drive, they reached Louisiana. Unique couldn't wait to see what the Dirty Dirty had to offer. Cezar booked them separate suites at the Historic French Market Inn. The place was absolutely breathtaking. Unique couldn't have been happier. After they checked the car in with the valet service, she and Bigg headed in.

"Hi, my name is Edward Whitaker. I'm here to check in," Bigg lied, using one of his alias names.

"OK, let me look that up sir," the desk clerk chimed. "I'm sorry sir, your check-in time was for 3 o'clock as you can see it's 5:30. One of your rooms has already been taken but the other room is still available."

"So, what you're saying is that I'm going to have to sleep in the same room with him?" Unique asked, appalled.

"Yes ma'am, that's the way it looks."

"Oh hell naw! I can't believe this shit!"

"Don't mind her, we'll take it."

This turn of events had thrown Unique for a loop. She didn't know how she was going to survive three days with Bigg, let alone share a bed. Standing in the elevator on their ride up to the room she turned to him and said, "While we're in this room together there will be no funny business. We will not be having sex so don't even try it."

"Who said anything about having sex?"

"I know how ya'll niggas think."

"There you go with that shit again. Evidently me fuckin' you is on your mind. Don't beat around the bush, ma, all you gotta do is ask." Walking up on her, he continued, "You want me to fuck you, Unique?" Her back was up against the elevator wall, pinned by his body, as they exchanged breaths.

"Boy please, you better get away from me." Unique gazed into his eyes, barely able to breathe.

"That's what I thought." He grinned, backing up. "Trust me, fuckin' you ain't even on my mind. Besides … you wouldn't know what to do with this dick anyway. I'm too much of a man for you to handle. Continue to fuck with these lil' locs, ma, 'cause a nigga like me would tear your shit up and have you begging for more."

"Negro please, you and that jailhouse dick of yours can kiss my ass," Unique spat as they got off the elevator and walked toward their room.

"You know what? You and that mouth of yours gon' get you fucked up."

"Just open the door."

"That's real talk. I'm gon' end up fuckin' you up before the weekend is over." He inserted the key into the door.

"Whatever." Unique rolled her eyes as she entered their lavish suite.

The room was quite elegant. The style of it was very dark and sensual. One king-sized bed sat in the middle of the floor, while a desk and armoire adorned the wall. Walking farther into the suite, they saw a couch, mini bar, full bath and Jacuzzi. Plopping down onto the bed, Unique kicked off her shoes and turned on the television. She was so into the Style Channel that she didn't even notice Bigg undressing. Then out of no where she caught a glimpse of chocolate flesh.

Quickly turning her head toward him, Unique saw that Bigg had stripped down to his boxers. Holding her breath she tried not to let the words escape that filled her mind. *Prison did a body good*, she thought. Even though Bigg was tall, his body was ripped with muscles. His arms and legs were full and his abs held a perfect six pack.

She ran her eyes over his upper torso and noticed several different tattoos. Across his stomach he had the name "Dontay" written in an arch. His left arm had "Bigg Entertainment" written with money and smoke formed around it. On his right forearm was a scripture and on his hands he had "Bigg" tattooed on one and the other, "Upps." As he turned around she also noticed that he had a huge gash going across his left shoulder blade. It looked like someone had beaten him with a belt or cane badly. But what really caught her eye was a tattoo of man blowing his brains out.

Ignoring Unique's blatant stares, Bigg continued to undress. He stepped out of his boxers and walked past her like she wasn't even in the room. Unique eyed him hungrily and bit into her lower lip. There was no denying it — she wanted Bigg in the worst way. His thick ten and a half inch dick called her name as he bopped toward the bathroom door.

"What are you doing?" she finally asked with a dry mouth.

"What does it look like I'm doing? I'm about to take a shower."

"You couldn't have taken off your clothes in the bathroom?"

"No, why? Is my dick bothering you or something?" He grinned devilishly.

"Boy please." Unique waved him off, rolling her eyes.

"Admit it, Unique. You want me."

"Bigg, get over yourself. The only person who wants you is a nigga named Stud on cell block eight."

"I see you got jokes," he said, stepping closer. Standing directly in front of her, Bigg rubbed his manhood. Unique looked into his eyes and tried her best not to notice his erection but it was very hard not to, being that his dick was damn near smacking her in the face.

"Touch it. I know you want to," he whispered.

Unable to resist a big dick, she took her hand and softly slid it from the tip to the shaft. Unique had never seen a dick so big in her life. Bigg was truly living up to his name. Not only did he have length and width, the muthafucka was heavy as well. The man had a dick the size of an anaconda. Gazing into each other's eyes, they continued to slide their hands up and down his mammoth penis.

"I knew you wanted a nigga." He laughed, taking his dick from her hand.

Feeling stupid, Unique snapped back to reality and said, "Whatever, nigga! I was trying to not to hurt your feelings."

"Quit frontin'. You know you want to drop them draws."

"Boy please, you better get yo' ass away from me."

"You can join me in the shower if you want," he suggested, standing in the doorway of the bathroom giving Unique a

Keisha Ervin

perfect view of his muscular ass.

"I'll pass," Unique said, focusing her attention back to the TV.

"Yeah a'ight, whatever, ma. Keep lying to yourself."

"Bigg, shut the fuck up and concentrate on not dropping the soap!"

In the  Middle

Not having to meet up with Cezar's new connect, Jackson, until Saturday afternoon, Bigg and Unique spent the entire day Friday sightseeing and shopping. Bigg himself had spent well over ten grand. Unique thought she could shop a lot but Bigg spent money like it was flying off trees. Shopping at the stores in Canal Place, Unique made an impromptu stop at the Gucci store. Bigg hadn't even noticed that she stopped until he began talking and realized he wasn't getting a reply back. Retracing his footsteps down the block, he found Unique sitting inside the store surrounded by sales attendants and boxes of shoes.

Looking up at him, she smiled. Unique was in shoe heaven. Laughing at her excitement, Bigg headed over to the men's section of the store. Finding nothing for himself he returned to Unique's side. She was in deep thought. Unique sat thinking if she should get the fifteen hundred dollar large, black, horse bit leather bag or a pair of nine hundred dollar patent leather boots. She really wanted both but only had enough for one. Cursing herself for not bringing more money she put the Gucci bag back. Hanging her head low, she walked over to the counter.

"Will that be all for you today, ma'am?" the sales attendant asked.

"Yes." She nodded with a sad look on her face.

Unique pulled out a thousand dollars in cash and paid for her shoes.

"I'm ready," she said gloomily to Bigg.

They continued their stride down the street. Noticing a change in her demeanor, Bigg became concerned. It was unlike Unique to pout, so seeing this side of her made Bigg care for her even more. He saw that she really wanted the bag but wasn't able to purchase it. Spotting a little café up the block, Unique suggested that they stop.

"You go ahead, let me stop at this store right quick," Bigg said.

"OK."

Unique took the bags they had accumulated back to their suite. She freshened up and headed back to the café. Fifteen minutes later Bigg met back up with her as promised. Approaching her, he watched as she sat cross-legged, sipping on a latte, talking on her cell phone. The rays coming from the sun seemed to be glowing upon her peanut butter skin. Grabbing his pants, Bigg adjusted the hard on that had grown. Getting himself together, he approached the table and sat across from her.

"Tone! Will you listen?! I don't want to talk about this right now!" Unique spoke firmly into her cell phone while looking at Bigg. He turned his head in the other direction pretending as if he weren't listening, but he was. "I'm tired of hearing about you and your other hoes! It's nothing! Just be honest!" She paused for a moment. "Look, can we talk about this when I get home? Hello? Hello? Oh, I know that muthafucka did not just hang up on me!" Unique slammed her Nextel shut. "My bad, I didn't know if you wanted anything but I ordered you a mocha latte," Unique said, pretending as if nothing happened.

"Thanks but a nigga like me needs something stronger than that. So, that was your man of five years on the phone?"

"Yeah."

"Seem to me like that nigga stressing you out."

"It's nothing. I just hate when people lie to me."

"So, what you want to do after this?" Bigg changed the subject.

"We can go back to the room because I'm getting tired."

"That's cool. I'm kind of getting tired, too."

"I see you went back to the Gucci store. What did you buy?" Unique suddenly perked up.

"Just a little something, something." He smiled.

"What is it? Let me see."

Without permission she took the bag from his hand. Bigg didn't mind, though. Pulling the large black box out of the bag, she sat it upon the table. Quickly Unique lifted the top off and unfolded the paper. She expected to find a shirt or a pair of pants but instead she was greeted with the same Gucci bag she picked up at the store. Looking over at him she wondered if it were some kind of joke.

"It's yours. I hope you like it." Bigg smiled showing off a perfect set of thirty-twos.

"Like it? I love it! I can't believe you went back and got it for me."

"After I saw how bad you were pouting I had to get it for you."

"I was not pouting."

"Yes, you were."

"No, I wasn't, but thank you. It was so nice for you to do

Keisha Ervin

this for me. When we get back home I will pay you your money."

"Your money is no good with me, ma. It was a gift; just enjoy it."

"Well thanks again. I can't wait to wear it," Unique said excitedly as jolts of electricity graced the sky. Out of nowhere rain began pouring down.

"Oh, shit it's raining. We ain't even got an umbrella."

"I know my hair is gonna mess up, plus I got on these heels," Unique whined, looking down at her satin Prada kitten heels.

"I got you." Bigg stood up taking her hand.

"What are you going to do?"

"Just slip off your shoes and put them in the bag. I'm gonna carry you back."

"Are you sure?"

"What I just tell you? I got you."

Unique gazed into his light brown eyes and knew that she could trust him. She placed her shoes into the bag and quickly leaped into Bigg's strong arms. While securely in his embrace, Bigg ran the block back to the Inn. Unique hid her face in the crook of his neck the entire time. The smell of his cologne sent chills up her spine; he smelled so good. Bigg was wearing Jean Paul Gaultier, which was one of Unique's favorites.

Then, suddenly, Unique had the insatiable temptation to kiss Bigg's neck. The combination of rain drops falling upon her skin and the feel of his arms wrapped around her body took Unique to a place of complete tranquility. She wanted to be with Bigg in every way imaginable. Without any warning, she began licking and sucking on his neck as he carried her in his arms. Bigg didn't know what to do. He hadn't expected for Unique to go there with him. Loving the feel of her tongue against his skin, he slowed his pace. Bigg didn't want the moment to end.

By the time they made it back to the suite, they both were hot, horny and wet. Not wanting to, but knowing he should, Bigg put Unique down. Looking into each other's eyes they wondered what was next. He watched as she stood before him shivering wet with anticipation. Not able to control his feelings any longer, Bigg grabbed the back of Unique's neck and pulled her close. *Fuck all the bullshit*, he thought. The sky shown colors of orange and pink hues as Bigg hungrily kissed her lips. Returning the feeling, Unique kissed him back with as much intensity.

At that moment Bigg didn't want anything but Unique. He had to have her. Her skin felt like silk as he ran his hands up her shirt and caressed her back. Subconsciously Unique's lips released a moan. Realizing what was going on, she abruptly stopped their kissing session.

"Why you stop? What's the problem?" he asked, confused.

"I'm trippin'. We can't do this," Unique confirmed, pulling down her shirt.

"Come on, ma. Stop with the games. You want a nigga as much as I want you."

"Thanks for the purse, Bigg, but I can't fuck wit' you like that."

"What the fuck you mean you can't fuck wit' me like that?" he questioned, eyeing her erect nipples.

"I came here to do a job. Nothing more, nothing less. You're a cool guy and all but me and you are on two different levels right now—"

"You know what? I'm about sick of you and your bullshit!" Bigg cut her off. "You too fuckin' confused for me! You think you know everything and don't know shit! But let me tell you something, these lil' games you playing gon' get yo' feelings

Keisha Ervin

hurt, you keep on fuckin' with me! You know what, for the rest of the trip, don't say shit to me!" He stormed off, leaving Unique standing alone.

$ $ $

After their argument, Unique locked herself in the bathroom. It was the only way she could avoid Bigg. She ran herself a nice, hot, bubble bath. With nothing but complete silence surrounding her, Unique closed her eyes and let the day's events replay in her mind.

She knew that she was wrong for treating Bigg the way she did. An apology was what was needed, but being pig-headed, Unique let her pride get in the way. *Fuck him*, she thought. It wasn't like he was her man, she reasoned with herself. Needing someone to talk to, Unique picked up her cell phone and called Kay Kay.

"What up?" Kay Kay playfully answered on the first ring.

"You silly, what you doing?"

"Nothing, fixing dinner for me and Arissa."

"Oh, where is Kiara?"

"Ripping and running the streets as usual."

"That don't make no damn sense. You need to make her come and get her child."

"Arissa is my niece. Somebody gotta take care of her and you know Kiara ain't. But anyway, what you doing?"

"Shit, ready to come home."

"Why? What happened?"

"Nothing," Unique lied.

"Come on, Nique, this is me you're talkin' to. I know something happened or else you wouldn't be sounding like that."

"I don't know, girl, it's just that I've been thinking a lot lately —"

"Hold up. What, Arissa?" Kay Kay said, cutting her off.

"Auntie, I'm hungry," Unique could hear her little cousin say in the background.

"OK Arissa, here I come. I'm fixing dinner right now. Go finish watching Raven. By the time that goes off dinner will be done."

"OK!"

"Now back to you. What you thinking about?"

"About life and shit." Unique avoided telling Kay Kay the truth. *Love is forbidden* was their number one rule, she remembered. Unique had made it up herself. There was no way in hell she was going to tell Kay Kay that she was catching feelings for Bigg.

"Nique, are you high?"

"Naw, girl." Unique laughed. "I've just been thinking that I need a change, that's all."

"A change? Like what?"

"I don't know. I just need something to happen. I mean, come on Kay, there's got to be more to life than this. I'm tired of hiding behind clothes and cars. After a while that shit don't mean nothing when you come home to an empty house." She shrugged knowing fully well what she needed was love.

"I don't know what to tell you, boo. All I can say is that you're young, beautiful and smart. What more can you ask for? We got all these hoes out here trying to be like us."

"I guess, but anyway, what's going on up there?"

"Shit. I just met this nigga yesterday. His name is Tommy. He looks like he workin' with something. I think I can trick a couple of grand outta his ass."

"That's what's up, drain that nigga."

"Oh, I got this! Don't even trip but oh I forgot to tell you—"

"Forgot to tell me what?" Unique interrupted, knowing

something was wrong.

"Aunt Syleena's nurse called. She said that your mom had another setback yesterday."

"What? Why didn't you call and tell me?" Unique yelled, pissed.

"I didn't want to worry you. Plus the nurse said that they had it under control."

"What kind of setback did she have?"

"The nurse said that Syleena had another fit. She said that Syleena was fighting with the orderlies again. This time it got so out of hand that that she sprained her wrist. My bad Nique, I should've called you."

"I knew I should've stayed home." Unique began to beat up on herself.

"Don't even start, Unique. There was nothing you could do anyway."

"How could you say that? She needed me and I wasn't there!" Unique yelled into the phone, really wanting to say, "I needed her and she wasn't there."

"Come on, Nique, you have to let this fantasy that Syleena is going to get better go. I know that this may hurt but Syleena is never going to be the mother that you want her to be."

"Did they say anything else?" Unique asked, ignoring her comment.

"Only that she was asking for you."

"She really asked for me?"

"Yeah, but Nique, don't go getting your hopes up."

"I hear you," Unique mumbled as her bottom lip began to quiver.

"I'm sorry I had to say it like that but it's the truth. I don't want to see you hurt over this any more than you have to."

"It's cool, let me get off this phone. I'ma call you when we

Keisha Ervin

get on the road."

"I know you, Nique, don't be down there stressing over your mom. Try to have some fun."

"I will," Unique lied.

Closing her cell phone shut, Unique tried her best to will back the tears that were forming in her eyes but couldn't. At any moment she felt as if her life were going to spiral out of control. Yes, Kay Kay was right, Syleena was never going to be the mother that Unique and Patience deserved, but she was still their mother. There was no way that she could give up on her.

Unique placed her hands over her eyes and cried uncontrollably. At that moment she didn't care whether Bigg heard or not; then she remembered he left the suite. Crying for herself and her mother, she prayed to God that their life would somehow get better. All of her life Unique prayed that her mother would make a full recovery but as the years continued to pass it became more and more apparent that it was never going to happen. Praying for a miracle, Unique wished that somehow she could regain her life back and start over from scratch. No playing men, no stealing cars, no tricking herself for the highest bidder — if she could she would wish that all away.

On the other side of the door, Bigg sat on the bed smoking a blunt filled with Purple Haze. He was trying his best to calm his nerves. He thought that he was alone in the suite and had no idea that Unique was in the bathroom crying until he began to hear muffled noises. He turned down the television and listened for the sound again. Not hearing anything, he turned the volume back up. *I'm high and tripping*, he told himself. Then suddenly the sound became more apparent. Bigg went over to the door and knocked.

"What?!"

Keisha Ervin

"You a'ight?"

"Yeah!"

"You sure?"

"Damn, what did I just say?"

Thinking that her crying was over him, Bigg apologetically replied, "I'm sorry. I ain't mean to hurt your feelings earlier—"

"Nigga please, this ain't got nothing to do with you! Just leave me alone, OK!" Unique shouted, holding her chest with one hand and wiping her nose with the other one.

"Yo', I was just tryin' to help yo' funky ass! Hurry the fuck up! I got to get in there, too!" Bigg shouted back, banging on the door.

Seeing that the old Unique was back, Bigg shook his head and returned to his spot on the bed. No matter how hard he tried to understand her, Bigg couldn't quite get a grip on who the real Unique was. Was it the tough, hardcore girl from the block or was it the vulnerable, insecure girl that had presented herself over the past two days? Never in his life had Bigg met a girl who was so pretty but acted so mean.

Once Unique pulled herself together she got out of the tub, lotioned up and put on an all-black La Perla chemise. She grabbed her toiletries and opened the door only to find Bigg standing there. Not even acknowledging his presence, she slid past him. Ignoring her, too, Bigg walked into the bathroom and shut the door. Unique lay in bed with the covers pulled up to her head counting down the minutes until Bigg joined her. Even though he annoyed the hell outta her she still liked being in his presence. The way he nurtured and took care of her made Unique feel safe and secure. Twenty minutes later, after showering, he bopped out of the bathroom smelling so fresh and so clean.

Unique pretended to be asleep. As he pulled the covers

back, Bigg gazed over her well-toned back. Immediately his dick began to rise. He wanted to feel the touch of her skin again. Just as he was about to give in to his desires, Unique's words from earlier crept back into his head. *I can't fuck wit' you like that. I'm here to do a job, nothing more nothing less. We're on two different levels.*

Fuck that bitch, Bigg thought to himself. He turned off the light and stared at the wall. He had plenty of hoes back home on his jock. He didn't have time to chase after Unique. Unbeknownst to him, she was on the other side of the bed thinking the very same thing.

5
Stop 'n Go

Saturday, the day of their meeting with the connect, Unique and Bigg tiptoed around the hotel room trying their best to avoid one another. Not a single word had been spoken except for hello, yes, maybe, and no. With just an hour until the meeting started, Unique slipped into her champagne-colored, open-back Luca Luca cocktail dress. On her feet she wore a pair of champagne-colored Alexander McQueen heels and her hair was pulled up into slick ponytail. All though she wasn't one, Unique looked every bit a top model.

Bigg, being the thug he was, opted to wear a black and red LRG jacket, matching T-shirt, jeans and black Prada tennis shoes. His black and red Phillies hat was cocked to the side as usual and the only jewelry he rocked was a pair of five-carat diamond earrings. Catching glimpses of him out of the corner of her eye, Unique couldn't deny that the boy had style.

"You ready to go?"

"Yeah," she replied, grabbing her purse.

The ride over to Jackson's place was a quiet one. Neither of them said a thing. Both Bigg and Unique were too headstrong to admit when they were wrong. After a twenty minute ride they pulled up to Jackson's mansion. The man was doing the damn thing. Trying to be nice, Bigg got out of the car and opened the door for Unique.

"Thank you," she said as she got out of the truck.

"Ay, let me holla at you before we go up in there."

"What is it?"

"When we get in there, let me do all the talkin', OK."

"Why? What you think I can't handle myself?"

"I know more about this kind of stuff than you do. If we were stealing a car I would let you handle it, but we're not."

"Oh, I see, you tryin' to play me?"

"I'm just stating the facts, ma. Stick to stealing cars. I got this."

Before Unique could come back with a snappy remark of her own, one of Jackson's henchmen approached them. Without a word he walked up on Bigg and patted him down. Once he saw that Bigg wasn't packing any heat, he checked Unique.

"Can you open the briefcase please?" the guard asked after seeing that both of them were cool.

"No problem," Bigg replied as he placed the silver briefcase he was carrying on top of the hood. Opening it up, he revealed well over eighty thousand dollars.

"Thank you. Mr. Smith will see you now."

"Come on." Bigg grabbed Unique's arm and began to walk.

"Don't touch me," she hissed, pulling her arm away. Walking in front of him, Unique made sure that she was the first one to speak to Jackson.

"I'm glad you all could make it." Jackson greeted them with a warm smile.

Jackson wasn't at all what Unique expected.

She expected to meet a man dressed in loud colors with

Keisha Ervin

about five or six golds in his mouth. Instead she was greeted by a middle-aged man with sunkissed skin. Jackson was about six feet tall, medium build with sandy brown curly hair. If Unique would have been into older men she would have gotten on him.

"Nice to meet you sir, I'm Unique." She smiled, extending her hand.

"If I'm being forward, forgive me, but Unique you are absolutely breathtaking," Jackson said, taking her hand into his.

Instead of shaking her hand he gently placed Unique's hand up to his mouth and kissed it. Watching while Jackson fawned over Unique, Bigg became jealous. The veins in his neck were thumping overtime.

"And you must be Bigg?"

"Nice to meet you, man." Bigg shook Jackson's hand.

"If you two will follow me, dinner has just been served."

Walking throughout the mansion, Unique admired Jackson's interior design. The walls were a deep chocolate brown. All of the furniture was brown, tan or mahogany. Huge ceiling-to-floor windows adorned the walls. Entering the dining area, Unique was greeted with a long mahogany table. Twelve chairs were strategically placed around it and Jackson's best china was delicately placed on top. Wanting to show a united front, Bigg politely pulled out Unique's chair for her. Still pissed, she glanced up at him and gave him a tight lipped, "Thank you."

"So, how was the drive down?" Jackson asked as the maid poured them all a glass of red wine.

"It was cool. Kinda long, but cool. Unique slept the entire time," Bigg joked.

"A girl has to get her beauty rest." Unique smirked, rolling her eyes at him.

"Would you like a glass of wine, ma'am?" the maid asked Unique, ready to pour.

"Yes. Fill it up, please."

Unique let the warm wine coat her throat. Suddenly the sadness she felt over the past twenty-four hours seemed to melt away.

"Have you done any sight-seeing yet?" Jackson asked, continuing the conversation.

"Yeah, we went over to Canal Place yesterday," Bigg answered.

"Good, good. So, let's get down to business. What we talkin' here Bigg, candy or sneakers?" Jackson was speaking in code.

"I hear your candy is sweet," Bigg rubbed his chin, "but I also hear your sneakers are fly as hell."

"Really, well that's good to know. How many pairs would you like?"

"About ten of them thangs."

Not knowing what the hell they were talking about, Unique became frustrated and irritated.

"Look, I don't mean to be rude or nothing but I went to the mall yesterday. Can we discuss this in layman's terms? My man Cezar wanted us to come down here to set up something with you and frankly I don't have time to beat around the bush. So can we please get to the point?" Unique stated firmly.

Studying her for a second, Jackson didn't reply. He simply looked at Unique as if she had lost her mind. Anger wasn't even the word to describe how mad he was. Jackson had never been so disrespected in his life. Leaning back in his chair, he clasped his hands together, looked at Bigg and said, "Is this your friend?"

"Yo, my bad. I don't know what her problem is."

Keisha Ervin

"Should I assume she has a wire on?"

"Nah man, it ain't even that kind of party," Bigg reasoned, glaring over at Unique.

"I'm gonna leave you two alone," Jackson replied, getting up.

Once they were alone, Bigg grabbed Unique by the neck and yelled, "What the fuck is yo' problem? Have you lost your fuckin' mind? You trying to get us knocked?"

"Nigga, you better get your hands off of me!" She pushed his hand away.

"Nah, fuck that! I should kick yo' inexperienced ass! Look, you might be pretty and all but yo' ass gon' get us killed up in here talkin' that nonsense! You know what? As a matter of fact, get the fuck out! Your ass is through!"

"What the fuck you mean I'm through?"

"Beat it! Take yo' ass back to the car! I got it from here!"

"Go back to the car? Nigga please, like I give a fuck! Get your chips and dip or whatever the fuck you were talkin' about and hurry the fuck up! I don't want to be here no way!"

Feeling embarrassed but trying her best to disguise it, Unique walked out of the room with her head held up high. As she walked back to the car she bypassed Jackson. She smiled at him and said goodbye but he only ignored her. Unique couldn't believe that she had really played herself. Just as she hit the front door she heard Jackson say, "And make sure she stays out."

Willing herself not to cry, Unique hurried to the car.

$ $ $

Over an hour passed by and Bigg still hadn't returned to the car. The entire time Unique sat there alone, she replayed the conversation over and over again in her mind. She thought that coming hard and direct was the way to handle a man like Jackson but evidently she was wrong. Trying to out-do Bigg had almost cost her her life. *How stupid can you be?* she thought as tears fell from her eyes. *Get the fuck out! You trying to get us knocked?* she remembered. *You might be pretty.*

"Damn, he did say I was pretty, didn't he? So, that nigga has been checkin' me," Unique said out loud and smirked. Hearing Bigg's voice she wiped her eyes, hoping he wouldn't notice she had been crying.

"Once again, sorry for the little inconvenience earlier. It was nice meeting you," he apologized once again giving Jackson dap.

Pulling Bigg close, Jackson whispered into his ear, "Call me before you leave. I have something I would like to discuss with you."

"A'ight," Bigg responded, wondering what Jackson could possibly want to discuss. Back in the truck he gave Jackson one more head nod, then peeled off. Turning the volume down on the radio he looked at Unique and shook his head.

"Don't be shaking your head at me," she snapped.

"Look, I don't even feel like arguing wit' you," Bigg shot, getting on to the highway.

"Then don't be lookin' at me like that!"

"See that right there," he said pointing to her mouth, "that's your problem, your fuckin' mouth! You talk too much! I told you before we got in there to let me handle it but nah, you just had to do things your way!"

"Whatever! I don't want to hear that shit." Unique rolled her eyes. "I fucked up, OK!"

"You damn right you fucked up!"

"You know what, fuck you! I ain't gotta apologize to you! You ain't nobody!"

"Whatever, Unique."

"Yeah, whatever Bigg!"

Twenty minutes later Unique and Bigg were still going at it as they entered their hotel suite. Holding her by the arm, Bigg opened the door and yanked her into the room.

"Get yo' ass in here and sit the fuck down!" he ordered, pushing her down onto the bed.

"Oww, nigga that hurt! Don't be grabbing me like that!" Unique snapped, rubbing her arm.

"Don't you know you could've gotten us killed? You could've fucked up the whole deal with that shit you was talkin'!"

"Fuck that deal!"

"Fuck that deal? Bitch is you crazy? Yo', I can't even deal wit' you right now! I can't wait to get back to St. Louis so I can get the fuck away from you!"

"Are you done? 'Cause nigga I can't wait to be away from you, either!" Unique yelled, looking him square in the eyes.

"You know what, just shut the fuck up talkin' to me!" Bigg barked, slamming the bathroom door behind him.

$ $ $

By the time Bigg made it out of the bathroom, Unique was knocked out asleep on the foot of the bed. Securing the soft cotton towel around his waist, he walked over to her. It never failed. No matter how mad she made him he could never stay mad at her for long. Lightly touching her face, Bigg brushed her hair to the side, revealing Unique's pretty slanted eyes. He then gently took the remote from her hand and pulled the covers back. Letting his towel fall from his waist, Bigg lifted Unique's limp body up. As if on cue she wrapped her arms around his neck. After he laid her down, Bigg grabbed her hands so he could release her grip only for Unique to hold on even tighter.

"Don't leave me," she whispered in her sleep.

"I won't," he said seriously.

Bigg didn't know what it was about her but from the first moment he laid eyes on Unique, he was hooked. Even though she played tough, he knew that a softer side lurked deep inside. Since she wouldn't let go of his neck, Bigg slid his way into bed, lying down next to her. Now face to face, he gazed at her.

To him she was gorgeous. Focusing his eyes elsewhere, he rested them upon her full breasts and slim waist. Instantly his dick began to rise. Bigg couldn't take it anymore. His body was telling him he had to have her. Even though she was still in a deep sleep, Unique's body naturally responded to Bigg's advances. She touched him back while scooting closer. Once she was where she wanted to be, Unique rested her head directly in front of his.

Bigg held her tight and kissed her forehead. Making his way down he then kissed her eyes, nose, cheeks and chin, all before kissing her lips. He then brought her face to his. Slowly he kissed her mouth. Coming out of her sleep, Unique wrapped her left leg around his while moaning his name.

"Bigg," she whispered softly, barely able to speak.

"Yes baby?" he said in between licking and sucking her lips.

"I'm sorry."

"I know."

"Bigg?"

"Yes."

"Make love to me."

"Are you sure? 'Cause once we go there ain't no turning back."

"I know." She gazed sleepily into his eyes.

Fully awake, Unique knew exactly what she was saying. She was tired of the wham-bam thank you ma'am sex she had been having since she was 17. Unique wanted to feel what it felt like to be loved and wanted. Looking into her big brown eyes, Bigg placed his warm body onto hers while parting her legs with his. Her face was in his hands as he kissed her passionately. Bigg couldn't get enough of Unique's lips. They were soft and moist — just how he liked them. After kissing her lips he feasted on her tongue for a while then sucked on her bottom lip.

Running his hands down her thighs, Bigg pushed her dress up. At that moment there was no other place in the world that he would rather be than between her knees, kissing her lips and caressing her body. Desperately wanting to feel him inside of her, Unique wrapped her legs around Bigg's back, pulling him in closer. He then took off her dress, unsnapped her bra and threw it across the room.

As he kissed her neck the burning desire to explore her honey-colored breasts took over him. Taking one into his hand while massaging the other, Bigg wrapped his lips around Unique's hardening nipple. Excited, he circled his tongue around each one as she bit into her lower lip. Once he had her where he wanted her, Bigg made his way down.

He found her inner being and swiftly inserted one of his fingers inside of her warm, wet slit. One finger, two fingers, three fingers, four. Shamelessly, Unique rotated her hips to the rhythm of Bigg's finger strokes. Before she knew it his mouth was exploring her clitoris. Unique arched her back and held onto Bigg's head as it shifted from side to side. Driving his tongue in and out of her pussy, he caused her to cum immediately.

"Bigg!" she cried.

"What? Ain't no turning back now," he mumbled into the lips of her pussy.

"I don't want to turn back!" She squealed in sheer agony. "I want you to fuck me!"

Bigg locked eyes with Unique while holding both of her thighs. For a second she wondered if she was making the right decision. Bigg wasn't just any nigga. Unlike most dudes, he kept her on her feet. Being with him caused her to ponder life and the decisions she had made thus far. Up until then, love didn't mean a thing to her. It wasn't even in her vocabulary but now Bigg had her questioning love and everything it stood for.

He had her actually pondering loving him, which was a first for Unique. The only thing she loved was her family, the finer things in life and money. Interrupting her thoughts, Bigg inserted his rock hard dick inside of her tight, warm walls. Shocked but pleased, Unique tilted her head back. Her eyes rolled into the back of her head as she begged for more. The feeling of pleasure and pain took her mind and body to new heights of ecstasy.

As he rocked deep and slow inside her treasure chest of love, Unique tantalized his neck with her tongue. The taste of his skin on her lips could only be defined as heavenly. Pushing her legs back, Bigg began thrusting his dick in and out of her at a feverish pace. He had slept with a lot of chicks in his day but none could compare to Unique.

Her pussy was one-of-a-kind. Turning over onto his back, Bigg let Unique get on top. She slid up and down his long rod until her entire body began to shiver. Jolts of electric currents ripped throughout her stomach and pelvic area. Tenderly he pinched her nipples causing her to moan even more. Drenched in sweat, Unique continued to ride Bigg until she felt his body stiffen. It was time; he was reaching his peak.

"Fuck ma, I'm cumming!" he yelled, trying his damnest not to scream.

"Ooh … Bigg … you feel so good!" she cried.

Bigg held onto her waist tightly as juices dripped from her valley. Unique's body began to convulse. Cumming too, she took Bigg's finger into her mouth and sucked. She came all over his still rock-hard dick. Pulling her back down onto his chest, Bigg brushed her hair from her face and said, "Ain't no turning back now, ma. You're mine."

What Goes Up Must Come Down

A couple of days passed since the Louisiana trip and Unique and Bigg had been inseparable ever since. Every minute and hour of each day that passed was spent together. Bigg couldn't get enough of Unique. She was the chick that he had been searching for his entire life. Unique still wasn't quite sure, though.

Her guard was up and naturally it bothered Bigg, but trust didn't come easily for Unique. She wasn't totally sure about him yet. Even though they were an official couple, Unique still hadn't ended things with Tone. They hadn't really talked since she came back home, but he still wanted things to work out between them.

Bigg, on the other hand, trusted her, so one night on his way over to her house he decided to be truthful about a few things. After a ten minute drive he was there. Dressed simply in a Jamaican-colored Triple Five Soul jacket, Polo shirt, baggy Cavalli jeans and shell-toe Adidas, Bigg knocked on the door. Not wanting to seem pressed, Unique slowly answered the door.

"Come here," he said, wrapping her up in his arms as soon as he saw her.

Unique wanted to play hard to get but she loved spending time with him. He lit up her day every time she saw him. Without hesitation he took her into his arms and kissed her lips passionately. Barely able to breathe, Unique kicked the door closed. Kissing him back with just as much intensity, she held his face and led him over to the couch. Bigg took a seat with her still positioned on top of him. They went at each other like two wild animals. After ten minutes of nothing but kissing, Unique finally came up for air and let his lips loose. After staring at each other for a minute they broke out laughing.

"Damn, I've been wanting to do that all day," he said, still eyeing her swollen lips.

"I know, me too." She grinned.

"How was your day?"

"It was cool," Unique answered while skimming over his body with her eyes. Bigg's look alone could make any heterosexual woman want to cum on herself. Helping him out of his jacket, Unique continued to place small kisses all over his face.

"What you got to eat up in this muthafucka?" he asked, lifting her up and carrying her into the kitchen.

"You high, ain't you?"

"You can't tell," he laughed.

"Niggas. And I don't mean that a good way." Unique laughed, too. She warmed them both up a plate of pork chops, mashed potatoes and corn that was left over in the refrigerator. Once the table was set they sat down and ate.

Bigg took a bite of the food and said, "You fine and you can cook. I'm really gon' have to wife you now." It was his first time eating Unique's cooking.

"Whatever," she replied, not able to hide her smile. "But Bigg, with all seriousness, doesn't it scare you that things are moving so fast between us?"

"Nah, not really. Ever since I put my hand on yo' thigh I knew you didn't want to get rid of me," he chuckled, taking another bite of food.

"An-y-way, I do. I ain't never clicked this well with a guy."

"That's because the nigga wasn't me."

"Whatever." She rolled her eyes. "I never asked, do you have any kids?"

"Yeah, I got a lil' boy."

"How old is he?"

"He's 3."

"Hold up. How can you have a 3-year-old son and you were locked up for seven years?"

"Come on Unique, don't play dumb."

"Eww, you are so nasty." She playfully hit him in the chest. "You was doing it like that in jail? Who is the chick? It better not be anybody I know."

"Nah, you don't her. Her name is Carmella."

"Why aren't you still together?"

"Shit just didn't work out but, ah, I gotta go take a piss. I'll be right back."

"A'ight lil' nasty." She laughed. As Unique continued to eat she heard the sound of Bigg's cell phone ring. His phone was in his jacket pocket so she went through his pocket to retrieve it. As she searched for the phone she ran across a bottle of prescription pills. *Depakote? My mother used to take this, didn't she*, she thought.

"Baby, let's run up to Blockbuster. I want to rent some movies," Bigg said, reentering the kitchen. Caught off guard,

Unique jumped, dropping the bottle of medicine on the floor. "What you doing?" he asked, eyeing her suspiciously.

"Nothing."

Not believing her, Bigg walked closer. Spotting the pill bottle he shouted, "What the fuck you going through my shit for?!"

"Nah, nigga, don't try to turn this around on me. The real question is why you lie to me?"

"What you talkin' about? I ain't lie to you."

"Yes you did! My mother took Depakote. I know what that shit is for! Don't tell me you're crazy, too!"

"I suffer from manic depression, Unique."

"Excuse me? Say that again?"

"I was gon' tell you—"

"Ah uh," Unique cut him off. "I'm not going through this shit wit' you, Bigg! It's bad enough I had to deal with my momma, now you?! I did everything for her! Fed her, bathed her, and guess what, she left me! I can't risk you leaving me, too! How the fuck could you do this to me?!"

"Do what to you? I was gon' to tell you!"

"Let me fall for you and tell me when?"

"When the time was right."

"When the time was right?! Nigga the time wasn't gon' ever be right! I told you everything! I was totally honest with you! You knew about my mother and how fucked up my childhood was! I told you how that shit nearly killed me when my mother left us for good! I can't afford to lose you like I lost her! "

"I promise I ain't going nowhere, I'm gon' hold you down. I ain't never gonna leave you."

"Yeah, OK, and I guess I'm boo boo the fool," Unique sniffled, rolling her eyes.

"Calm down, shorty. I ain't going nowhere." Bigg gently

Keisha Ervin

took her hand, easing her onto his lap. "I told you, you mine now. I got mad feelings for you, girl. I ain't going nowhere. Besides, it ain't even like that. I ain't had an episode in a while."

"What the fuck is an episode?"

"See, you think that being manic depressive is the same as being schizophrenic, but it isn't."

"Well what is it then?"

"Manic depression is an illness that affects changes in your mood, thought and behavior. When I have an episode, that means that my creatine levels are at an all time high. I'm not stable when I get like that. Sometimes it can last for hours, sometimes weeks. But as long as I take my medication I'm cool. But I'ma be honest wit' you. I don't like taking that shit."

"Why?"

"'Cause it makes me feel like I'm dependent on a drug or something. I mean, you know what I do. I see these fiends out here and how they can't go a day without getting a hit. That's how I am. If I don't take my medication my ass will straight go seven thirty on yo' ass."

"Don't lie to me, Bigg. You swear you're taking your medication?"

"Yeah, I swear." He placed his right hand up to God. "Look, I'ma be real wit' you, Unique. I had a fucked up childhood. My ole' bird used to beat the hell out of me and my ole' dude used to sit back and let her. My moms was manic depressive, too. Every time her ass would flip and have an episode and beat the dog shit outta me, my pop would tell me that she didn't mean to hurt me, and that it was her illness that made her do it. I hated my mother for that shit. That bitch used to tell me I wasn't shit and that I wouldn't amount to nothing. She told me she wished I was dead."

"For real?"

"Yeah. She died though while I was locked up. Me and my ole' dude still speak from time to time."

"At least you know who your father is," Unique said, staring off into space.

"It's cool, ma."

"No, it's not because I know how that shit feels to have your mother not give a fuck about you and for your daddy to not be there for you. But it's cool. I got you. I don't even wanna talk about it anymore. What's your son's name?" Unique asked, trying to forget the thought of her own mother.

"Dontay."

"Ahh, that's cute. I bet he looks just like you." She smiled, easing up a bit.

"Yeah, that's my lil' man," Bigg said, rubbing his stomach. "A nigga full as fuck." Reaching out and grabbing her by the waist, he pulled her close. "Empty my plate for me, would you? I'm ready to go to bed."

"Do I look like my name is Moms Mabley? And I didn't say that you could spend the night."

"You don't want me to spend the night?" he asked, staring intensely into her eyes.

"I don't make it a habit of allowing strange men into my house, let alone my bed," she joked.

"First of all, I'm not a strange man. I'm yo' nigga so get it right. And from now on your door will always be open to me."

Looking at him like he was crazy, Unique rolled her eyes, got up from the table and emptied her plate. As she walked past him she turned off the light, went into her bedroom and climbed back into bed, leaving Bigg sitting alone in the dark. Laughing at her strong will, he followed her into the bedroom. Bigg kicked off his shoes and climbed into bed with her. Not able to lay next to him and not touch him, Unique turned over, placed her head on his chest and fell asleep to the sound of his heartbeat.

$ $ $

As time continued to fly by, Unique and Bigg grew closer and closer. Nothing could break their bond. Their connection and commitment to one another grew stronger and stronger every day. Bigg's playa days were over. He was finally at a point in his life where he was ready to put his pimp cup down. No other chick could compare to Unique. She was the total package — beautiful, smart and confident.

Unique was the kind of chick that he wanted to stay in the house for. At night he wanted to rub her back and massage her feet. There would be no more kickin' it in the club until the wee hours of the morning. Bigg wanted to be with Unique; only she could satisfy his every need. She even made him think about attending church — that's how much he dug her. The only woman he wanted, or needed, was Unique and after four months of being together, he decided to tell her just how much she meant to him.

The setting was perfect. They would enjoy a nice night on the town together. Bigg wanted to give Unique flowers so he went to a florist to find the prettiest flowers he could find. He ended up choosing white roses because the florist told him that they meant humility, innocence and purity. The flowers fit Unique perfectly because even though she played hard, she possessed a lot of childlike qualities.

Bigg showed up to Unique's place at exactly 7 o'clock on the dot. As he knocked on the door he held the dozen white roses in hand. Unique couldn't believe her eyes when she opened the door to find Bigg standing there with flowers. She had received plenty of roses from guys before but never white

Keisha Ervin

roses.

"Thank you, baby," she gushed.

"You're welcome." He smiled as he handed them to her. After she put the flowers into a vase filled with water, the two headed out hand in hand.

"So where are we going?"

"It's a surprise," Bigg explained.

And he didn't lie either. A surprise is exactly what Unique got. First they attended a concert at the Fox Theater. Alicia Keys was performing. Bigg had the hook up so they had front row tickets. Alicia Keys sang her heart out that night. She went through a playlist of her old and new songs. Just as she was about to perform her hit song *"If I Ain't Got You,"* Unique got the surprise of her life.

"I want to dedicate this next song to my boy Bigg and his girl Unique," Alicia announced to the crowd before singing.

Unique couldn't believe it. She was in absolute heaven. The night couldn't get any better. After the concert, they had a lovely dinner at the Steak House. The meal was extraordinary. By the time dessert came, Unique couldn't eat another bite. Since they weren't yet ready to go home, Bigg suggested that they take a walk on the Riverfront.

He couldn't have picked a better night to tell Unique that he loved her. The midnight sky was filled with stars and the moon was in full bloom. Unique and Bigg had a perfect view of the Mississippi River. They stood along the shore gazing at the water and different casino boats as they floated along the waterfront. With his arms wrapped around Unique, Bigg softly whispered into her ears the words, "I love you."

You would have thought that Unique would've answered back with an "I love you" as well, but she didn't. To admit that she loved Bigg was a big thing for her and Unique wasn't sure if she was ready to do that just yet. Admitting to Bigg that she

Keisha Ervin

loved him would be letting her guard down and Unique knew that once she did this, she would be opening herself up to heartbreak. *Love is forbidden* is what she continued to tell herself. *You cannot love him. I know you don't want to end up like your mother*, is what her inner voice kept on saying.

"Unique, did you hear me?"

"I heard you," she turned around and replied. Face to face they gazed into each other's eyes. Once Unique took a glimpse into Bigg's light brown eyes she knew she couldn't deny him. No matter how much she tried to tell herself that she didn't love him, she did. "I love you too, Bigg," Unique whispered back, feeling like she was losing a piece of herself in the process.

As if he could read her mind Big assured, "I promise I'm not gon' let you down."

Unable to speak, Unique allowed her heart to open up to the thought of being loved by someone. She tried her best to blink back the tears that had formed but it was no use. She couldn't contain her feelings. Tears streamed down her face at lightening speed. Gently, Bigg took her face into his hands and kissed her lips. There on the Riverfront with the stars twinkling up above, Unique gave her heart and soul to Bigg and promised that from that day on, she would love him forever.

$ $ $

Fast forward two weeks — Unique and Bigg weren't even speaking. Her biggest fear had come to fruition. One night while she and Bigg were asleep in bed, his cell phone rang, so Unique, being the chick she was, answered it.

"Hello?" she spoke in a raspy tone.

"Speak to Bigg."

Keisha Ervin

"Who is this?" she asked, fully awakened by the female voice.

"Brittany, who is this?" the girl shot back.

"This is his girlfriend, Unique."

"Unique? Bigg ain't tell me he had a girlfriend!"

"Well, bitch, I'm tellin' you! Don't call this phone no more!"

"You mean to tell me you not gon' let me speak to Bigg?"

"What part of the break down don't you understand? Are you dumb or something? Bigg is my man!"

"If Bigg was so much your man I wouldn't be calling him. So instead of yellin' at me you need to check your man!" Brittany spat.

"You know what, you about right," Unique snapped, hanging up the phone. With a smack upside the head Unique woke Bigg.

"What the fuck is yo' problem?" He jumped, turning over.

"Who the fuck is Brittany?!"

"You lost your muthafuckin' mind? Don't put yo' hands on me no more, Unique!"

"Nigga, fuck you! Like I said, who is Brittany?"

"Go head wit' that, man. Just let that shit go. She was a jump off. Don't even trip."

"You know what Bigg, I ain't got time to be playin' wit' you! How can I trust you when you got hoes calling yo' phone and shit!" Unique shot, putting on her clothes and preparing to leave.

"Ahh, here we go. What the fuck you want me to say, Unique? That we used to fuck around? OK, I used to fuck her, are you happy now?"

"Whatever Bigg, I don't even care."

"Where you going?"

"I'm going home! I ain't got time for this shit! I'm through fuckin' wit' you!"

"Ma, ma, ma, calm down."

"Fuck you, nah, I'm not calming down!"

"So, you not gon' even listen to your man? It ain't even what you think," Bigg said truthfully.

"My man? Nigga, you ain't my man! My man wouldn't have other chicks calling his phone all times of the night!"

"You know what? You actin' real silly right now!" Bigg snatched the covers from off of his body and got out the bed.

"I can't believe I trusted you! I knew this shit was gon' happen!"

"Oh, so now you don't trust me?"

"What you think?" Unique rolled her neck and folded her arms across her chest.

"Humph, it's all good." Bigg shook his head, rubbing his chin.

"What is that supposed to mean?"

"Look, ma, I ain't gon' argue wit' you. If you don't trust me then maybe we shouldn't be together."

"How you gon' break up with me? You the one got hoes calling your phone, not me!"

"What are we even arguing for? You gon' think what you want to think anyway." Bigg got quiet for a second. "You don't trust me?"

"No!"

"Then step!"

"You're telling me to step?" Unique repeated in disbelief.

"I ain't for repeating myself! Get the fuck out! You should-n't have answered my muthafuckin' phone in the first place!"

"You know what Bigg, fuck you!" Unique yelled, slamming his front door behind her.

She couldn't believe that Bigg was actually trying to play her but it was all good because Unique wasn't gonna let any man bring her down. She hadn't seen nor heard from Bigg since their argument so instead of trippin' off of him, she got on the grind. Heartache wasn't gonna come between Unique and her paper. At least that's what she tried telling herself.

On the real, Unique knew she was wrong for reacting the way she did. Her biggest fear in the world was that if she fully gave Bigg her heart that he would end up hurting or leaving her. Unique just couldn't afford for that to happen. She wasn't about to sit around and wait for heartache.

It was Saturday afternoon and she had just returned home from yet another job out of state. In a mad rush to check her voicemail, she left her bags by the door. After putting her pin number in, Unique learned that she had no new messages. Hurt that Bigg hadn't called, she slammed the phone down. Needing to hear his voice she picked up the phone again but her pride wouldn't allow her to dial a single digit so she hung the phone back up.

"Unique?"

"Yeah. Did Bigg call me while I was gone?"

"Nope!" Patience replied, coming down the steps, eating an apple.

"Did my package get here?"

"Yep, it arrived this morning. Everything's there. I put it in the safe like you asked."

"Cool, you want to go to the mall? I don't feel like sitting in the house all day."

"Yeah."

"A'ight, get dressed then." Quickly, Unique and Patience jumped into the shower, lotioned up and dressed.

On the upper level of Nordstrom where all the major designer clothes were located, Unique held a pair of L.A.M.B. capris in hand when her cell began to chirp.

"What up?"

"Girl, where you at? I just tried calling your house," Zoë talked into the phone, popping gum in her ear.

"At the mall," Unique said, switching the tag on the pants from two hundred and fifty dollars to forty.

"Why you ain't call me? I would've went wit' you."

"My bad, I'm wit' Patience though. I needed to spend some time with her since I ain't seen her in a couple of days."

"That's cool but uhmm, I was calling to tell you that yo' boo's group is performing down at Toxic tonight." Just the mention of Bigg caused Unique's heart to go *pitter patter*.

"Oh, for real." She tried to sound unfazed.

"You ain't gotta front. I know you wanna go."

"Girl, please. I ain't fuckin' wit' Bigg right now. I might pop his ass if I see him."

"Whatever, Unique. You know Bigg got you wrapped around his finger."

"Never that, sweetheart."

"Nique, you ain't got to front with me. I know you feeling Bigg and that's cool. Ya'll make a good couple."

"You mean that?"

"Yeah. Everybody can see that ya'll love each other. Ain't no need trying to hide it."

"You know how it is though, Zoë. I can't really be with Bigg until I cut some things loose." Unique hinted to what they did for a living.

"I feel you, but if you really love him then you got to do you before another bitch come and take your place."

"Girl please. Bigg ain't crazy — he know I'll kill his ass."

"So, are you going?"

"Yeah, I'ma go."

"A'ight then, I'll be at yo' house around 11."

"One."

With a huge smile spread across her face, Unique

approached the cash register and purchased herself and Patience six pairs of BCBG heels. She also bought the L.A.M.B. capris. Calling her beautician, Miesha, she made an impromptu appointment to get her hair flat-ironed. By the time she finished getting her hair done and her nails filled in, it was dark out.

After dropping Patience off at her best friend Chantell's house, she rushed home, showered, applied her makeup and then stood in front of her walk-in closet. Unique hadn't seen Bigg in over a week so she grabbed one of her come-fuck-me dresses and put it on. Standing in front of her full-length, three-way mirror, she eyed her physique from every angle. Hearing Zoë outside blowing, Unique gave herself the stamp of approval and walked outside to meet her girl.

"You trying to hurt somebody tonight, ain't you?" Zoë teased as Unique got into the car.

"Nah," Unique replied, playing it off.

"Yeah right, you're trying to make sure that Bigg notice that ass."

"Oh, he gon' notice me a'ight. I'm gon' make sure of that."

As Unique and Zoë approached the door of the club, they were greeted by a slew of people they knew. After saying, "What's up," to a couple of people, they both headed inside. Zoë headed for the bar to get a drink while Unique searched for Bigg. It was hard to spot him because of the neon lights but she quickly noticed Cezar, NaSheed and Bigg's other partna, Chris. NaSheed and Chris were a part of Bigg's rap group called St. Louis' Finest.

As soon as his cash flow picked back up, Bigg reopened his entertainment company, Bigg Entertainment. Chris and NaSheed's first single *"Money & Hoes"* was already in heavy rotation on every radio station across the United States. They also pumped D for Bigg on the side. They were his number one workers and closet friends.

Bigg and his boys were well on their way and Unique felt threatened by this. In a short amount of time, Bigg had made his way back on top. Shortly after they returned home from Louisiana, Bigg quit working for Cezar and set up his own thing. Jackson was Bigg's connect. With Jackson as his connect, Bigg had no other choice but to do the damn thing. His top two recruits were, of course, Chris and NaSheed. Besides Cezar, he trusted them the most. Money was pouring in left and right.

Financially stable, Bigg made it clear that he wanted Unique to quit stealing. The man was willing to take care of her and give her whatever she wanted but Unique could never see herself living off of a man.

Spotting him in the back of the club by the bar, she stopped dead in her tracks. There he was, leaning against the bar with some chick that Unique didn't recognize.

The girl had her arms wrapped around his neck and was whispering something into his ear. Unique couldn't believe what her eyes were seeing. Even though Bigg wasn't touching the girl back, she was still pissed. Her whole point of coming to the club that night was to apologize for the fight they had. Pulling her shoulders back, Unique held her head up high and took her place right beside her man.

"Come on Bigg, I miss you," the girl whined, biting down on his ear.

"Ah, uhmm!" Unique coughed, clearing her throat.

"Unique, baby, what you doing here?" Bigg asked as he pried the girl's hands from around his neck.

"Uh ah." She placed her hand in front of his face. "That's not important right now. Who is this?"

"Hi, I'm Brittany." The girl spoke in a perky voice with her hand stuck out for a handshake.

Keisha Ervin

"Excuse me?"

"What? Is there a problem? Bigg, who is this?" Brittany eyed Unique up and down.

"Oh, so you're the lil' chick that I talk to over the phone?" Unique said, piecing everything together. *Whap*!!! Unique slapped Bigg dead in the face. "So you lied to me?! You *have* been fuckin' wit' her!"

"Yo', chill! What the fuck is your problem?! You on some ole crazy shit!" Bigg yelled, grabbing Unique by the neck and trying to block her next hit.

"Nah, nigga let me go!"

"Kill all that noise, ma. It ain't even what you think."

"It ain't what I think?! You got this bitch, the same bitch that we argued about, hanging all over you but it ain't what I think?! Let another nigga even look my way and you go crazy!" Unique yelled, swinging her arms wildly and trying her damnest to hit Bigg again.

"Who you calling a bitch?" Brittany snapped, getting into Unique's face.

"You! Do you see anybody else standing here? As a matter of fact, both of ya'll some bitches!" Unique swung her fist, hitting Brittany in the mouth and causing it to bleed immediately.

"Oh no you didn't just put your hands on me!" Brittany snapped, grabbing an empty beer bottle.

"Yo', you better fall the fuck back," Bigg warned, taking the bottle out of her hand.

"Fall back? Nigga please, your hands were just all over my ass so don't even try it!"

"Bitch please. I wasn't touching you. I told you I had a wife when you walked yo' retarded ass over here! Don't get it twisted, ma, you wasn't nothing but a jump off, a one night stand. That's it."

Keisha Ervin

"Why is you lying, Bigg? You know you told me you love me. I was your wife, not her."

"Yo' Bigg, what the fuck is going on, man? You know we can't have no fighting in the club," one of the bouncers said.

"My bad dog, I got this."

"A'ight man, check yo' girl."

"Answer me, Bigg. Why is you lying? You know you said you wanted me to be your girl," Brittany continued.

"Bitch, what the fuck don't you understand? I don't want you!"

"You know what, Bigg, this is really amusing but I am so not beat." Unique laughed. "If you wanna be with the bitch, be with the bitch."

"Yo', shut the fuck up and quit talkin' out the side of your neck," Bigg ordered, grabbing Unique by the arm and walking away.

"So it's like that, Bigg? You just gon' leave me for her?! Nigga fuck you!" Brittany continued.

"Yeah, yeah, whatever. You couldn't suck dick anyway," Bigg shot over his shoulder.

"Your lil' girlfriend looks like she's mad. You better go talk to her," Unique said sarcastically, but really on the inside she was hurting like hell. Ignoring her, Bigg flagged down the bartender.

"Ay, let me get a Hennessy and Coke. You want anything?" he asked Unique.

"Yeah, an apple martini."

The bartender had their drinks ready in a matter of seconds. Handing Unique her drink, Bigg tried to gaze into her eyes to see what she was thinking, but Unique wouldn't even look his way. The man was stuck. Bigg didn't know what to say or do.

"Are you ready to listen to what I gotta say now?"

"No. I don't even care anymore." Unique turned her back

to him and took a sip of her drink.

"Why you bullshittin'? Me and her was just talkin'. It wasn't even nothing. I ain't even been fuckin' wit' that girl. As a matter of fact, I haven't talked to her since I went to Louisiana wit' you and you know how long ago that shit was. I don't know why she called me that night. You know I love you."

"What's love got to do with it?" Unique shot, trying to sound sarcastic.

"Oh, so, now we on some ole Ike and Tina shit?" Bigg joked, trying his damnest to make her laugh but she wouldn't. Unique gave him a look of pure disdain. "Come on, ma, don't look at me like that."

"I ain't got nothing to say to you, Bigg. I actually came here to apologize to you and then I see that shit. I can't trust you so I'm through fuckin' wit' you."

"Stop lying. You don't mean that." Bigg hoped and prayed to God that she didn't.

"Just leave me alone. I don't want to talk to you." She placed her hand on his chest trying to push him away. Unique was undeniably hurt. Bigg played it cool on the outside but it felt like a piece of him was dying on the inside. If Unique left him for real he didn't know what he would do. To make matter worse, Tone was making his way through the club to speak to her.

"What's up, ma?" he asked, sweeping Unique off the floor and giving her a big bear hug.

"Hey Tone. What's up?" Unique's voice cracked. She didn't know what to do. On one side of her stood Bigg, the man she loved, and in front of her stood her drunk ex-boyfriend that she was still stringing along.

"Damn, a nigga ain't seen you in a minute."

"But like I was saying, we need to go home and talk about this." Bigg continued to talk as if Tone wasn't there. Fading him out, Unique didn't reply.

"How you been?" she asked.

"Fuck how I been. How you been? Lookin' all good and shit."

"On the grind. Trying to stay focused and in good health."

"I feel you. You healthy a'ight, that ass ain't changed a bit." Tone spun her around so he could get a good view of her butt.

"Yo', who is this nigga?" Bigg questioned, pissed.

"Bigg this Tone, Tone this is Bigg." Not expecting it to be Tone, Bigg stood silent for a second. He was finally face to face with the man who had Unique's heart before he did.

"What's up man?" Tone put his hand out for a handshake. Instead of speaking, Bigg gave him a funny look and a pound.

"Ay, Bigg, let me holla at you for a minute," Cezar called out.

"I'll be right back." Bigg tried kissing Unique on the mouth but instead she played him and turned her face. "Yo', don't make me fuck you up."

"Whatever." Unique rolled her eyes.

"I got to tell you, ma, you lookin' good tonight. You making a nigga want to take you home and do some thangs," Tone continued.

"Come on Tone, cut it out."

"I'm for real. A nigga been missing you like crazy."

"Is that right?" She smirked.

Bigg was only a few feet away from Unique as he held a conversation with Cezar. While talking he kept his eyes on her at all times. He could tell that something was up with Tone. Never before in his life had one person given off so many bad vibes. Checking his waist, he made sure that his burner was on him.

"I know you miss a nigga, too," Tone said, caressing Unique's cheek.

Keisha Ervin

"Tone, please. It was nice seeing you again but I gotta go."

"Let me just talk to you." He grabbed her arm.

"What is it? I said I gotta go."

"I'm sorry."

"Sorry for what?"

"You were right. I was cheating on you but I swear to God I was just fuckin' them girls. I was gon' get right back."

"That was then. It doesn't even matter now."

Unique didn't know it but Bigg was standing right behind her. "Come on, I'm ready to go," he said, interrupting their conversation.

"What the fuck is the deal? Who is this nigga? Is this your man or something?" Tone asked, agitated by Bigg's presence.

Unique took one look at Bigg and said, "Nah, he ain't my man and neither are you so why are you questioning me?"

"What the fuck you just say?" Bigg's questioned, about ready to slap the shit outta Unique.

"Did I stutter, muthafucka?"

Snatching her up by the arm, Bigg dragged Unique out the club and yelled, "Do you want me to beat yo' ass up in this muthafucka? 'Cause I will! I'm about two seconds away from slapping the shit outta you!"

"Haven't I told you about grabbing on me?"

"And haven't I told you about your mu-tha-fuck-in' mouth! Learn how to close that muthafucka sometime!"

"If you was on your job maybe I wouldn't have to bitch and complain!"

"I swear yous the most ignorant bitch I've ever met in my life. You make a nigga want to cheat on you with some of the nonsense you be talkin'."

"Nigga, you ain't got to be with me and call me another bitch if you want to!"

"You know what, I'm tired of arguing wit' you. Get the

fuck out my face," Bigg shot, pushing her away with force and almost causing her to fall.

"So that's it? You don't want to talk any more?" Unique questioned, hurt and turned on all at the same time.

"Don't play stupid wit' me, ma! I'm tired of talkin' to you! You hard headed! Got me at the club arguing wit' you over some dumb shit! I ain't got time for that! Take yo' silly ass home!"

"Ain't nobody playin' wit' you, Bigg! You're the one that started all this shit to begin with! Now you wanna get mad?"

"Like I said, I ain't for the arguing."

"Fuck you then, it's over!" Unique spat, walking away.

"What the fuck is going on?" Zoë questioned, running out the club to see what happened.

"Nothing, man."

"What did you do to her?"

"I ain't do nothing."

"Yeah, right. I saw you wit' that skank bitch Brittany. Bigg, you playing yourself if you gon' try to throw another chick up in Unique's face. At least let the chick be some competition. Now go after her. You know how dramatic she is."

"I am, but after I have one more shot of Hen."

7
Just Me & U

"Yo' Unique, open up!" Bigg yelled through the door.

"What the fuck do you want?!" she yelled back.

"Just let me in so I can talk to you!"

"Nigga, I ain't got shit for you! Go holla at that bitch you was talkin' to at the club!"

"Man, I told you we was just talkin'! You was talkin' to another nigga, too!"

"So!"

"Open the door!" Bigg yelled, pounding his fist up against the door.

"You better stop banging on my door before I call the police!"

"You better open this goddamn door before I kick this muthafucka down!"

"Bigg, yo' scary ass ain't gon' do shit!"

"What?!" He banged again with even more force.

Taking the chain off of the door, Unique swung the door open to Bigg's surprise. Immediately his dick began to rise once he saw what Unique had on. She wore nothing but a

Hello Kitty tank top and a pair of lace boy shorts. Her under-wear was so tight that it crept up her voluptuous ass whenever she walked. Holding his dick, Bigg knew right then and there that he would say whatever he needed to say so he could see her ass slap against his thighs that night.

"Now what the fuck do you want?!"

"Don't play wit' me, Unique," he spoke calmly.

"Don't play wit' you! Nah, nigga, don't you play with me! You the one trying to play me crazy! That was Brittany, the same Brittany that called yo' phone last week!"

"Baby, why would I be in another bitch's face when I knew you would be up in the club?"

"Quit lying. You ain't know I was gonna be back today."

Bigg grabbed her waist and continued to plead his case. "I'm gon' be honest wit' you. I used to fuck wit' Brittany before I got wit' you. Once you and I got together I swear to God I broke things off with her."

"If that's the case why was she all over you at the club and why is she still calling your phone?"

"I don't know why she called my phone that night. I haven't talked to that girl in months but after you left like that I was pissed. There I was being faithful to you and the first time some shit pops off, you up and say it's over."

"What else was I supposed to do?"

"You were supposed to listen to your man. Now, what's up wit' you and ole boy?"

"Nothing. I've been stop fuckin' wit' Tone," she lied.

"You better not be lying to me," Bigg warned.

"I'm not."

"You still my baby?"

"Get the fuck off of me, Bigg. I ain't forgot you called me a bitch," Unique protested, trying to sound convincing but the sight of him was turning her on to the fullest. His red STL

Keisha Ervin

baseball hat rested on his head tilted to the right. An oversized red and black BAPE T-Shirt rested on his chest. Baggy shorts hung low off his waist and a pair of red and white Air Force Ones were on his feet. Last but least, an iced out platinum chain brought out the thug in him that she loved.

"You called me a bitch, too." He laughed.

"Shut up. Ain't nothing funny."

"I'm sorry but you pissed me off with that shit you was talkin'."

"Yeah, OK, whatever. I thought ya'll had a show tonight anyway?"

"We did but the money wasn't right so I told ole boy to come and holla at me when they had their shit together."

"Whatever, Bigg, you're probably lying." Unique waved him off.

"Look I'm done! The shit is played! I don't want to talk about it no more! Where baby sis at?" he asked as he let her go.

Looking at him like he was crazy, Unique rolled her eyes. She knew she was pushing it but if Unique didn't put her foot down now she knew that little stuff like this would continue to pop up. Walking over to the refrigerator, Bigg took out a Heineken. He needed something to quench his thirst. Once the door was locked, Unique followed him into the kitchen.

"Just because you're done talkin' about it doesn't mean that I am. And she's over Chantell's house, if you just have to know."

"I don't want her hanging around that fast-ass girl. You know she tried to holla at Chris once."

"Don't be trying to change the subject, nigga."

"What more is there to say, Unique? We had a show, the shit got canceled so me and the fellas stayed around and kicked it. It's not my fault that the bitch walked up on me talkin' in my ear and you happened to see it. What was I supposed to do?"

"You was supposed to tell the hoe that you had a woman and to step off!"

"Come here."

"No."

"Come here, Unique!" Bigg demanded. She knew he wasn't playing anymore so she slowly walked over to him. Bigg took her hand and placed her on his lap.

"Don't start trippin' now, ma. You know that I love you. Don't let all this other bullshit cloud yo' judgment. If you can't deal with these around-the-way bitches how you gon' act when shit really get poppin'?"

Bigg had a good point. Whenever a female approached him Unique would spaz out. She hated the sight of another woman staring him in the eyes or being close to him. Bigg was the man that she wanted to marry, and his life would become hers so she had to get her act together quick. Besides that, Unique was suffering from a serious case of dick deprivation. Turning around, she straddled him.

"I'm sorry but don't let me catch you with that bitch again," she warned.

"You won't. I promise," he whispered, kissing her neck and palming her ass at the same time. "Ay, but I ain't playin', if I ever catch you lookin' at that nigga Tone I'ma kill you and that's my word," he said seriously.

Ignoring him, Unique took his face into her hands and kissed his lips passionately. She enjoyed the feel of his lips pressed against hers as she wrapped her arms around his neck. Running his hands up and down her spine, Bigg pushed her tank top up and off. Ever so lightly he tickled her nipples with his tongue while fondling her breasts.

"Ahh," Unique moaned as she arched her back. Watching

Keisha Ervin

as her nipples grew from every lick, Bigg sucked harder. He then trailed kisses down her stomach as he continued to caress her breasts with his hands.

"You know we gon' have to work on that mouth of yours," Bigg whispered in between kissing her lips.

"Whatever." Unique smirked, sucking on his bottom lip.

"Raise up."

Unique did as she was told and lifted up so that Bigg could take off her panties. She unbuckled his shorts, pulled them down around his knees and knelt to the floor. She then made sure that his already erect dick was as stiff as it could be by stroking him up and down. Holding his waist, she placed him in her mouth and went to work.

"Oh my God!" Bigg moaned as he watched her lips slide up and down his dick. He hated to admit it but Unique could suck a mean dick. She had his eyes rolling into the back of his head and everything. Looking down at her he watched as her lips slid up and down. Bigg couldn't take it anymore. The sensation was becoming too much for him to handle.

"Hold up baby, I ain't ready to cum yet," he panted, lifting her head up.

Unique straddled him, smiling at a job well done. Gently guiding her, Bigg sat her all the way down onto his dick. Licking her lips she began to ride him slowly. As she rode him Bigg held her waist making sure that every inch of his fat dick went as far in as it could possibly go.

"Ooh, baby, I can feel you all the way up in my stomach!" Unique whined, gaining speed while screaming in pleasure. "Shit, Bigg, I can't breathe!"

"You like that dick?" he demanded to know, smacking her ass.

"Yes!"

"Say you like it."

"I like it," Unique moaned, biting down on her bottom lip as Bigg pumped roughly.

"I can't hear you. Say you like daddy's big dick!"

"I like that big dick!"

"You gon' quit talkin' shit?"

"Yes!"

"You want daddy to fuck you?"

"Yes baby! Fuck me!"

Bigg found her spot and began to target it with every stroke. Bucking and moaning, Unique couldn't contain her emotions; Bigg was driving her crazy.

"Ooh, Bigg, you feel so good! I could just bite you right now!" Unique growled, feeling like a mad woman.

"You wanna bite me?" He smacked her ass.

"Yes!" She licked and sucked his bottom lip.

"Ride that dick!" He smacked her ass again. "That's right!" He smacked her ass even harder. "Show yo' man what you workin' wit'!" Bigg ordered, smacking her ass over and over again.

"Baby, what you doing to me? Ahh, I'm gon' cum!"

"I wanna see you cum. Cum for me, baby," Bigg ordered, pumping harder.

Grabbing onto his shoulders, Unique let out a thunderous moan as her body began to convulse. Bigg held her tight and continued to pump slowly while she regained her composure. Cumming too, he licked and sucked her breasts.

"Fuck!" he yelled, regaining speed. Tracing his lips with her tongue, Unique kissed him passionately while he came inside of her. Bigg caressed her ass cheeks and kissed her back.

"That was a good nut, baby," Unique said while placing soft, sensual kisses on his neck.

"I know. It's all over my thighs and shit," he laughed.

Keisha Ervin

"Come on, let's go take a shower."

Doing as he was told, Bigg picked Unique up, carried her into the master bathroom and turned on the shower. Leaning her up against the wall, he prepared her for round two.

$ $ $

The next morning, Bigg was awakened by Unique hitting him upside the head with a pillow.

"Wake up, sleepy head," she giggled.

"What time is it?" Bigg asked, turning over and not paying her any attention.

"It's *time* for you to wake yo' punk ass up!"

"Girl, you better gon' wit' that shit. Wake me up in another hour." He turned back over.

"No, you have to get up now." She hit him again.

"Why?" Bigg questioned with his face buried in the pillow.

"'Cause I'm hungry. I want to go out to eat breakfast."

"You better take yo' ass in that kitchen and fix you something to eat."

"Get up, Bigg," Unique whined, pulling the covers off of him and exposing his mocha-colored back.

"I'm gon' kick yo' ass you keep on playin' wit' me." Bigg sat up, rubbing his eyes.

"You can kiss my ass." She grinned and bent over. Bringing her ass toward his face, Bigg kissed it and then smacked it as hard as he could.

"Oww, nigga that hurt," Unique yelled, dancing around the room and holding her butt cheek.

"I told you to quit fuckin' wit' me," he laughed.

"I can't stand you."

"Come here." Smiling, Unique walked back over to him. Gently, Bigg kissed her lips slowly. "I love you."

Keisha Ervin

"I love you, too but, ay, close your eyes. I got a surprise for you."

"What kind of surprise? It's too damn early in the morning for a surprise. A nigga tired and wanna go back to sleep, ma."

"Quit bitchin' and close your eyes."

Not wanting to, Bigg played along. Before she returned to the room, Unique made sure Bigg's eyes were closed by peeping her head through the door. Ready to show him her surprise she squealed, "Open your eyes!"

In front of him was a breakfast tray with a plate filled with scrambled eggs, bacon, sausage, hash browns and sliced strawberries. Over to the side was a champagne glass filled with mimosa. Unique had only cooked for Bigg that one other time so breakfast in bed was a huge surprise and treat for him.

"Come here, lil' dude."

"Ah uh." She smiled, swaying her head from side to side like a little girl.

"Just come here, man," he demanded. Unique grinned from ear to ear and climbed into her king-sized bed with him. She sat Indian style in front of him. Bigg loved being this close to Unique. Just the sight of her face brightened up his day. Moments like this he knew that he could live the rest of his life with her but being the nigga he was, he had to keep it gangsta.

"You know I can't live without yo' big head ass, right."

"Fuck you." She laughed, mushing him in the head. "I can't live without you either."

"You love me?"

"Yeah, I love you," Unique answered truthfully. "Why you actin' all mushy? You know a bitch got a rep to protect."

"Shut up." Bigg playfully mushed her back in the head. "But, nah, for real. When you gon' quit bullshittin' and be my wife?"

Caught off guard by the question, Unique sat silent and unsure of how to answer.

"I know we've only been together for a while but I got mad feelings for you, ma. I'm sick of the fact that you only call me your man when you want something. I want you to be my wife not just my girlfriend or the person that I fuck on a regular. So, I'm coming to you right now as your man, asking you to marry me."

Staring into his eyes, Unique couldn't fight back the tears that stung the brim of her eyes. There was no way that she could play tough in this situation. Bigg was asking her the ultimate ride or die question. Unique loved Bigg and there was no denying that, but her life constantly got in the way of her happiness.

"Are you for real?"

"I'm dead serious. I told you, you was gonna be mine. I want you to be my wife but first you gotta quit this whole stealing cars bullshit."

Without hesitation she said, "You ain't said nothing but a word. It's a done deal. I'm gon' tell the girls that I'm out. I'm sick of the shit anyway."

"A'ight, then. Now answer my question."

"What?" she asked confused.

"Will you marry me?"

"You really want to marry me?" she asked, still unsure.

"Yeah, what you thought I was playin'? I know you try to act all hard and you try to push me away but it's gon' take more than that for me to leave you alone."

Unique sat and pondered her answer. Checking herself she knew that there was nothing to think about. Bigg was her man and she loved him to death so the only logical answer was yes.

"Yes, Bigg, I will marry you."

Keisha Ervin

"That's what I'm talkin' about, now drop them draws and hop on daddy's dick," he said, hugging her.

For the rest of the weekend, Unique and Bigg spent their time together. Lying in bed with Bigg making love into the wee hours of the morning was fun but Unique had business that needed to be tended to. First, she had to meet with Cezar to tell him that she was out of the business. Second, she wanted to officially end things with Tone and third, she had to meet with the girls to divvy up the money one last time.

"What's on your agenda for the day, lil' lady?" Bigg asked, pinning her up against his truck.

"I'm going over to Cezar's place first to talk to him and give him his cut. Then I'm going over to Kay Kay's house to give the girls their share of the money from our last job," Unique replied, conveniently leaving out the part about meeting with Tone.

"A'ight, call me later then." Bigg kissed her gently on the forehead.

Arriving downtown at Cezar's Brownstown-style home, Unique stepped out of Bigg's cranberry red Range Rover and walked into Cezar's house. He knew that she was on her way over so the door was already unlocked. She found Cezar seated on the couch reading the newspaper in his favorite robe.

"Have a seat," he said. Sitting down in a chair across from him, Unique waited for Cezar to acknowledge her presence. "So, how much you got for me?"

"I got forty grand." She handed him a yellow envelope, already ready to leave.

"Good." He put the money down beside him. "I might have ya'll a job up in VA in a few weeks."

"I wanted to talk to you about that. After today, this will be your last time seeing me."

"And why is that?" Cezar asked, putting down the paper.

"Because I'm out; I can't do this shit no more."

"Oh, really? So when did you come to this conclusion?"

"I've been thinking about it for a while but I made up my mind once Bigg asked me to marry him."

"And let me guess, you said yes." Cezar smirked.

"As a matter of fact, I did."

"So, that nigga finally locked you down?" he said more to himself than her. "Look, ma, I ain't got no problem wit' you marrying Bigg. That's my boy, but you fuckin' with my paper. You and the girls have brought me in a nice piece of change. I don't know if I can let you go that easily."

"I'm sorry to tell you, but you don't have any other choice." Unique stood her ground.

"What do Kiara, Kay Kay and Zoë have to say about this?"

"I haven't told them yet. I'm getting ready to go meet with them now."

"Well, tell them that I would love to keep them on my payroll."

"I will but who are you going to get to run things now? You know Kiara's not reliable and I think Zoë might feel the same way I do, so that only leaves Kay Kay."

"What do you think? Do you think she can handle running things?"

"Yeah, Kay Kay's a smart girl; she can do it but look, I gotta jet."

"A'ight everything's set. I hope everything works out for you and my boy."

"It will."

"I hope not." Cezar smirked.

"Let me hurry up and get away from you before I hurt you." Unique laughed.

$ $ $

Keisha Ervin

Stepping up to Tone's door, Unique adjusted the shades on her eyes and knocked.

"Who is it?"

"It's me, Unique."

"What you doing here?" Tone asked, opening the door and looking like he was still half asleep.

"I came to talk to you about the other night. Can I come in?"

Being a gentleman, Tone stepped to the side and let her in. Unique looked around to see if everything was still the same. It was. Tone was never big on furniture so only the bare necessities were in his place. One thing that stood out, though, was a picture of he and Unique. It was a large black and white photo that they took a year ago. It hung over his mantle.

"Look, I ain't gon' take up too much of your time but I need to talk to you."

"You cool, let me go put on a shirt though." Tone had on nothing but his boxers.

"You're all right. It ain't like I ain't never seen you in your drawers before. I just wanted to tell you that I am with Bigg and whatever me and you shared is over now."

"Really?" Tone closed the door behind them.

"Yeah, I'm getting married."

"Damn, I always though it would be you and me."

"Nigga, please. You cheated on me the whole time we were together." Unique laughed.

"Even though I cheated I did have feelings for you."

"Oh, so you're finally admitting it?" She hit him playfully on the arm.

"I mean you know ... but you sure you want to be with that nigga? He seems like he kinda crazy. Oh, I forgot, you like them crazy niggas."

"Bigg's cool. I love him." Unique blushed like a school girl.

"Did I just hear Unique Alexander say she loved something besides Gucci, Fendi and Prada?" Tone joked.

"Shut up. It was nice seeing you but I gotta burn out."

"It was nice seeing you, too, ma," Tone said as he opened the door for her. "Can a nigga at least get a hug before you go?"

"Sure, one last hug couldn't hurt." After hugging Tone goodbye, Unique hopped in the Range Rover and sped off.

$ $ $

Thirty minutes later, Unique was at Kay Kay's house. They all sat in the kitchen awaiting Kiara's arrival.

"If she ain't here in the next five minutes then she just gon' be shit out of luck," Unique spat, pissed off.

"She knows what time we supposed to meet up. She just being silly," Zoë added.

"What's been up with her lately? She has been acting crazy for a minute now. I mean at first I thought the bitch was just going through something, but now she just get on my nerves."

"Well since I get on your nerves so much don't say shit else to me," Kiara said, entering the room.

"Yo', don't even start it today, Ki, I'm not in the mood," Unique warned.

"Whatever. You got my money so I can get up out of here?" Kiara sniffled, wiping her nose.

"Yeah, let me hurry and give you yo' cut before I end up saying something I'm gon' regret. Oh, but before I do, I got something to tell ya'll. I have some good news and some bad news."

"What?" Kay Kay asked.

The good news is that I'm getting married." Staring

around at their faces she saw that all of their jaws had dropped. Nobody said a word. Only silence filled the room.

"Congratulations girl!" Zoë exclaimed, running around the table to hug Unique. Hugging her back, Unique watched as Kiara and Kay Kay exchanged disapproving looks. She could tell that they were not happy for her.

"First of all, who is crazy enough to want to marry you and where is your ring?" Kiara questioned, not missing a thing.

"If you would quit hatin' and shut the fuck up maybe I could tell you. Bigg asked me to marry him the other day and I accepted. I don't know when I'm getting my ring. I just know that it's going to be huge."

"Well, I wouldn't have said yes if the nigga didn't have me a ring."

"Get asked first then we'll have that conversation."

"I thought you said that you and Bigg were just friends?" Kay Kay asked.

"The whole thing between me and Bigg is complicated. I just know that I love him and he loves me."

"I heard that he still mess wit' his baby momma anyway," Kiara spat.

"Bigg ain't hardly fuckin' with Carmella no more so fall back! I don't even know why I'm entertaining this conversation with you! You're sorry you need to quit smoking that shit and get yo' self together!"

"Bitch, fuck you! You was the one that was all about fuck niggas, get money and love is not allowed! Now all of a sudden you marrying this nigga out the blue?" Kiara asked, furious.

"Kiara, we are getting older it's time out for all this shit! You can't be a block bitch forever! I know ya'll want to settle down and have kids and live a normal life just like I do. And Kiara, you really need to be getting your shit together! When is the last time you even saw Arissa? Instead of worrying about me you need to go and take care of your daughter!"

"Keep my daughter's name outta yo' mouth!" Kiara screamed, stepping up to Unique.

"Do it! I dare you!"

"Come on ya'll, that's enough!" Kay Kay yelled, pulling Kiara back.

"Unique is right. We are getting too old for this shit. I know that I want to go back to school and I can't do that with us going out of town every other week robbing niggas. Our cousin is getting married. Fuck all the dumb shit, it's time to celebrate." Zoë tried sticking up for Unique.

"But what about Cezar? What do you think he's gonna say about all of this?" Kay Kay questioned.

"I already talked to Cezar, he's fine. He told me to tell ya'll that if you want to continue on that ya'll can. Kay Kay, he wants you to take over."

"What?!" Kiara yelled.

"He wants me to take over for real?" Kay Kay asked astonished.

"Yep."

"What about me?" Kiara questioned.

"What about you? I've been tellin' you for the longest to get your shit together but you never wanted to listen. Everybody knows that you're not good with handling your business, Kiara."

"I can't believe this shit! You probably had something to do wit' his decision!"

"Look, I ain't got to explain myself to nobody! We had a good run, we made that nigga a lot of money but the shit is over for me! We have made a killing off of this shit! I would rather stop now while I'm ahead then for me to get knocked over some bullshit, you feel me? Now I've been saving up my money. Have you, Zoë?" Unique asked.

"Yeah, I have about two hundred thousand left," she answered.

"What about you?" Unique questioned Kay Kay.

"I got about one eighty put up."

"And you?" Unique asked Kiara.

"I've been saving all of my money," Kiara lied, knowing she had only ten grand left.

"OK then, that's that. We all get twenty-five thousand apiece today so everybody should be cool for a while. It's time to grow up, girls. Jersey was officially my last job," Unique said, giving everybody their cut.

"So you're really serious about this?" Kay Kay asked.

"Serious as a heart attack. I'm sick of this shit. I just didn't know how to tell ya'll."

"On the real, I'm getting tired of all the lying and plotting myself," Zoë agreed. After checking her money, Kiara grabbed her purse and left without saying a word.

"That's another reason I wanted to quit. I ain't got time for that dumb shit! That's my muthafuckin cousin and she gon' shit on me like that! Fuck her!" Unique snapped.

"Yo', that was fucked up," Kay Kay chimed in.

"It's all good. Like I said, fuck her. So what ya'll plan on doing?"

"I'm sorry, Kay Kay, but I'm out, too. Like I said, I want to go back to school. I want to take up graphic design." Zoë smiled.

"That's cool, ma. I guess it's just me and Kiara for now. What you gon' do?" Kay Kay asked Unique.

"I'm going to continue to save my money. My main focus is starting me a little business and giving Bigg a son or daughter within the next year."

"Look at yo' ole in love ass," Zoë joked playfully.

"I know, right. How her ole thug ass gon' be somebody's

Keisha Ervin

momma," Kay Kay continued.

"Fuck both of ya'll," she laughed. "But look, here are all the numbers to my associates. Sammy, up in Jersey, is a cool guy but Lou, down in Cali, can be a bitch sometimes. They will help you set up everything." Feeling her two-way going off, Unique pulled it from off of her waist and scrolled through it. It was Bigg telling her to come up to the studio because he missed her. "Yo', ya'll wanna roll up to the studio wit' me to see Bigg?"

"Nah, I'm about to head over to my mom's house to eat," Kay Kay said, rubbing her flat stomach.

"You know yo' ass can fuck up some food, wit' you lil' ass," Unique teased.

"Don't hate!" She laughed, grabbing her purse.

"Hell, I ain't got nothing else to do. I'll roll wit' you," Zoë said.

"We'll take my car. I got to go pick up Patience from school."

$ $ $

Walking into the studio, Unique searched for her man through the sea of men and cloud of weed smoke that was in the air. Bottles of Hennessy and Patrón were scattered everywhere throughout the room. Unique stood for a minute and watched as NaSheed spit a verse into the mic. Bobbing her head to the beat, she returned her eyes to finding Bigg.

"Damn, these niggas sho'll do know how to spark up," Zoë replied, coughing and grabbing her chest.

"Right, give a nigga some Hennessy and Coke and they don't know how to act. I can't find Bigg though," Unique yelled over the noise and loud music.

"You a'ight?" a fine caramel brotha asked Zoë, grabbing

her hand.

"Yeah, I'm fine." She blushed, gazing into his eyes.

"Do you know were Bigg is?" Unique asked.

"He's over there." The guy pointed in Bigg's direction. He was already eyeing her. Smiling to herself, Unique approached him.

"What's the deal, ma?" Bigg said, taking her hand and leading her onto his lap.

"You, daddy." Unique kissed his lips.

"What's up, big brother?" Patience smiled.

"You, baby sis, I ain't seen you all weekend. How did you do on that chemistry test you had? I ain't forget."

"I don't know, I won't get my test scores back until tomorrow." Patience felt embarrassed in front of the room full of men.

"A'ight, you betta have an A or I'm not gon' get you that new Hermes bag you want."

"What about me?" Unique asked.

"Don't even trip. I got something even better for you."

"Oh, for real?" She lifted up so that he could go into his pocket.

"Yo', turn that shit down," Bigg yelled to the sound man. "I got something to say."

"What you got to say, nigga? You messed up my flow," NaSheed joked.

"Nigga, yo' flow was already messed up." Laughing, Unique watched as Bigg pulled out a small black box. Inhaling deeply, she looked over at Zoë who was giving her the thumbs up.

"Ya'll know this my lady and I love her to death. This my nigga and I would die for her. That's why I asked her to be my wife the other day. I ain't have a ring to give to her at the time but she still said yes. That's the kind of pull yo' boy got," Bigg laughed. Everybody in the studio laughed, too. "But I told you that I got you, ma, and that all you had to do was trust me and you did." Bigg opened the box to reveal a flawless five-carat princess-cut yellow diamond ring. Placing the ring on her finger, he watched how her eyes lit up.

"Baby, it's beautiful," Unique gushed.

"You're beautiful," he replied back.

"Are ya'll done so I can finish spittin' this verse?" NaSheed asked, fucking with Bigg.

"Nigga, get yo' ass back in the booth before I give yo' ass a five dollar fine!" Bigg joked.

"Congratulations, Nique!" Patience happily hugged her sister.

"Thank you, Patience. I can't believe you surprised me like this." Unique turned her attention back to Bigg.

"What did you expect from yo' man? I wasn't going to let you walk around telling people you were engaged without having an engagement ring."

"I know, you just took me by surprise."

"Yo', Zoë over there all in my man Legend grill."

"I taught her well." Unique smiled looking over in their direction.

"So, Legend, you got a woman at home waiting for you?" Zoë questioned, licking her lips.

"Nah, ma. I'm a single man."

"Good but not for long."

"Oh, straight," he said, taking out his cell.

"Yeah, so go ahead and put my number in that phone 'cause from now on I will be the only chick calling you." She smirked.

"You got a smart-ass mouth." Legend looked deep into her eyes. "I like that."

"I know you do." Zoë gazed over his tall, honey-colored

frame. Liking what he saw as well, Legend took her hand in his and made her put her number into his cell.

"I'm about to get up, but I'm gon' call you tomorrow, a'ight."

"You make sure you do that." Zoë eyed the thick bulge in his jeans.

Smiling, Legend caressed her cheek and left with one of his boys. "Where the ring at? Let me see it," Zoë said, walking over to Unique and Bigg, interrupting their kissing session. Unique smiled from ear to ear while showcasing her ring.

"You did good, my brotha. Nice choice."

"You know how I do."

"Whateva, Bigg."

"So what's up wit' you and my man?" he questioned, curious.

"Who, Legend?"

"Yeah, that's my homey, he cool peoples."

"What's the deal with him? He ain't got no woman, do he?" Unique asked, wanting to know.

"I don't know that man's business."

"He got a woman," Unique and Zoë both said in unison.

"Fuck it! If he do got a bitch it won't be for long." Zoë smirked, sure of herself.

"That's what's up."

"How long have you known him, Bigg?" Zoë questioned.

"Yeah, baby, I ain't never seen him before," Unique said.

"Yes you have, Nique. He been up here to the studio a couple of times to see me while you were here," Bigg answered.

"Oh, I must have not paid him any attention."

"That figures," Zoë laughed.

"Look, when Bigg is around I am only focused on him."

"That's right." Bigg slapped her ass.

"Whatever." Zoë rolled her eyes to the ceiling.

"But, yeah, that's my man, he cool peoples," Bigg continued.

"How did ya'll meet?" Zoë asked.

"I meet dude a couple of weeks ago at T Billy's. We was all down there playing pool, drinking and shit, when NaSheed introduced me to him. Dude was cool from the start and the fact that he out here trying to get this money like me was an A in my book so we been cool ever since."

"Oh, so when ya'll gon' set a date?"

"Shit, fuck a wedding, let's elope."

"Nigga, are you crazy? You will not catch me eloping," Unique replied with her face scrunched up.

"Why not?" he asked.

"Because, I want to have a big wedding and plus my momma has to be there."

"I feel you. Whatever you want you got it, shorty." Bigg kissed her on the forehead.

"Eww, ya'll are sickening!" Zoë pretended to throw up.

"I know right," Patience agreed.

"Ya'll some haters," Unique teased them both.

"You gon' be acting just like this once my man Legend get at you," Bigg told Zoë.

"Nigga, please. I'm gon' have Legend wrapped around my finger. Watch."

Catching 8 Feelings

Two weeks later, Zoë found herself questioning the game. Legend hadn't called her yet and she knew that she had laid down some superb game, so she didn't know what the hold up was. He had to be feeling her. She could tell by the look in his eyes. It wasn't like her hair, makeup and outfit weren't on point.

That day she sported her short black hair in soft beautiful curls that framed her oval-shaped face. Her high cheekbones, slanted eyes, thick eyelashes, cocoa skin and small frame gave her an exotic appearance. Zoë was very short and petite for her age. Most of the time, whenever she went to a club she got carded. But her supple breasts, round hips and bounceable ass were what always gave her away.

Men loved the fact that she was so small and cute. She only weighed one hundred and ten pounds, and kind of resembled the actress Malinda Williams. For the past couple of days, the fact that Legend hadn't called yet was eating at her ego big time. She told herself that once he decided to call her she either A) wouldn't answer the phone or B) was just going to blow him off. She dialed Vito's number.

"Hello?"

"What's good? What you doing?" she asked.

"Shit, what's good wit' you?"

"Nothing, I'm trying to see you tonight."

"For real? Where you wanna go?"

"I feel like playing darts. Let's head out to T Billy's."

"A'ight, I'll be there in fifteen minutes."

"A'ight." Zoë hung up.

Forty-five minutes later Zoë and Vito were standing in front of a dartboard laughing and talking shit to one another.

"I bet you fifty bucks you can't hit the bullseye," Vito teased.

"Nigga, please. You ain't said nothing but a word."

In front of the dartboard, Zoë closed one eye and focused her aim. She waved her arm back and forth and threw the sharp dart at the board. The dart landed directly in the center of the board. Happy, she jumped up and down.

"That was a lucky shot," Vito said, shocked.

"Whatever, nigga. Give me my money," she said with her hand out.

Vito reached down into his pocket and pulled out a fat wad of dough. Sizing it up, Zoë figured that he at least had about five or six grand on him. *Stunting ass nigga*, Zoë thought to herself. She knew Vito only bet her so that he could show off his money stack. Breaking her off a crisp fifty, he tried to hand it to her but instead Zoë peeled off five crisp one hundred dollar bills.

"I like this amount much better." She smirked, stuffing the money in her bra.

"I guess I'm gon' have to take my money back later." Vito licked his lips eyeing the cleavage that was pouring out of Zoë's blouse.

"Whatever," Zoë mumbled underneath her breath.

As Zoë withdrew the darts from the board she eyed a group of guys coming through the door. Breaking her neck to see if it was anybody she knew, she spotted Legend in the crowd. She bit down into her lower lip, excited to see him. Trying not to make eye contact with him, Zoë resumed her game of darts with Vito.

"Here, it's your turn to go first." She handed him the darts.

"I bet you I hit the bullseye," Vito boasted.

"Go baby!" Zoë said louder than she need to so that Legend could hear her. Feeling his eyes on her, she cheered Vito on even more. Just as she'd hoped, he hit the bullseye dead in the center. Zoë pretended to be happy and jumped up and down. She then hugged Vito around his neck.

"Damn baby, if I would have known you was gonna react like that I wouldn't have let you win the first time."

"Give me some money so I can get us a pitcher of beer," she ordered with her hand out.

Peeling off a ten he placed it in her hand and slapped her ass. Switching extra hard over to the bar, Zoë showcased her turquoise halter top, ultra low-rise Tag jeans and Kristen Lee wedge heels. Not one bitch in the spot had anything on her and she knew it. Not one strand of her short spiked hairdo was out of place and her nails and feet were perfectly French manicured.

"Let me get a pitcher of Bud Light," she said to the bartender.

"What you doing here with that nigga?" Legend asked, now standing beside her.

"Excuse me?"

"You heard what I said." He looked at her and licked his lips.

"Nigga, I gave you my number two weeks ago and you never called."

"Man, I lost my phone."

"Yeah, right, that's what all ya'll niggas say when you get caught up."

"You right, I ain't gon' even lie. What really happened was I got locked up." Legend grinned.

"Will you stop lying?" Zoë couldn't help but laugh, too.

"Nah, for real though, I was gon' get at you." Legend gazed deeply into her eyes to let her know that he was telling the truth.

Zoë wanted desperately to play him to the side but she couldn't. He looked and smelled even better than the last time she saw him. Legend's flawless skin complexion was one of honey and his brown bedroom eyes, kissable lips, mustache and chin hair and square jaw drew her in every time. He kind of put her in the mind of the rapper T.I. Since it was the summertime he rocked a black T-Shirt with Tony Montana's picture on the front, a pair of long LRG shorts and a pair of Nike sneaks on his feet.

An all-black Cardinals cap rested on his head tilted to the side, showcasing his low cut Caesar. Legend was a thug all the way. He even had a diamond grill on the bottom row of his teeth. It was the detachable kind. Shaking her head, Zoë tried to release the spell that his eyes had cast on her.

"Look, I gotta go. My date's watching me," she said, nodding her head toward Vito, who was shooting her daggers with his eyes.

"Oh, it's like that."

"Sorry playa, you shoulda called," Zoë replied, sashaying back over to Vito.

"Why was you all up in that man's face?" Vito questioned.

"Hold up, I'm grown. Don't come at me like that." She

checked him.

"Why you gotta be defensive all the time," he whined.

"Are we gon' finish playin' or are you gonna sit up here and bitch and moan?" Zoë rolled her neck, now aggravated by his presence.

"I swear to God if you weren't so fuckin' fine I would have been fucked you up by now." Vito grabbed a handful of her ass.

Easing his hands off of her ass, Zoë stepped back as she and Legend caught eyes. She and Vito continued to play another round of darts while Legend eyed her the whole time. The way he looked at her had Zoë feeling confused and wanted at the same time. Every time she looked over at Legend she felt a strong jolt of electricity run through her body. Needing some room to breathe, she told Vito that she was going to the bathroom. Since the entrance to the bathroom was out of Vito's eyesight, she leaned up against the wall outside of the restroom and caught her breath.

"You need me to get you something to drink? 'Cause you looking a little hot, ma," Legend teased.

"What do you want?"

"I want you," he whispered, standing in front of her with his hand pressed up against the wall.

"If you wanted me so bad you would've called."

"Look, I'm gon' be up front with you. I'm a very busy man but I make time for the things that are important to me."

"So, let me guess, I'm supposed to be important to you," Zoë said in a sarcastic tone.

Thinking for a minute before he answered, Legend said, "Yeah, you are."

Laughing, Zoë replied, "Ya'll niggas ain't shit."

"I'm being real, ma. There's something about you."

"Yeah, whatever." Zoë waved him off and began to walk away. Grabbing her hand, Legend stopped her.

"Come on, let's get out of here. I can tell you don't want to be here with that nigga. Look at him — he's a lame." Staring over at Vito, Zoë knew that everything that Legend said was true. Vito was nothing but a wanna-be gangsta.

"I can't do him like that."

"Why not? Fuck that nigga."

"'Cause it ain't right," she lied.

"Look, just tell him you have to use the pay phone. I'll be outside waiting in my truck."

"I don't know why I'm even considering going anywhere with you."

"'Cause, you want me just like I want you." He smiled, showing off his pearly white teeth.

"Ughh, all right here I come!"

"What took you so long?" Vito asked.

"It was a long line." Zoë ignored him, grabbing her purse off the stool.

"Where you going now?" he asked, irritated.

"I left my cell phone at home. I need to go outside and use the pay phone."

"Here, you can use mine."

"Nah, I don't want you knowing my business like that. I'll be right back."

Grabbing his dick as Zoë walked out the door, Vito whispered to himself, "I'm gon' putting a hurting on that pussy tonight."

Just as planned, Legend was parked out front in his all-black G-wagen. Zoë wondered if she had made the right decision as she hopped into the car. Too much about him screamed, *He'll break your heart*. Ignoring it, she told herself that she was in control and that he wouldn't get anywhere near her heart.

"So, where to, shorty?" Legend asked, as if he didn't

already know.

"Your place."

$ $ $

Zoë knew that she had no business being up in Legend's crib. Normally she wouldn't have thought twice about fucking a nigga so soon, but Legend was different. Something about him drew her in whenever she was around him and she hated it. Sitting on the edge of his leather butterscotch-framed bed, she glanced around the room. The brotha was smooth. He had candles lit and the melodic, soft, sensual sounds of John Legend filled her ears. *"She Don't Have to Know"* was playing in the background. Legend reentered the room with a bottle of Chandon and a bowl of strawberries and placed them on the nightstand.

"Let me get that for you," he said as he began to unbuckle the straps on her wedges.

"Nice move." She smiled. He took both of her feet into his hands and massaged them until she let out a subtle moan.

"Ooh, that feels good." After a ten minute massage, Legend got up and fixed them both a glass of champagne.

"Let's make a toast," he suggested.

"To what?"

"To me and you," he replied as he clinked glasses with Zoë.

"That sounds good to me."

"Here, take a bite." Legend placed a perfect, red, ripe strawberry to her mouth. As she bit down into the sweet fruit, juices dripped from Zoë's lips. Making his move, Legend swiftly licked every drop. He leaned her back onto the bed and continued to devour her wet lips. Zoë parted her legs wide.

"Damn girl, what you tryin' to do to a nigga?"

"What you talkin' about?" Zoë asked, confused.

Keisha Ervin

"You open up nice. Who taught you how to spread them legs that wide?" he joked.

"Don't play." Zoë laughed as he resumed kissing her lips. "Look, we can do this but don't mess up my hair," she instructed, breaking the kiss. Laughing a little, Legend continued to tantalize her tongue with his.

As he rose up her shirt over her head, Legend saw that she wore no bra. *Damn her titties sit up like that*, he thought. As he flicked his tongue across each of her nipples, Zoë's entire body began to shudder. With another strawberry in hand, Legend squeezed it and let the juices pour all over her breasts.

"Umm," Zoë moaned, biting down into her lip.

Licking and sucking until not a drop was left, he pulled her jeans down. Ready to taste the kitty, he snatched off her pink thong and threw it across the room. Legend grabbed two more strawberries from the bowl and pushed her legs back. He squeezed one of the strawberries until her pussy was covered with juices. For a minute he stared at her pink clit and admired the way it looked as it glistened underneath the light of the candles. As he lightly licked her pussy he felt her clit jump from excitement.

"You like that?"

"Yes," she moaned. Flicking his tongue across her clit he watched as it jumped again. Flicking his tongue even faster he watched as her clit danced around his tongue.

"Ooh, shit!" Zoë screamed, grabbing his head. She tried containing her emotions but Legend's tongue was driving her insane. From then on he was certified with a hurricane tongue. Zoë arched her back as he inserted two of his fingers inside her pussy. Working his fingers in and out, Legend licked her clit causing her to scream out his name.

"Legend!"

"Damn baby, you taste good." He licked again.

Keisha Ervin

With her eyes rolled back into her head she moaned, "Baby, I can't take it no more! Put it in!"

Paying her no mind, Legend parted her legs even wider. He grabbed the other strawberry and inserted it inside her pussy. Repeatedly he sucked the strawberry in and out causing enough friction to make her cum. He licked and sucked her pussy while eating the strawberry all at the same time. Then he began to massage her clit with his thumb.

"Fuck!" Zoë screamed as she eyed his head swishing around her pussy.

As he flipped her over, Legend licked and kissed her ass while still massaging her clit. Zoë came again all over his fingers then fell limp onto the bed. With a broad smile on his face, Legend got up and went into the bathroom to clean up. Breathing heavily, Zoë rolled back over. As she gazed up at the ceiling she tried her best to catch her breath. She had to prepare herself for some D. D as in Dick, that is. Back in the room, Legend took his place on the bed next to her and looked into her eyes.

"What?" Zoë asked after a minute of awkward silence.

"You're about the flyest chick that I've ever seen."

"Whatever." She laughed, waving him off.

"For real, I'm feelin' you." Not trying to hear him she grabbed his dick and massaged it through his shorts.

"Damn, ma, what you trying to do to a nigga?" he stressed. Just as she was about to unbutton his pants, he stopped her.

"What? What's wrong?" she asked confused.

"Look, I ain't tryin' to take it there wit' you just yet. I mean, what's the rush?"

"Ain't no rush ... I just thought ... you wanted to ... you know."

"I do but not yet."

"Why not?"

"'Cause, I wanna know that when I give it to you, you can handle it."

"Legend, please, I will have you speakin' in tongues." She laughed.

"I hear you talkin'." He grinned, licking his lips, liking her strong will.

"I'm for real." She started sucking on his neck.

"Come on, Zoë, chill." Legend pushed her up off of him. Looking into her eyes, he could tell that she was hurt. "Look, I'm feelin' you but I need to get to know you better before I take it there wit' you. I wanna know what's in your heart, Zoë. What makes you smile? What makes you cry? What ticks you off as well as what turns you on? I want to be your best friend as well as your lover so that when we do take it to the next level, I will not only be making to love your body but your mind as well. Let me just take care of you tonight," he whispered into her ear as he resumed stroking her clit.

Keisha Ervin

Ain't No
Holla Back Girl

9

"So, what you do last night?" Unique questioned Zoë over breakfast at Uncle Bill's.

"Nothing." She smiled slyly.

"Bitch, quit lying. I already know you was wit' Legend last night."

"How you know?"

"Don't worry about all that. I just know. Now tell me what happened."

"We just kicked it, that's all." Zoë blushed.

"Uh huh, I know you lying but it's cool. You ain't got to tell me."

"OK, OK, I'll tell you," Zoë said, ready to spill the beans.

"I knew yo' punk ass was lying." Unique grinned.

"OK, well first of all I went to T Billy's with Vito, not Legend."

"What? How did you hook up with Legend then?"

"While I was there with Vito, Legend and his partnas came

Keisha Ervin

through. You know I was looking fly, right, so a brotha was eyeing me kinda hard."

"An-y-way finish the story." Unique waved her off.

"Quit hatin'. Shit my two-way going off. Hold up."

"Who is it?"

"*Legend.* He just two-wayed me to say hi."

"Oh God, ya'll are so gay."

"Whatever."

"All right, finish tellin' the damn story!"

"OK, OK," Zoë giggled like a lil' school girl. "Well, when I went to go get us something to drink, Legend came up to me spittin' all this junk in my ear."

"It must not have been too much junk 'cause you left with him." Unique smirked with one eyebrow up.

"Shut up, Nique! An-y-way he got a sista all hot and bothered so when he asked me to leave with him, I did."

"You mean to tell me you just up and left with Legend and Vito didn't say anything?"

"Now see that's the funny part. I told Vito that I was going out to use the pay phone but really I left with Legend." Zoë cracked up laughing.

"Gurl you ain't nothing nice." Unique laughed, too.

"You want to hear the worst part?"

"What? You fucked him without a condom and now you think he gave you the dead man disease?"

"Nah, dumb ass, I'm finding myself catching feeling for this cat."

"Uh oh, somebody got a love jones."

"Yo', I'm for real! Dude got me buggin'. We were at his crib and shit last night and he ate me out and everything but never once did he ask to hit the pussy."

"Word? But the question is, did he leave you some cash?"

"Bitch, I ain't no hoe!" Zoë laughed.

"I'm just playin'. But for real, he on some other shit. You better watch him, Z. He might have yo' ass paying his bills in a minute."

"I know, right," Zoë agreed.

"What he say about not callin' you?"

"First he lied and said he lost his phone."

"Oh hell naw," Unique snapped, placing down her fork.

"I know, I know, even I was like negro please. But then he came up with that same ole tired ass line that all niggas use about how busy he was and that he was going to call me eventually."

"I don't know, Z, he seem like he might be on some bullshit."

"Girl please, as you can see I already got this nigga stuck. Shit after getting a taste of this pussy I won't be able to get that nigga off my back. But, on another note I am officially a UMSL college student."

"What? My girl going to school?"

"Yeah. I told you I wanted to go to school for graphic design."

"Well, I'm proud of you."

"You know with me going to school and everything my life is going to change drastically."

"Right, you can't keep on associating yourself with men like Legend."

"Girl, you know if his status ain't hood I ain't fuckin' wit' him," Zoë stated, laughing.

"I don't know what it is about having a thug-ass nigga rockin' your world but a bitch loves it," Unique joked.

"Have you heard from Kiara?"

"Nope. Have you?"

"Nah, I talked to Kay Kay though the other day."

"What she talkin' about?"

"Same ole same ole. She told me about this job that we could do out in VA but I told her that I wasn't fuckin' wit' her on that shit no more."

"Yeah Cezar told me about that. She probably gon' get Kiara to do it wit' her."

"Can you imagine the two of them stealing a car together?"

"I just hope they asses don't call me trying to get me to bail them out of jail."

"I'm full," Zoë said, looking down and examining her damage. She had consumed a stack of pancakes, four strips of bacon, two sausage links, two pieces of French toast, an omelet and to top it off, a diet Coke to cut down the calories.

"That is a shame. I don't know how your little ass can eat so much and never gain any weight."

"I get it from my momma," Zoë sang while doing a dance in her seat.

"You stupid," Unique laughed hitting her in the face with her napkin.

After leaving Uncle Bill's with a full stomach, Unique decided to head home. Once she got there she checked her messages and learned that Kiara had called with something important to tell her. Calling her back, Kiara picked up the phone.

"Hello?"

"You call me?" Unique asked with an attitude.

"Ay, Kay Kay, pick up the other phone. You there Kay Kay?"

"Yeah, I'm here. What's up wit' you, Nique?"

"Shit, so what's so important?" she asked, already knowing.

"We called you to tell you that Cezar got this job for us up in VA."

"I already know about it, but I told you and Kay Kay that I was done with that shit."

"You was for real?" Kiara asked.

"What, you thought I was playin'? Yeah, I'm dead serious. I'm done."

"So you really gon' leave me and Kiara hanging like that?"

"Look, Kay Kay, ya'll are two grown-ass women. I can't continue to hold ya'll hand and spoon feed you for the rest of your life. If ya'll want to continue doing the shit then do it. I'll support you fully, but I'm just not down with it anymore."

"First of all, we don't need you to help us out! We just thought that you wanted to get this money like we do! But shit, since it's like that, fuck you!" Kiara snapped, getting loud.

"You know what? I'm getting sick and tired of yo' mutha-fuckin' mouth! I've bit my tongue for a long time but now I'm gon' let yo' lil' ass have it! You're weak, Kiara! You wouldn't survive a minute without me and you know it! If you were smarter and thought with your head instead of your pussy, maybe I would've let you take over the business! But fuck that! I wouldn't let you wipe my ass let alone let run my business!"

"Fuck you, Unique! We don't need you!"

"Kay Kay, you quiet, you got something you want to say to me, too?" Unique asked, heated.

"It's just fucked up how you left us for that nigga you wit'. But it's cool though, ma, Kiara and I got this from now on."

"Oh, so, you siding with this bitch?!"

"Look, I'm trying to get this paper and Kiara is my sister so ... I guess I am," Kay Kay said slowly, making sure she was aware of what she was saying.

"A'ight then! Well fuck you too, Kay Kay! And Kiara, when I see you I'm gon' stick my size seven shoe all the way up yo' narrow ass!" Unique yelled, hanging up on them.

Keisha Ervin

Angry and hurt she paced the floor. She couldn't believe that it had gotten to this point with Kiara. They had grown up together, took baths, got their period and even double dated together and now they were practically strangers. She didn't want to fight Kiara because that was her blood but a good ass whooping was what she needed and Unique was just the person to give it to her.

For a minute she even thought about calling her aunt on Kiara but that would've been childish. What she needed to do was speak to Bigg. She needed his advice and his voice of reason at times like this so she picked up the phone and dialed his cell.

"What up?" Bigg said, bumping Jay-Z's *"Allure"* in the background.

"Hey baby."

"Yo' hang up, I'm pulling up right now." Unique hung up the phone and met Bigg at the front door.

"What's wrong wit' you? Why you lookin' like that?"

"I just got into it with Kay Kay and Kiara." She folded her arms, pouting like a 5-year-old.

"Why?" Bigg asked, kicking off his black and white Prada tennis shoes.

"They mad because I ain't fuckin wit' them no more on that stealing cars shit."

"Ma, if they can't support you and your decision, then fuck 'em," Bigg replied.

"But those are my cousins, Bigg. We grew up together. I'm the one that got them into doing the shit. Now I'm leaving them hanging just to be wit' you. I can see why they mad."

"What? You having second thoughts?"

"Nah, never that, you know that I ain't going nowhere."

"Well then, what's the problem? You gotta live for you and only you. You can't worry about what everybody else want you to do."

"I know but …"

"I know but nothing. You said that you were done with it so that's the end of it. Now go in kitchen and fix yo' man a sandwich."

"Negro please," she laughed, mushing him in the head.

$ $ $

Zoë sat in her platinum-colored Acura NSX thinking of Legend. For the life of her she couldn't figure out what was up with the guy. The two had been seeing each other for over a month but there was still a lack of communication. It wasn't because of Zoë's unwillingness. It was because Legend was showing traits of being a typical nigga. He swore up and down that he liked her and wanted to spend all of his time with her but his actions spoke differently. Either he didn't call or he didn't come by when he said he was going to.

Zoë didn't know what to do. Every time she got to the point where she thought she was over him he would do something sweet to reel her back in. They didn't even go together but whenever they did spend time with one another, he made sure that everything was all about her. He treated her like an absolute queen. It was nothing for him to send her on a shopping spree to one her favorite stores or for him to send her a dozen or more roses every day. Legend was real romantic in that way so the fact that he went without seeing her for days on end had Zoë confused.

She wanted to believe him when he said that he was busy but she couldn't help but feel like she was being played. Plenty of nights passed by where she held the phone in her hand daring herself to call him but her pride wouldn't allow it. Still, she continued to mess with him despite his lack of being

Keisha Ervin

there.

That day in particular, Legend had sent her to her favorite spa for a facial, massage, pedicure and manicure. The original plan was for the two of them to spend the day together since they hadn't seen each other in a week but at the last minute Legend had something more important to do. Zoë tried to play it off like she didn't care but every time Legend played her to the side it hurt like hell. He did promise that they would spend the rest of the afternoon together, though.

Zoë enjoyed the day of relaxation at the spa but knew her day would have been better if Legend had been there. His lack of presence was quickly forgiven when she walked to her car and found an envelope with her name written on it. Inside was a stack of one hundred dollar bills.

Smiling, Zoë shook her head and placed the money in her purse. On the way home from the spa, Zoë stopped at the Shell station on Lucas and Hunt by her apartment. Sweaty and hot, she flipped open her cell phone and called Legend to thank him but he didn't answer. She tried again three more times but still got no answer. Pissed, Zoë decided to try one more time.

"What up," he said, finally answering the phone on the fourth ring.

"Legend."

"What's good, ma?"

"What took you so long to answer yo' phone?!" she snapped. She could hear a bunch of niggas in the background and swore that she could hear a couple of female voices, too.

"'Cause I ain't hear that muthafucka ring. What's the problem now? Didn't you get the money I left on your car?"

"Yeah I got it!"

"OK, well what's the problem then?"

"Nothing. I was calling to tell you thank you and where are

you at?"

"I'm in the hood where the fuck I tell you I was at!" he shot, becoming annoyed with her nagging.

"Look, I ain't call to argue wit' you."

"I don't wanna argue wit' you, either."

"Good, so are we still getting together later?"

"Yeah but it's gon' be late."

"What you mean it's gon' be late? You said this afternoon, not tonight."

"Look, I gotta take care of some business, ma."

"You always gotta take care of some damn business! I'm sick of this shit!"

"Yo', chill wit' all that yellin' and carrying on! What the fuck I tell you earlier! I said I was coming through! Chill wit' all that noise man! I don't feel like hearing that shit today!"

As she held the phone away from her ear, Zoë couldn't believe that he came to her like that. The fact that she hadn't snapped back with a remark had her even more concerned. Not knowing why she felt the way she did, Zoë wanted to cry. She and Legend hadn't even fucked yet and he had her biting her words. No other man in her twenty-four years on earth made her feel the way Legend did.

"Hello?"

"Yeah, I'm here." She spoke softly into the phone.

"I'ma call you when I'm on my way."

"OK?"

"A'ight," Legend assured.

"A'ight," Zoë replied back, holding in the tears.

Hurt beyond words, she slammed her phone shut, hopped out of her car and went into the gas station. On the way out she got a few hollas from a couple of fellas in an Escalade but all she could think of was Legend. She tried to keep it gangsta but once Zoë's head started pounding, the tears she had been trying to hide began sliding down her face.

"Fuck that nigga," she sighed while wiping her cheek.

As she pumped gas into her car, the only thing on Zoë's mind at that point was getting home and taking a long, hot bath. Holding the pump with one hand, she placed the other to her forehead to wipe off the sweat beads that had formed. Suddenly Zoë's two-way began to vibrate. She checked it and learned that she had a message from Legend. It read: *I'll be there in a minute lil' lady.*

Fuck him, she thought as she released the clamp on the pump only to spill gas on her freshly pedicured feet.

"Fuck! Fuck! Fuck!" Zoë jumped up and down, pissed. Heated, she placed the pump back into the clip and hurried to the trunk of her car. In a mad rush to find a towel, she bent over into the trunk of her car.

"Damn jeans, your ass is fat," she heard a voice say from behind but ignored it.

"I know you hear me!" Legend shouted again.

Speak of the damn devil, Zoë thought as she recognized the voice. Standing up straight, she turned around and placed one hand on her hip while giving him the evil eye.

"Why you lookin' at me like that?" he teased with his head hanging out the window of his old-school candy-apple red Impala.

"Fuck you, Legend. I ain't got nothing to say to you."

"Ay, watch your mouth. I done told you about that shit already. Instead of getting smart you need to watch what you doing next time." He laughed as he stepped out of the car and wrapped his muscular arms around her waist.

"Ain't nothing funny! I just got my feet done!"

"'Bout time you got them crusty-ass feet done."

"Fuck you and where the hell you coming from, anyway? I thought you was in the hood."

"I was. I just left from my man's house over in Northwoods. I saw you as I was riding down Lucas & Hunt so I stopped. You look good as hell, ma." Legend rubbed her thighs and inhaled her scent. Trying her best not acknowledge his sex appeal, Zoë pushed him away from her.

"Get off of me. You hurt my feelings."

Ignoring her, Legend eyed her frame. The white Juicy wife beater, white hot pants and Michael Kors flip-flops made up her street chic outfit. Her short hair was styled to perfection as usual. Silver hoop earrings and a platinum chain with a heart pendant adorned her ears and neck. With a little hint of mascara and lip gloss, Zoë redefined beauty.

"How I hurt your feelings, lil' mama?"

"'Cause you always lying!"

"What I lie about now?"

"Don't play wit' me! You know damn well what you be doing! One minute it's, 'We gon' do this,' and then the next it's, 'I'm busy, something came up.' I ain't seen yo' ass all week! What, you got another bitch or something?!"

"Man, don't make me slap you. You know I got mad feelings for you."

"Yeah, that's what your mouth say."

"So, what's up? You still mad? 'Cause if not, I'm trying to see you tonight."

"I don't see why. You ain't been wanting to see me." Zoë rolled her eyes.

"Yo', what I tell you," Legend warned.

Happy to see him and not wanting him to leave, Zoë eased up some.

"My bad, I had a fucked up day," she apologized. *Did I really just say that?* she thought. *This nigga got me biting my tongue for real.*

"It's cool. Let me get that for you." He took the towel from her hand, grabbed her leg and wiped her foot. "You know you cute when you're mad, right?"

"Shut up." She playfully pushed him in the chest.

"So what's up? What you want to do today?"

"Ain't shit up. I told you, you hurt my feelings," she snapped, pulling her leg away, hoping he would kiss her ass some more.

"You're really mad?" Legend grinned, shocked.

"You damn right I'm mad."

"Why, 'cause I ain't seen you all week?" Staring him square in the eyes she looked at him as if he were dumb. "Didn't I just put over a grand in yo' pocket and send you to a five star spa?"

"Yeah but that shit don't mean nothing to me, Legend."

"Look shorty, I told you that I'm a very busy man. I thought that you of all people would understand that."

"I do, but damn."

"Look, I'm here now. That's all that matter so calm yo' lil' ass down. Ain't nobody tryin' to play you." Legend grabbed Zoë's arm and brought her over to his chest. Not wanting to but unable to control her feelings, she wrapped her arms around his waist. "That's better. I told you that I was gonna come through."

"I know," she replied, happy to be in his arms again.

"That's one thing that we gon' have to get straight right now. I am a man of my word. If I say I'm gon' do something, I'm gon' do it."

"Whatever. I'm still mad at you because today is Saturday I haven't seen you since last Saturday. Have you tried to come see me this week? Ah, no, muthafucka. And how many times have I talked to you? Twice, so you can save all that bullshit you talkin' for the next bitch," Zoë spat as she jumped in her car.

Legend smiled to himself, liking her strong will. He

jogged back to his car in order to follow her. He loved it when she played hard to get. Hurrying, he pressed the automatic starter button on his keychain and got into his car. Surprisingly, the distance from the gas station to her house was a short one. He pulled up right next to her and got out to open her car door. Zoë tried her damnest to still be mad at him but once they approached the door to her apartment, all the bullshit was put to the side.

"You still mad?" he asked, biting down on her neck while massaging her ass.

"Yep."

"I don't know why."

"'Cause Legend, you could've called or something," Zoë whined, not recognizing the sound of her own voice anymore.

"I know that I could've and I should've. I'm sorry. What more can I say?"

"Uh uh, don't do that to me," she moaned as he kissed her neck from behind.

"Do what to you? Make you feel good?" Legend's hands were roaming all over her body.

"Exactly."

"Why not? I know you don't want me stop." He licked her ear.

"Yes I do, it's that time of the month," she laughed, lying.

"Oh." Legend stopped immediately.

"See. Back up off me."

"Don't think I won't fuck you while you on yo' period."

"Boy, please. I don't even get down like that."

"So, if I wanted to fuck you I couldn't," he said all up in her face, backing her up into a corner.

Becoming flustered she stuttered, "N-n-n-no."

"That's what I thought." Legend laughed.

"You want something to drink?" Zoë questioned, trying to

play it off.

"Yeah, what you got?" he asked as he surveyed her apartment.

Zoë had a real Zen vibe going on in her place. Everything was white, tan and gold. In every room there were fresh flower arrangements ranging from yellow roses to daisies and tulips. Following her into the kitchen, the entire room was decorated in stainless steel. Zoë even had a see-through refrigerator. She loved her kitchen because it was where she spent most of her spare time. Cooking was something that she loved to do.

"I have bottled water, Fuze, Dr. Pepper and some Minute Maid Fruit Punch. Which one you want?"

"I'll have bottled water."

As she handed him his drink, Zoë wondered what was next. She barely knew Legend but thought of him every day. Feelings were running through her that she hadn't felt since she was a teenager. Zoë couldn't help it — she had to know how he felt. She searched his oval-shaped eyes for some kind of emotion. She hoped and prayed that he liked her as much as she liked him but Legend's facial features only showed lust.

"Why you lookin' at me like that?" he asked, snapping her back to reality.

"I wasn't looking at you," she lied again.

"You need to stop lying so much. Your nose is gonna grow like Pinocchio." He smiled, placed down his drink and moved toward her. Hugging her, he picked her up and began to carry her.

"What are you doing?" she asked, perplexed.

"Where is your bedroom?"

"Down the hall and to the right. Why?"

Legend didn't say a word as he placed Zoë down and gently began to peel off her clothes. While undressing her, he made sure to kiss and caress her skin. Loving the feel of his mouth on hers, she moaned. Fully exposed, Zoë prayed that the moment wouldn't end. Making his way up to her lips, Legend massaged her ass while saying, "I want you to go in the bathroom, take a hot bath and put on your sexiest negligee. I gotta make a run right quick. I'll be back in less than hour."

Running his tongue all around her mouth, he made sure he had Zoë nice and hot.

"Less than an hour?"

"Less than an hour," Legend assured.

"Don't be on no bullshit, Legend. I ain't playin'." Zoë looked him dead in the eye.

"I promise."

$ $ $

Four hours later, Zoë sat on her bed alone with the phone in her hand. Every minute that passed by she cursed herself for believing Legend. The nigga was full of shit and she knew it, but it was something in his foreplay that drew her back to him every time. What really tripped her out was the fact that they hadn't even fucked yet and he had her so sprung. "I got to leave this nigga alone," Zoë said out loud.

Gazing across the room, she felt like an absolute idiot for preparing such a display for him. Right after he left, she hurried and took a bath, lotioned up and put on a lavender Agent Provocateur negligee, just like he wanted. Strategically she placed ten tea candles all around her bedroom. The sounds of Kem danced around her ears as the light from the candles showcased her bronze-colored skin.

After another hour and a half, Zoë picked up the phone and called Legend's number for the umpteenth time, only for him not to answer. With one of her arms folded underneath

Keisha Ervin

her breasts, she slammed the phone back down and sighed. To make matters worse, Legend had the keys to her apartment. She gave them to him thinking he would be right back so she wouldn't have to get up and open the door.

Zoë started to wonder if he would he even come back at all. All the what ifs Legend had placed in her head were starting to drive Zoë crazy. She honestly didn't know how much more she could take. A minute later her fears were put to rest when she heard the sound of the front door opening. Instantly her entire body began to tremble with anticipation. She couldn't wait to see his face again. All of the anger she felt suddenly disappeared. Hearing his footsteps nearing the door, she smoothed down any of the wrinkles that appeared in her nightgown. Quickly she wondered what her reaction should be as the doorknob turned. Deciding to go with angry, Zoë rolled her eyes at Legend as soon as he entered the room.

Amazed beyond words, Legend couldn't believe that she had gone through all the trouble of lighting candles and setting a mood for him. He hadn't expected her to go all out. Legend figured by the time he got back, Zoë would be asleep. He looked at her and wondered if he should apologize or leave. Making the decision for him, Zoë said, "Leave my keys on the dresser and get out."

Ignoring her request, Legend slid off his clothes and shoes, placed his gun on the nightstand and got into bed with her.

"Are you hard of hearing? I said get out!"

"Ma, I'm sorry."

"I don't want to hear it, Legend. Just get your shit and go."

"Look, I said I was sorry. Let me make it up to you."

"I don't think so. You better get yo' ass on," Zoë shot, turning her back to him.

"Yo', what the fuck I tell you about yo' mouth," he

snapped, flipping her back over.

Getting on top of her, Legend positioned himself in between her thighs. The smell of his freshly cleansed body drove Zoë insane. To her, there was nothing better than a man that looked and smelled good. Lying so close that they exchanged breaths, she relished the feel of him rubbing and touching her thighs.

Zoë knew she was a fool for giving in to Legend so easily, but getting physical with him was the only way she felt close to him. It had become their routine. He played her, she played mad, they'd argue and then he would please her so well that she would forget about the entire situation. Sometimes she wondered if it was all a game to him. Tracing his finger from her cheek to her lips, Legend watched as Zoë hungrily took it into her mouth.

Licking and sucking his finger, she moaned as Legend toyed with her nipples with his other hand. Zoë knew she couldn't turn back so she opened her mind and let the moment be. There were so many things that she wanted him to do to her. It seemed as if her entire body craved his touch. Feeling the same way, Legend bit and pinched her nipples until they were nice and hard. In one swift move, he replaced his finger with his tongue and placed on a condom. Gazing into her eyes, Legend slowly rubbed his dick against Zoë's vaginal lips.

"Put it in for me," he instructed.

Doing as she was told, Zoë grabbed his dick and slowly eased all nine inches inside of her. Zoë was tight as hell. Legend felt like he was fucking a virgin. As he enjoyed the newness of her pussy, he playfully teased her by pushing himself all the way in, hitting bottom, then pulling out over and over again. It took everything in Legend to hold his cum back; he wanted to bust a nut so bad. Zoë couldn't believe it, they were actually having sex and the feeling was so good. Legend held her waist tight as he slowly pumped in and out. He wanted to make sure that after their first time together, she would want no other.

Zoë thought she was losing her mind; he felt so good. The way he stroked and kissed her lips had her dripping wet with desire. At that moment all expectations were left at the door. The only thing she wanted was for Legend to make her cum. As her first orgasm neared she became dizzy. With her head spinning and her body covered in sweat, Zoë came long and hard. Just getting started, Legend flipped her over onto her stomach.

"Wait, wait, baby, I can't cum again yet." She moaned, trying to pull herself together.

"Fuck that. I'm about to tear your shit up."

And with that said, Legend began hitting it from the back doggystyle. Holding her waist with his hands, he rotated his hips in a circular motion, hitting all four of her corners.

"Legend … baby … ooh stop … you hitting my spooooot … SHIT!!!" Zoë screamed as her thighs began to shake.

"Ah, uh, you … gon' … take … this … dick!"

Grinding hard but slow, Legend continued to hit her with the death stroke. The tightness of her pussy had him going insane. He could feel cum building up in the tip of his dick but being the nigga he was, he held it back. Legend had a point to prove.

"Ooh baby, I'm getting ready to cum again!"

"Gon' and get that shit off, boo," Legend moaned.

"Cum with me!" she demanded. Screaming his name, Zoë came all over his dick.

Cumming too, Legend had to bite down on his lip so he wouldn't scream out like a bitch. Still not done pleasing her, he pulled out and slid his way down in between her thighs.

Keisha Ervin

Tasting the creamy cum that pooled in her wetness, he flicked his tongue across her clit at lighting speed.

"Legend!" she screamed, cumming again for the third time.

"Shh, baby, let me taste you," he said, holding her thighs in place.

"Ooh, I hate you! I hate you!" she moaned as she held onto his head.

Legend wiped his mouth and made his way back up to Zoë's lips. Without saying a word he kissed her lips. Roughly, Legend cupped her chin with his hand and tantalized her tongue with his. He hoped that the words he couldn't convey with his mouth came through with his heart. Hating him and loving him all at the same time, Zoë kissed him back with much intensity.

"You hate me?" he questioned out of nowhere.

"What?" she asked confused.

"You said you hated me."

"I don't even remember saying that," Zoë lied, making light of the situation.

"Yeah, right. Don't ever let that shit come out yo' mouth again," Legend snapped, pushing her away and getting out of bed. Turning over on her side, Zoë knew she was wrong for allowing Legend to fuck all of his mistakes away. Every time she came in contact with him, he played chess with her heart and each time she lost. But being with Legend was like a high she couldn't come down from. As she pulled the covers over her body, Zoë knew that she could only play the fool for Legend for so much longer.

Six Months 10 Later

"That's the only information you have?" Federal Agent Lansing asked.

"Yeah, I told you dude been chillin' since he got engaged," NaSheed answered, smoking a cigarette.

"I don't believe this! We brought you in six months ago and you have yet to give us any information!" Federal Agent Lansing yelled, slamming Bigg's file down onto his desk. "I know McClain is up to no good! Good behavior my ass! He should have never been released from prison in the first place! We thought bringing Agent Johnson in would help, but he hasn't dug up anything either!"

"I'm telling you, Bigg ain't been fuckin' wit' that dope shit no more, man. The dude has gone completely legit."

"McClain didn't start that record company with clean money. He got the money from selling dope. You should know. We caught you transporting his product!"

"Man, why you gotta keep bringing up old shit." NaSheed blew smoke in the agent's direction.

"Looka here you cocky son of a bitch, if I don't have some

Keisha Ervin

hard evidence on Kaylin McClain soon, your ass is gonna be serving fifteen years for drug trafficking!"

"Calm down, man. I told you I'd get you something on him."

"You better because your ass is on the line!"

"Agent Lansing, Agent Johnson is here," Officer Carter said, peeking her head through the door.

"All right, send him in. Agent Johnson, I hope you have some good news. You have to have something on McClain."

"Sorry, the guy has been untouchable so far," Legend replied.

"I don't believe this shit! What the fuck have you been doing this whole time? You have been in McClain's circle for almost six months and you mean to tell me all you've witnessed is some moving violations?"

"What can I say? Bigg is good. He hasn't slipped up once since I've been on the case."

"Well that's not good enough! Do you know how that will make me look if I can't get him in?! Do I have to take you off this case, Johnson? 'Cause I can see traffic duty in your future if I don't have McClain soon!"

"Nah man, just give me some more time to get next to him. If he won't tell NaSheed, his partna of fifteen years, nothing, what makes you think he gon' be quick to talk to me?"

"I don't care! I want him in!" Agent Lansing banged his fist on the table. "Do whatever you have to do! I want McClain in handcuffs by April or else," he continued to yell as he exited his office.

"Yo', you better get on your job 'cause I ain't going to jail for nobody!" NaSheed ordered.

"You better calm down, nigga! Didn't nobody tell yo' dumb ass to sell twenty kilos of cocaine to an undercover cop! I will arrest Bigg when it's time and not a minute earlier!" Legend

Keisha Ervin

declared, unsure of what his next move would be.

$ $ $

"I'm a hustler, I'ma I'm a hustler homey, I'm a hustler, I'ma I'm a hustler homey, Nigga, ask, Nigga, Nigga ask about me, Nigga ask, Nigga, Nigga ask about me," Unique sang along with Cassidy while driving Bigg's pearl-white Navigator through the city.

It was the middle of winter and she was on her way home to prepare dinner for Bigg. The little bit of sun that had peeked through the clouds earlier that morning was now starting to fade away and Unique couldn't wait to snuggle up with Bigg in front of the fireplace. Things couldn't have been better. He kept her laced in the illest snakes, pushing hundred thousand dollar cars. They were the '05 Bonnie & Clyde or Bobby & Whitney— they held each other down. Unique was a rider and Bigg was a roller. Together there was no stopping them.

Bigg was on the come up and had figured out a way to go legit. No more selling coke for him. His record company, Bigg Entertainment, had just inked a deal with a major record label for fifty mil and Unique was more than ready to jump on the money train. Getting home to Bigg was the only thing on her mind, but first she had to see who was following her. Looking through her rearview mirror, she noticed that the same black Ford Taurus she spotted earlier was still behind her. Curious to see if she was being followed, she made a left onto Kingshighway Boulevard. The Taurus made a left, too, which prompted Unique to speed up.

She looked through the rearview mirror again and read the license plate number. It read 555-JZH. Repeating the number over and over again, she placed it into memory. She didn't know who was following her but it had to have something to do with Bigg since she was driving his car. The windows on the Taurus were tinted so she couldn't see the driver's face, but she did make out that there were two men in the car.

Riding down Natural Bridge, she made a quick turn onto Ridgedale, then onto Myron. Cutting onto a couple more side streets, she shook the Taurus and hopped on the highway heading to Bigg's studio. A little shaken but never scurred, Unique grabbed her purse and headed into the studio to tell Bigg what happened.

> *"Money over bitches that's all that stay on my mind*
> *Two or three bitches on my arm at all time*
> *Hustlin' ain't the same, the game way to serious*
> *Sickest flow, now ya know, leave ya hoe delirious*
> *Muthafuckas out here bitin' my adlibs*
> *Come to the Lou my nigga see where I live*
>
> *I'm on the grind all day*
> *Hustlin' the block flippin' keys that's how I make my pay*
> *The kid been in the game for far to long*
> *Nothin' holdin' me back my will too strong."*

"What you think?" Chris asked from inside the booth.

"Yo' nigga that was some heat!" Legend shouted to Chris.

"Do it again," Bigg instructed, taking a swig of Patrón.

"Why? We got what we needed right there."

"It wasn't good enough! Do it again!"

"Here this nigga go." Cezar laughed while sparking up a Cuban cigar.

"I ain't gon' be in this hot-ass booth all day, man! I got shit to do!" Chris shouted.

"Just do the verse over and quit bitchin'!" Bigg yelled back.

"Chill out, dog," Cezar said, sensing Bigg's frustration. Holding his head in his hand, Bigg shook his head and tried his best to clear his mind.

"My bad, take five."

"You was spittin' some straight fire though, dog," Legend said as Chris came out of the booth.

"Yo', I was feeling that shit. It was like I was in the zone or something."

"Shit, you were."

"That nigga NaSheed still ain't showed up?"

"Nah, that nigga ain't here yet." Bigg leaned back into his chair. "I don't know what's up wit' dude."

"That nigga a'ight, don't even trip." Legend tried to smooth the situation over.

"I don't know, man," Bigg replied.

"What up, Nique?" Chris spoke as he saw her come through the door.

"What's up, Chris?" Unique strutted over to him dressed simply in a black fitted velvet blazer, Citizens of Humanity jeans tucked inside a pair black patent leather Gucci boots and in her hand she held the Gucci purse Bigg bought her in Louisiana. Her hair was pulled back in a sleek ponytail with swoop bangs showcasing her brown eyes. With a smile on her face, she gave Chris a hug. As usual the studio was filled with smoke. Holding her chest, Unique coughed and said, "What it do, Legend? Where my girl at?"

"She at home studying, she got a test tomorrow."

"A'ight, tell her I'ma call her tomorrow if you talk to her."

"I will."

"What's good, mommy?" Cezar spoke.

"Nothing. Just visiting my boo." Unique planted a wet kiss on Bigg's lips.

"What you doing here? I told you I was gon' meet you at

home," he said, clearly agitated with her presence.

"Well hi to you too, muthafucka." Unique matched his attitude. "I came to tell you that some niggas was just following me."

"Word?" Chris said, shocked.

"Yeah, some niggas in a black Ford Taurus with tinted windows but you know I shook they ass." Unique smiled.

"You all right?" Bigg finally asked.

"Yeah, I'm good. I just want to know what's going on. Do I have to carry my nine wit' me now?"

"Look at yo' trigger happy ass," Legend laughed.

"Nah, you good, ma. I told you, I got you."

"Well, since you're so *busy,* I'll leave." Unique rolled her eyes at Bigg.

"Sit yo' ass down. You ain't going nowhere."

"I don't have to stay. I see that I'm not welcomed."

"Just sit down and wait until we finish this session and follow me home."

"Damn, did you ask me if I wanted to stay or did you tell me?"

"Unique, I ain't the mood to be playing with you. SIT DOWN!"

Checking her, she rolled her eyes, sucked her teeth, folded her arms and plopped down on the couch next to Legend. Anybody else would've gotten cussed out or even cut for talking to her like that, but Bigg was her man and he was only trying to keep her safe. Turning his back on her, he resumed the recording session without NaSheed.

"What the fuck is his problem?" Unique whispered to Legend.

"I don't know." He shrugged. Looking over at Bigg, Unique knew that there was more to the situation then what met the eye. Silently she prayed that his disorder wasn't returning, because if it was, Unique knew that at any moment all hell could break loose.

"Ya baby momma not actin' right
She let me beat the pussy up, now you cryin' dialin' my number can't sleep at night
St. Louis' Finest no other can do it better — "

"What's really good?!" NaSheed interrupted with a bottle of Chandon in hand and a crew of niggas not too far behind.

"This nigga," Chris whispered under his breath inside the booth.

"Where the fuck you been?" Bigg questioned.

"Calm down, money. I was chilling wit' my peoples. I'm about to get my drink on." NaSheed took a swig of champagne from the bottle then passed it to Bigg.

"Get that shit out my face! You knew we had a session. You could've done that later."

"Chill wit' that shit. I'm here, ain't I?" NaSheed waved Bigg off which was a huge mistake.

"Nigga, who the fuck you think you talkin' to?" Bigg barked.

"Bigg, calm down," Unique called out. She knew that Bigg was a time bomb just waiting to go off, if given the chance.

"Shut up, Unique! Mind your business!" Bigg warned.

"What's up wit' your man?" one of NaSheed's people asked.

"Nigga, what you say?" Bigg challenged the dude. "You better get yo' boy, NaSheed. Matter of fact, don't bring these bummy-ass niggas to my studio no more! Ain't nobody supposed to be in here but the staff and us anyway! From now on, I don't want nobody in here that I don't know!"

"What the fuck is yo' problem, dog?" NaSheed questioned, barely able to stand up straight.

"Nah, nigga! What the fuck is yo' problem? You been late to the last couple of sessions. When you do show up, you either drunk or high off that X! What, you an E head now, nigga? I'm tryin' to run a business. Keep that block shit on the block!"

"You buggin', man. You need to chill 'cause the shit ain't even that serious. Smoke a blunt and relax." NaSheed waved him off again.

Yoking him up, Bigg barked, "Nigga, I'm about tired of yo' shit!"

"Bigg, let him go!" Unique yelled, grabbing his arm.

"Get the fuck off me!" Yanking his arm away from her caused Unique to stumble and fall to the floor. "Yo', I'm sorry, baby," Bigg said, catching himself.

"Nah, see, this is what the fuck I be talkin' about!" she snapped, getting up. "Can't nobody talk to you when you get like this! I ain't none of these nigga! You ain't gon' talk to me crazy! Kill him for all I care!" Unique grabbed her purse and left. Letting go of NaSheed's collar, Bigg sat back down and lit a Cuban cigar.

"What the fuck is yo' problem, NaSheed? You need to lay off them pills and shit, dog," Chris stated.

"Ya'll niggas be trippin'. I ain't got time for this shit, I'm up."

"Don't come back until you get yo' self together." Bigg blew out a breath of smoke.

"You know what Bigg, fuck you," NaSheed said as he left.

"Yeah, a'ight nigga, fuck you too," Bigg yelled after him.

"Yo' boy trippin' for real." Legend shook his head.

"That's yo' boy," Chris replied, shaking his head.

"Fuck that nigga. Let me call this big head girl before I choke her." Bigg picked up his cell phone and dialed her number. He let the phone ring until the voicemail picked up.

Hanging up, he called again only to find out that she had turned off her phone.

"I swear to God, I'm gon' fuck her up."

"Nique ain't answering the phone?" Legend asked.

"Nah, the session's over. Lock up, I gotta go find this chick."

$ $ $

"Nique!" Bigg yelled as he entered his home. No one answered back. "Nique, I know you hear me!"

Bigg turned on the light switch in his bedroom and found Unique sound asleep in his bed. He turned the light back off, smiled and went into the master bath to take a shower. Bigg placed his head underneath the steamy hot water and tried to forget the day's events. He had been under a tremendous amount of stress lately.

The Feds were all over his back, watching his every move. NaSheed was trippin' not showing up to recording sessions, wasting Bigg's time, money and patience. The only sane thing he had in his life was Unique, and the way things were going between them lately, he was sure he was gonna lose her, too. It seemed like every day Unique and Bigg were arguing over petty, ignorant shit. With both of them being pig-headed, neither was willing to back down. Bigg could feel it in his heart that if something else bad happened, he would most definitely lose his mind.

After a ten minute shower, he dried off, lotioned up and put on a pair of boxer-briefs. Reentering the room, Bigg hopped into bed and fell asleep as soon as his head hit the pillow. Fifteen minutes later he was awakened with a thundering smack across the face. Hopping up, he immediately grabbed his nine from underneath his pillow and aimed it in the direction of the hit.

"Put the gun down! Wit' yo' scary ass!"

"What the fuck is yo' problem? What you hit me for?"

"'Cause of that shit you pulled earlier!"

"Hit me again and I'm gon' fuck you up!" Bigg promised as he turned back over, pissed.

"Nigga, you ain't gon' do shit!" Unique kicked him in the leg as hard as she could.

Sitting up, Bigg pushed her with all his might onto the plush carpet that lay below. With a loud thump she landed on the floor. Unique recovered quickly though and climbed back into bed throwing bows left and right. She missed, trying to hit Bigg in the face, giving him enough time to grab her hands. Pinning her down onto her back, Bigg placed all of his weight onto her while roughly pushing her thighs apart with his legs.

With her hands in his, he kissed her deeply. Running his tongue across her lips he stopped to suck her bottom lip. Bigg then let one of her hands go so that he could trace his free hand down her side. Once he reached her center he played in the wetness that already lay in between her thighs.

"Ahh," Unique moaned, arching her back. Bigg couldn't wait to devour her body as he gazed down upon it. Noticing that she had on nothing but a white tee, he became even more aroused.

"Why you got on one of my T-shirts?" he asked as he kissed her breasts through the shirt, leaving wet marks around her nipples.

"'Cause … you weren't here … ooh … and I wanted to feel like … you were here with me," she moaned, trembling from his touch.

Licking her breasts, Bigg ripped the T-shirt down the middle, exposing her full breasts. He took them both and pushed

Keisha Ervin

them together, running his tongue back and forth across her swollen nipples. On a sexual high, Unique rubbed Bigg's head and bit into her bottom lip. They locked eyes with one another as he placed kisses from her breasts up to her mouth.

Bigg swam in a sea of wetness as he entered her. He almost broke down and busted a nut on his first stroke, but Bigg was gangsta, he wasn't going out like that. He had to put it down on Unique. The two intertwined their fingers as they rocked to a hard but slow, steady beat. Already beginning to feel weak, Bigg buried his face into the crook of Unique's neck. She held his hands tight and cried out in ecstasy as he circled his hips slow and hard, in and out of her wet slit repeatedly. Unique could already feel herself cumming.

"Bigg, Bigg, wait … I'm not … ooh … I'm not ready to cum … cum yet," she stuttered.

"You love me?"

"Yes. You love me?" she asked as she kissed and bit into his soft skin.

"Without a doubt."

Wrapping her legs around him as they kissed, Unique and Bigg continued to make love into the wee hours of the morning.

Keisha Ervin

11
I Can Feel It in the Air

"Look Bigg, that's the new Louis Vuitton denim mono-gram purse that I was telling you about!" Unique replied excit-edly as they walked hand and hand in Frontenac Plaza. "Ooh please, can I get it?" she begged.

"I don't care, Nique. Here, hurry up and go get it so I can hit up the Nike store." Bigg handed her three thousand dol-lars. "You know the new Jordans came out today."

"Thank you, baby." She smiled, kissing his cheek.

"Yeah, whatever, just make sure you get on them knees later on tonight," he joked.

"Fuck you." Unique laughed while walking into the store.

Standing outside the Louis store, Bigg pulled out a Black & Mild to ease his weed fix until he got back to the car. He and Unique had already spent over ten grand hitting store after store. After lighting the Black & Mild, he inhaled then exhaled the sweet smoke slowly. Bigg had been on edge the past cou-ple of weeks. It seemed like if it wasn't one thing it was anoth-er with him. NaSheed was clowning, not showing up to ses-sions and Bigg swore that he felt as if he were being watched.

More than ever he was drinking and smoking to calm the nervousness he felt. Bigg hadn't taken his medication in weeks so he was really over the edge. Anything anybody said to him out the way, he flipped out. Even Unique had to be put in check a couple of times.

Studying his surroundings, Bigg knew that something wasn't quit right; he could feel it in his gut. Suddenly he noticed a white van with the words "Forget Me Not Florist" written across the side. Any patron walking down the street wouldn't have thought twice but Bigg knew better.

The van stuck out like a sore thumb amongst the Mercedes Benzes, Lexus trucks and Bentley coupes. Plus, the fact that every other minute the window would roll down about five inches and a camera would peek through sealed Bigg's suspensions. Bigg shook his head knowing well it was nobody but undercover cops photographing him. *They're probably the muthafuckas that were following Unique*, he thought. With a smile on his face, Bigg put his middle finger up at them. Tapping on the store window, he signaled to Unique to hurry up. Five minutes later she walked out with a huge smile spread across her face.

"Come on, we gotta go home," he confirmed, grabbing her hand and cutting their shopping spree short.

"Why? We just got here."

"Don't look, but across the street it's a van with some undercover cops in it, taking pictures of us."

"Why would the police be taking pictures of us, Bigg?" Unique asked with an attitude, snatching her hand away.

"Don't make me be beat yo' ass out in this muthafucka. Don't say shit while we in the car. They probably got it bugged."

Unique seethed with anger as she got into the Lexus truck that Bigg had bought for her birthday. As they rode down the highway heading home, Bigg looked through the rearview mirror every five minutes to make sure he wasn't being followed. Out of nowhere he signaled to Unique to check the truck for bugs. Doing as she was told she began to search the car for anything suspicious.

Gliding her hand across the interior above the window, she felt a bump underneath the suede ceiling. Unique needed something to tear the material with so she used a pocket knife that was in her purse. In less than a minute she had torn a hole into the suede material revealing a listening device. Showing it to Bigg he shook his head in disbelief and hit the steering wheel, heated.

Unique then climbed into the back and searched her cream leather seats. She searched the headrest, seat and floor, only to find nothing but something told her to keep going. Running her hand underneath the seat, she found a small tracking device. Unique threw the bug out the window and climbed back into the front seat.

"Now that that's taken care of, what the fuck is going on?"

"I don't know!" Bigg barked.

"Well you need to find out!"

"They probably got my phone tapped, and yours, too," he thought out loud.

"Mine! Why the fuck would my phone be tapped?"

"'Cause you my girl and they know that I be at yo' house so watch what you say over the phone from now on."

"What are you going to do, Bigg?"

"I'm gon' keep on doing me. I ain't letting the po-pos or nobody else come between me and paper."

$ $ $

"How much you got?"

Keisha Ervin

"Only fifteen thousand," Kay Kay spoke.

"What the fuck am I supposed to do with fifteen thousand dollars?"

"The job was only worth sixty-five grand, Cezar, damn," Kiara snapped.

"Watch yo' mouth!" Cezar shouted, upset. "Ya'll haven't been pulling your weight since Unique left."

"Fuck Unique, we don't need her."

"You need somebody 'cause this shit ain't working."

"I'm sorry, Cezar, don't pay her no mind. I'll think of something," Kay Kay apologized, preparing to leave. Seeing that Kiara wasn't behind her she asked, "You coming?"

"Yeah, here I come. I got to go use the bathroom."

"A'ight, meet me at the car." Once Kiara saw that Kay Kay was out of sight, she turned her attention toward Cezar.

"You know that I've missed you, right?" she purred with a devilish grin on her face.

"Is that right?"

"Yeah, can I show you how much I've missed you?" Kiara kissed his stomach as she began to unbuckle his pants. Getting down onto her knees she took his thick, hard dick into her hand and began to suck.

"Shit," Cezar moaned.

"You like that, baby?" Kiara moaned as she deep throated his dick.

"Yes!"

"I knew you missed me."

"Damn right I missed you," Cezar moaned, grabbing her hair.

"Since ... you ... missed me ... so much ... let me get some work," she asked in between sucking.

Shocked by her request, he pushed her head away. "Get the fuck off me!"

Keisha Ervin

"What's your problem? Don't act like we ain't done this before!"

"I should've known you were up to something!"

"Why you trippin'? I just need a little fix."

"You better get yo' ass up outta here with that shit," Cezar barked, infuriated.

"Come on, Cez, hook a bitch up."

"Now I see what Unique meant. You are irresponsible. What about your daughter, Kiara? Do you think about her while you smoking that shit?"

"Don't talk about my daughter!" she yelled, thinking of Arissa.

"Get the fuck up outta here!"

"I don't need you or my cousin, fuck both of ya'll," Kiara screamed as she grabbed her bag and left.

Still heated, Kiara made sure the coast was clear before opening her purse. Kay Kay was parked two houses up so she couldn't see her. Taking the last bit of cocaine she had in a small Ziploc bag, she sniffed it up each nostril. Immediately she felt relaxed. Now that she was calm, Kiara plotted her next move. All of a sudden a sinister grin appeared on her face. Her cousin wasn't the only one who got her way with men. The next time Kiara saw Bigg she was sure to get her way with him.

$ $ $

In a matter of weeks, things in Bigg's life had gone from bad to worse. Bigg's manic depressive episodes had returned. He had done nothing but drink and pace the floors for the past couple of weeks. Unique had never seen him like this before so she didn't know what to do. Seeing him in such a state hurt her heart in the worst way. When he was this way, Bigg was no

Keisha Ervin

good to anyone, not even himself. His decision making wasn't the same when he was having an episode. He tried being strong but really, he was at his weakest during times like these.

Bigg wouldn't accept any calls from anyone and he barely wanted to talk to Unique, either. She had seen this too many times before, dealing with her mother, but her mother never had guns in the house. Bigg's sawed-off shot gun stayed by his side at all times and Unique was forbidden to go anywhere outside of the house. She tried explaining to him that she needed to go home to check on Patience but he wouldn't listen.

To make matters worse, his son Dontay was over for the weekend. Unique tried to get him to take his medication, but each time she brought it up, Bigg would only go off and tell her to leave him alone. He could smell it in the air; something was brewing beneath the surface. Sitting alone in his four-cornered living room, he sat in his favorite lounge chair puffing on Purple Haze.

Visions of the Feds busting the doors down danced in his head over and over. At that moment, Bigg didn't trust anything with a pulse. Something in the back of his head kept on telling him to tighten his circle, but who was out to get him? He couldn't figure out. Hearing breathing behind him he quickly turned, cocked and pointed his gun.

"Bigg!" Unique screamed.

"What the fuck I tell you about creeping around this muthafucka!" he yelled, un-cocking his gun.

"Bigg, it's getting late. Come to bed," she pleaded. "You haven't slept in days."

"Shh ... they watching," he said drunkenly and out of his mind.

"Who?"

"You don't see them?"

"Nobody's outside, baby, you're scaring me," she said, looking around the dark room, feeling crazy herself.

"Dontay sleep?"

"Yeah, baby. I think you should let me take him home, though. He doesn't need to be around you right now."

"Don't tell me my son don't need to be around me!" Bigg yelled, frightening her.

"I'm sorry, you're right. Dontay does need to be here with you."

"Come here." Taking a seat in his lap she sat sideways and hugged his neck tight. "I saw the devil last night. He sat right there across from me in that chair and told me that I was going to die."

"Baby, please take your pills 'cause it's only going to get worse if you don't."

"I ain't takin' them fuckin' pills, Nique! That shit fucks wit' your brain! I ain't no fiend! I ain't tryna to get hooked on no drug!"

"But Bigg, you can't stay cooped up in here for the rest of your life."

"You don't understand, ma. Every time I close my eyes I see niggas out to get me. It's always the same thing. I'm out and this dude approaches me. I go to shake his hand but his handshake ain't matching his smile. I can tell the nigga ain't right."

"You think somebody you know a snitch?"

Ignoring her question and without any warning, Bigg hopped up and dropped Unique to the floor. He grabbed his gun and headed over to the window. Somebody had just pulled up next door. Peeking through the blinds, he watched the car carefully with his finger on the trigger. Not knowing what to do, Unique sat on the floor with her hands up to her face, crying.

Her mother's episodes were never like this so she didn't know what to do. Reasoning with Bigg didn't work so the only thing she could do was sit idly by, praying that the old Bigg would come back to her soon. Not moving until the car eased out of the driveway, Bigg turned around to find Unique sobbing uncontrollably.

"What the fuck are you crying for?" Unable to stop, Unique continued to cry. "I swear to God if you don't shut the fuck up I'm gon' kill you," Bigg said menacingly with a cold blank stare in his eyes.

He had told her plenty of times before that he would kill her but those times were chalked up to him just playing, but not this time. Unique could tell that this time was different. Seeing Bigg like this brought back all the memories of her childhood. Holding her breath, Unique willed herself not to cry. Bigg saw the fear in her eyes and smiled.

He hadn't felt this much power in a long time. Too much shit was going wrong for him and he couldn't quite bring it all back together. At any moment he felt as if his mind would explode. Sitting back down, Bigg picked up his last bottle of Grey Goose and continued to drink.

"Niggas think they gon' get me? Ya'll niggas can't see me," Bigg said out loud to the demons seated before him. "You want me come get me! Stupid-ass niggas! I ain't scared!" he whispered as he stared at the gun resting on his lap. "I'll take my own life before I let you take it."

"Bigg," Unique said just above a whisper.

"What?"

"I need to use the bathroom, is it OK that I get up?"

"Why the fuck you asking me some dumb-ass shit like that, Nique! Go use the muthafuckin' bathroom!"

Bigg had already forgotten about dropping her to the floor

and threatening to kill her. Easing her way off the floor, she kept her eyes on him and the gun at the same time. Once she hit the steps she ran as fast as she could. Unique couldn't take it anymore. She had to get up out of there. Packing things for herself and Dontay, she prepared to leave.

Once packed, she went into Dontay's room. There he was, peacefully asleep. He looked just like Bigg. Dontay possessed the same mocha-colored skin and oval-shaped face that his father had. Unique couldn't wait to have a son of her own. By the time she made it back downstairs, Bigg had finally dozed off to sleep.

Unique walked over to Bigg and took a look at the man she was in love with. "Bigg, I'm going home," she whispered quietly with tears streaming down her face while holding his sleeping son in her arms.

"You see them, Nique? They think they slick, trying to creep up on me."

She bent down and kissed him on the cheek. "Bigg, I love you but I can't stand to see you like this anymore."

Bigg opened his eyes, thinking he was dreaming, but her words and her close presence startled him. "Not now, Nique. I ain't got time for this shit!"

Bigg's booming voice startled his sleeping son. Climbing down out of Unique's arms, Dontay stood by her side and held her hand.

"I can't help you if you won't let me, Bigg, so I'm going home." Seeing a duffle bag sitting by the door, he realized that she wasn't playing.

"So you just gon' leave me like this?"

"I don't want to but you need some help and evidently I can't give it to you." Hating the sound of her voice, Bigg told himself that he didn't care if she left or stayed.

"Fuck you, Unique! You just like my mother and that bitch

Carmella! The first chance you get you gon' leave. Well fuck you then! Leave!" He turned his head and closed his eyes. A minute or two passed by before Bigg reopened his eyes and turned, only to find Unique still standing there. "What, you can't hear? Get the fuck out! Leave!"

Hurt beyond words, Unique's chest began to heave up and down as her lips trembled with fear. She felt the tears rising in her throat but she still tried to hold them in. Looking up at her, Bigg knew that he was wrong but at that moment he didn't give a fuck. Not wanting to, but knowing she had to, Unique turned her back to Bigg, grabbed her keys, held tightly onto the little hand that was inside of hers and left.

It took Unique approximately twenty minutes to get to Carmella's house. It was the middle of night and all of the lights were out. Only talking on the phone a couple of times, she didn't know how Carmella would react seeing her on her doorstep with her son. Stepping up to the door, Unique knocked quietly, not wanting to wake Dontay who fell asleep during the ride. It took a minute but she finally came to the door.

"Who is it?"

"Carmella, it's me, Unique."

"Is everything all right?" she asked, opening the door.

"Yes and no."

"Come in, it's freezing outside."

"I'm sorry I didn't call first. Bigg wouldn't give me your number."

"What's going on?" she asked, taking Dontay from Unique's arms and laying him down on the couch.

"Bigg is having an episode and I didn't want Dontay to be around him while he is like that."

"Thank you. I'm glad you brought him home."

"Well it's late, let me get home." Unique bit down on her

lip, unsure of what else to say.

"Wait, there's something I want to talk to you about."

Puzzled, Unique wondered what Carmella could possibly want to discuss with her. The two had nothing in common besides loving Bigg. To Unique, Carmella was nothing but a square broad that wasn't down to ride for her man. Curious, she followed her into the kitchen and took a seat at the table.

"Would you like a cup of coffee?"

"Yes please, I could use it."

"I know how you feel. I used to be just like you."

"What do you mean by that?" Unique questioned, getting defensive.

"I didn't mean it like that. I meant that I used to feel like I needed to save Bigg, too, but no matter how hard I tried, I never could."

"I just don't know what to do," Unique said, letting her guard down.

"There's really nothing you can do, Unique. Bigg has to help himself first before anybody can help him. I tried getting him to take his medication but he wouldn't and I got tired of the highs and lows that came along with being with him."

"I can't get him to take his medication, either."

"And you won't be able to until he gets over his fears."

"I don't get it though, why won't he take it?"

"I guess he never told you what happened."

"No, what happened?"

"When Bigg was 12, his mom started to notice that something wasn't quite right with him. You know, he would start spazzing out for no reason and she never understood why. Well back then, nobody knew what being Bipolar was, so she sent him to a mental institution instead of to a doctor. The facility she put Bigg in was like something out of a horror flick. Bigg said they put him in a straight jacket and tied him

Keisha Ervin

down to his bed at night. They shot him up with all kinds of different experimental drugs. Now mind you he was only 12 years old," Carmella explained, handing Unique her cup of coffee.

"The orderlies beat the fuck out of him because he talked back. You know that long gash on his back came from when he was in that mental institution. One of the orderlies beat him so bad with a belt that the skin on his back opened up. He had to get stitches and everything. They even did shock treatments on him. He told me that he cried for his mother and begged her to let him come home but she wouldn't. You know that bitch was evil."

"I know." Unique nodded her head in agreement. "Bigg told me about his mother."

"Yeah, I'm glad her ass died before I had Dontay 'cause ain't no way I would've let her come around him. But anyway, he was there for a month and after he got out, Bigg said he was like a walking zombie. They had him hooked on so many drugs that he didn't know which way was left and which way was right. It took him another month to get the drugs out of his system."

"I wonder why he never told me that," Unique said with tears in her eyes.

"He probably didn't want you to worry since your mom is in a mental institution."

"How you know about my mom?"

"Well, I did do a little background checking on you once I found out you and Bigg were serious."

"I see." Unique nodded, knowing she would've done the same thing.

"I couldn't deal with it, Unique, but you're stronger than I am when it comes to his illness. Bigg loves you. I've never seen him happier. Even when we were together he was never

Keisha Ervin

this happy."

"I love him, too, it just got a little hard tonight. It all reminded me of my mother and how she used to be."

"Well you're about to be his wife, Unique. You gotta hold him down."

12
Cold

With Bigg gone, nothing in Unique's life was the same. She knew that he needed her but he wouldn't listen to anything she had to say. With the television on and turned down, she turned the volume up on the stereo and sang along to Mary J. Blige's *"Don't Go."*

"Every day is not perfect day, for you and I somedays
Somedays things are just not right, that doesn't mean
that I don't love you
And boy you know it's true, I cannot always please
you."

"Unique, Unique!" Patience screamed, scaring the hell out of her.

"What?" Unique asked, holding her chest.

"Turn on the news! They're talkin' about Bigg."

Unique knew that something bad must have happened so she rushed over to the television and turned the volume up.

In other local news, federal investigators searched the offices of Bigg Entertainment, the record label home of local rappers St. Louis' Finest, as part of an ongoing investigation of CEO Kaylin McClain, better known as Bigg. The authorities are reportedly investigating whether or not money from drug trafficking helped Mr. McClain break into the music industry. The authorities are also looking into a number of attacks as a part of their allegations. St. Louis City Officials also seized computers and documents during the raid. We'll have more on this story during the nightly news.

"Shit!" Unique said, grabbing the phone, dialing Bigg's cell but getting no answer. She hung up and called Zoë.

"Hello?"

"Are you watching the news?"

"No, I'm waiting on Legend. We're going out on a date but he's late for some reason."

"Bigg's studio just got raided by the Feds."

"For real?" Zoë replied nonchalantly knowing the code — *Don't say shit over the phone.*

"Yeah."

"Have you talked to him?"

"No. I tried calling his cell but he didn't pick up."

"Damn, that's fucked up. You want me to come over there?"

"Yeah but I don't want to fuck up your plans."

"It's cool, ma. Let me call Legend and see what's up." Clicking over, Zoë dialed his cell.

"Hello?"

"Where you at?"

"I got caught up fuckin' with this nigga Gary. How about we get together tomorrow?" he lied. Legend was really at the police station going through evidence found in Bigg's office.

"OK, but you could've called," Zoë said with an attitude.

"I know, baby, I'm sorry. I'll make it up to you tomorrow, I promise." Thinking about the things he did with his tongue, she smiled as she clicked him off and resumed her conversation with Unique.

"Well, I'm free so I'll be over there in like thirty minutes. We can go out and have drinks or something."

"A'ight one," Unique said, hanging up.

Dialing Bigg's phone once more, she left him a message telling him to call her ASAP. Across the way, Bigg sat on a bar stool at T Billy's as if nothing had happened, sipping on a bottle of Hen. Once Chris heard about the raid on the studio, he decided it was best to get Bigg out of the house before he hurt himself or someone else. Surveying the crowd, Bigg knew that they were all watching him but he didn't give a fuck. They could all suck his dick as far as he was concerned.

Beep...Beep went the sound of Bigg's cell phone but he didn't care. He saw Unique's number flashing across the screen of his phone but he couldn't talk to her. He was still mad at the fact that she had left him. To him, Unique left him at the one time he needed her most. The first chance she got, she up and ran out on him. In Bigg's mind that was looked upon as betrayal and he couldn't forgive her for that so soon.

"Sup, Bigg," Kiara playfully whispered into his ear.

"What's up, Ki?"

"Shit, I heard what happened. You a'ight?"

"You know a nigga straight. The Feds ain't got nothing on me." Bigg played it off.

"Where my cousin at?"

"She at home I guess."

"Uh oh, do I detect trouble in paradise?"

"We cool."

"Just cool? You and Nique used to be great. You know, honestly, I never saw ya'll together anyway."

"Why you say that?" Bigg asked, walking dead into her trap.

"It's nothing." She smirked, waving him off.

"If you got something to say, say it."

"I shouldn't be the one telling you this, but my cousin is foul."

"What you mean, Unique foul?"

"Are you sure you want to hear this?"

"I ain't got time to play wit' you, Kiara! Just tell me what the fuck is up!"

"OK, OK, damn. Calm down. You not gon' like this but … Unique and Tone are still fuckin' around."

Feeling his heart drop out of his chest, Bigg stared ahead showing no emotion on his face. He learned at an early age to never let his true feelings show. *Always keep your feelings close to your heart*, his father would say.

"I'm sorry, Bigg, I shouldn't have told you."

"Man, get the fuck outta here. I don't believe that shit. Unique hasn't had any contact with that nigga in almost a year."

"Sorry Bigg, but I have proof."

"What kind of proof?"

"Tone showed me these pictures the last time I saw him here," she said, reaching into her purse. "Here." She handed him the photos.

The first photo showed Unique getting out of Bigg's Range Rover and heading into Tone's house. The second one showed them coming out together with Tone having nothing but a pair of boxers on. The third one showcased Unique hugging and Tone smiling.

"When I saw them, I took 'em 'cause I didn't want him putting my cousin's business out there in the street," Kiara continued, making the situation worse.

He couldn't believe it — Kiara was actually telling the truth. Unique was fucking Tone. The blood in Bigg's body was past the boiling point. First the Feds were watching him, then his studio gets raided and now his girl was playing him. He couldn't take it anymore. Bigg was about to snap. Seeing that her plan was working, Kiara tried her best to hide the wicked grin that was slowly creeping onto her face.

She knew that taking the pictures of Unique and Tone would pay off sooner or later. It was just a matter of the perfect time and place and she couldn't have planned it better if she tried. Kiara knew that some shit was about to go down when they all returned from New Jersey so the day of their last meeting together, she followed Unique. Unique never had a clue.

"I can't believe this shit."

"I'm sorry, Bigg," she said sympathetically. "Is there anything I can do to help?" Kiara traced her finger down his cheek, getting in his face.

"You and Unique are cousins, why you telling me all of this?"

"'Cause Unique living foul and I don't condone that shit. How she could play a fine nigga like you, I'll never know."

"And you never will," Bigg replied, pushing past her.

"Ah nigga, you should be thanking me!"

$ $ $

Less than ten minutes later, Bigg was at Unique's building banging on her door. He had been standing there for five minutes before he realized that she wasn't there. Taking his phone out of his pocket he dialed her cell but she didn't answer that either. Already heated, he assumed that she was with Tone. Walking back to his car, he decided the best thing to do was wait.

$ $ $

"You feel any better?"

"A little, I won't be OK until I know Bigg's OK though." Unique said as she and Zoë rode back to her house.

"Girl, everything's gonna be a'ight. You and Bigg have made it through plenty of other shit. Ya'll gon' make it through this, too."

"I keep on telling myself that." Unique began to speak but felt a vibration coming from her purse. It was her two-way going off. "Damn, he just called me and I missed it. I'll call him when I get in the house."

"You want me to stay for a little while?" Zoë asked as they pulled up to Unique's building.

"Nah, I'm cool, but thanks anyway," she replied, mustering up a smile.

"OK, I'm gon' holla at you tomorrow then."

"A'ight," Unique said, in a hurry to get out of the car and in the house. Quickly noticing Bigg stepping out of his Range Rover, a smile a mile wide appeared on Unique's face. "Bigg," she gushed as he approached her.

"What up, Bigg?" Zoë spoke, rolling down the passenger side window.

"You fuckin' that nigga?!" he barked, getting into Unique's face and pinning her up against the car.

"What?" she asked, caught off guard.

"You heard me! You still fuckin' Tone?" He yanked her up by the neck.

"Bigg, stop!" Zoë yelled.

"Bigg, what are you talkin' about? You trippin', baby. Come in the house so you can get some rest," Unique pleaded, trying to remove his hand from her neck.

"Fuck you! I ain't going nowhere wit' you!" Bigg yelled, back-handing her face as tears fell from his eyes onto her hands. Jumping out of the car, Zoë raced to help her cousin. "You been fuckin' that nigga behind my back this whole time?"

"What the fuck are you talkin' about, Bigg?" she asked, unsure of what to do because of his mental state.

"I know you been fuckin' that nigga! I saw the pictures, bitch! I told you if I ever caught you wit' that nigga I was gon' kill you! How the fuck you gon' play me like that?" Bigg continued to cry as he looked her in dead in the eyes.

"Bigg, I don't know what you think you saw but you need to let her go! Unique ain't fuckin' Tone!"

"Baby, let's just go in the house and talk about this. Somebody's been lying to you."

"Why the fuck would yo' cousin lie to me?" he yelled, throwing her body up against the car.

"My cousin?"

"Yeah, Kiara!"

"Kiara told you that shit?" Zoë asked, shocked.

"She told me everything! Your game is up!"

"I don't know what you're talkin' about, Bigg! I swear!" Unique assured.

"Yeah, a'ight, keep lying! I can't believe you! I'm out here watching my back thinking these niggas is out to get me when all along I should've been watching you! Snake-ass bitch! How the fuck you gon' play me like that? I was planning on marrying you!"

"What is going on out here?" Jeffery, the doorman, questioned.

Keisha Ervin

"Nigga, mind yo' business," Bigg snapped.

"How dare you speak to me like that! I'm calling the police!"

"Jeffery, please don't! He didn't mean it!" Turning back to Bigg, she continued, "Baby, please. Don't do this! We still can get married!"

"I knew you was a sleazy bitch! Got me out here in these streets grindin' for you and that's how you do me! That's a'ight though 'cause I'm done fuckin' wit' yo' trick ass!" He pushed her with all this might causing her neck to jerk back.

"Bigg, look what you did! Are you OK?" Zoë asked, examining Unique for injuries.

"I'm OK. Bigg, wait! Let me explain!" she begged, holding her neck and trying to reach for his hand.

"Fuck you! Don't touch me! I trusted you!"

"Fuck me? No, fuck you! After all we've been through you gon' say fuck me?" Unique yelled, trying to break loose from Zoë so she could hit Bigg.

"Ah uh, Z! Let me go! This nigga done lost his mind!"

"Zoë, take her in the house! She's making a fool out of herself." Bigg walked away, ignoring her.

"Oh, so, I'm a fool now? After all I've done for you, you gon' do me like this? I was the one who took care of you when yo' retarded, depressed ass needed help! Me, Bigg! Not Cezar, not Kiara, not Chris, not NaSheed! Me! And you gon' have the audacity to accuse me of some bullshit I didn't even do! NIGGA FUCK YOU!"

Unique knew that she was hurting him but she didn't care. Bigg had made a fool out of her. Watching him as he left, Unique cried what seemed to be a million tears because she knew that this time she had fucked up.

$ $ $

Keisha Ervin

Back in his car, Bigg called Chris.

"What up?"

"Where you at?" Bigg asked, smoking a blunt.

"I'm still down here at T Billy's, where you at?"

"I'm leaving Unique's house."

"You should come back down here, it's poppin', man."

"Is Tone there?"

"Yeah, why?"

"Make sure he don't leave, I'm on my way." Bigg hung up, not waiting for his reply.

Racing up the highway bumping 50 Cent's *"Ski Mask Way,"* he pulled up in front of T Billy's. Bigg placed his burner in the waist of his pants and took one more pull off the blunt before putting it out. Not even turning his engine off, he instructed one of the bouncers to watch his truck. Bigg searched the bar until he found Tone sitting at the bar wit' two hoes by his side.

Walking up to him, he got in Tone's view. "Let me holla at you, man."

"Can it wait? I'm busy," Tone replied, ignoring him.

"Nah, nigga it can't! Niggas is telling me you fuckin' my girl. You fuckin' my girl, dog?" Bigg yelled, causing a commotion.

"What the fuck you talkin' about?"

"Yo' Bigg, what's up?" Chris asked.

"This nigga been fuckin' my girl!"

"Don't nobody want yo' girl," Tone replied waving him off, trying not to show how afraid he was.

"So it ain't true?"

"I ain't fucked Unique in almost a year. I thought I loved her but on the real she wasn't nothing but backseat back shots to me," Tone laughed.

"What the fuck you say?" Bigg asked, turning beet red.

Keisha Ervin

"It ain't my fault you fell in love with a slut! I mean, Nique is mad physical. Mommy does know how to work it in bed." Tone cracked up laughing.

Before anyone knew it, Bigg had pulled his gun from his waist and began beating Tone mercilessly. He hit Tone in the head with the butt of the gun repeatedly while words of venom spewed from his mouth.

"She a slut, huh? Nigga, do you want to die? I will kill you! Pussy-ass nigga!"

"Yo' Bigg, chill!! Don't do this shit here!" Chris pulled him off of Tone.

"I'm gon' kill him! That's my word — you dead nigga," Bigg yelled as he continued to stomp Tone. Blood was flying everywhere, on Bigg's shirt, jacket and shoes.

"Nigga chill!" Chris demanded, pulling Bigg away.

"Let me go!" Bigg barked, out of breath. Fixing his coat, he walked out of the bar with his face screwed up.

"Go home!" Chris said as he pushed Bigg into his truck. Without another word, Bigg put his foot on the pedal and speed off.

Ghetto **13** Affair

It had been two weeks, three days — exactly four hundred and eight hours since Bigg left Unique in a million pieces. For the first time in her twenty-five years on earth, Unique felt heartbreak. She never knew that a man, a mere human being, could cause so much pain. Without Bigg she couldn't eat, sleep, think or breathe. Unique didn't realize it but she had allowed herself to need him.

Every time she let a tear fall down her cheek she remembered her number one rule — *Love is forbidden*. Love is a funny thing and sometimes it sneaks up on you when you least expect it. That night at Club Plush, Unique fell in love with Bigg. Without one word, as soon as she laid eyes on him, she loved him. She loved everything about him and to not have him in her life was tearing her up inside.

Loving him had her calling him at all times of the night praying to hear the sound of his voice. It had her crying herself to sleep at night, riding past his house to see if he was home, leaving voicemail messages proclaiming her undying love and begging for forgiveness. Unique was a mess and so

Keisha Ervin

was Bigg. Every time she called he held the phone in his hand dying to pick it up. At night he would drive past her house wanting to see her.

Already reeling from his battle with depression, being without Unique caused his condition to worsen. She was the only one who could get through to him and without her he became sicker by the day. Unique knew that people thought she was crazy for being with Bigg. She knew that they called her a fool for loving him. She had a college degree and her own money, but yet and still, she wanted to be a hustler's wife.

But only she could live her life, only she could feel her heartbreak. No one else had to sleep in her bed at night so she didn't care. The love that she and Bigg shared would never go away. Unique hadn't forgotten about Kiara, though. She just wasn't strong enough physically to handle her but once she got her swagger back it would be on and poppin'. Two weeks, five days — exactly four hundred and fifty six hours into their breakup, she lay in a deep, comatose, tear-stained sleep. Feeling something touching her arm she jumped up, frightened.

"It's me," Bigg whispered.

"Oh, you scared the shit outta me," Unique said, holding her chest and still shaken up.

Bigg turned on the lamp beside the bed and took off his jacket and Timbs before climbing on top of her. Unique smiled on the inside for the first time in weeks. Noticing that her eyes were swollen from crying caused Bigg to feel terrible.

"How did you get in here?"

"Patience let me in. You didn't hear me ringing the bell?"

"No. Do you want me to turn off the light?"

"Nah, I wanna look at you," Bigg said, looking into her eyes for the first time in weeks.

Her hair was sprawled across the pillow, and her peanut

Keisha Ervin

butter-colored skin looked good enough to eat. As he gazed into her eyes, he traced his index finger across the scar under her right eye. Unique sighed. More than anything over the past couple of weeks she had missed the touch of Bigg's skin against hers. He too had been missing her like crazy. Bigg missed the way her mouth turned up on the end revealing a slight smile even when she wasn't. Hugging his back tight, Unique inhaled his scent causing more tears to flow down her cheeks.

"I missed you," she cried.

"Stop crying. You know I can't stand to see you cry." He spoke almost above a whisper.

"I can't."

"I talked to Tone."

"And?" Unique wiped her eyes.

"He told me ya'll weren't fuckin' around."

"So, you gon' believe that man's words over mine?"

"I'm sorry, I should've trusted you." Placing soft kisses on her tear-drenched face, Bigg himself tried not to cry. He held her face in his hand as he gazed into her almond-shaped eyes. He saw that she missed him and needed him but he still wasn't sure.

"You love me?"

"Yeah."

"No, do you really love me?"

"Yes!"

"Do you need me?"

"I need you, Bigg, you know that. You got me going crazy here without you. You don't have any reason to be insecure. I know where I wanna be. I know I made a mistake and I promise that I'll do whatever it takes to make it up to you. Unless you got your heart set on breaking up with me." Unique cried even harder, barely able to breathe. Not able to forgive and for-

Keisha Ervin

get that easily, he got up and began putting his shoes back on.

"Where are you going?"

"I'm going home. I can't deal with this right now."

"What you mean you can't deal with this right now?" She sat up. "What the fuck you come over here for then?" she yelled, feeling stupid for baring her soul.

"I thought I was cool but I'm not."

"I said that I was sorry, what more do you want from me, Bigg?"

"I don't want anything but you, that's all I've ever wanted!" he said, now fully dressed.

"You not gon' leave me like this! You gon' stand here and you gon' listen to me!" Unique pushed the covers off of her body and followed him.

"Kill all that noise, Nique. You gon' wake Patience up."

"Nah, fuck that. You not gon' leave me!" she yelled, mushing him in the head as he walked down the steps.

"I'm gon' fuck you up if you touch me again," he turned and warned her. "Don't start no shit."

"Don't start no shit? Nigga, you started it by coming over here making me look like a fool!"

"How I make you look I fool?" he asked as he left out the front door.

"Tell me you need me, Unique! Tell me you love me, Unique! What the fuck was that shit all about, Bigg? You know you hurt me, too!"

"My bad, I'm sorry for coming over here. It won't happen again." He pressed the open button on the elevator door and got in.

"Ah uh, I'm not through talkin' to you." Unique hopped on the elevator, too.

"What the fuck are you doing?"

"We gon' finish this!"

"I'm through talkin' about it," Bigg spoke nonchalantly.

"You know what? I ain't got to beg for your forgiveness! Fuck you! You can have your stupid-ass ring back, too!" Unique yelled, throwing her engagement ring at him.

"Whatever, ma," Bigg replied as he pocketed the ring and got off the elevator.

"Yeah, whatever! Fuck you, too, you big head muthafucka! I'm sick of crying over you! I've never loved anyone the way I love you and this is how you do me!" Unique followed him through the lobby and to his car parked outside.

"It's always about you, ain't it? It was about you when you was out there stealing cars for no reason. It was about you when you lied to me about Tone and it's about you now since you're so hurt. Did you ever stop to think that I might be hurting too, Unique?"

Not able to speak, she stood outside in front of him in a tank top and panties at 3 o'clock in the morning during the middle of winter.

"I love you more than you know! I told you to leave that nigga alone but did you listen? No! I asked if you were you still fuckin' wit' him and you said no, knowing damn well you hadn't ended things with that nigga! So you only got you to blame for how you feelin' since it's all about you anyway." Slamming his car door shut, Bigg started up the engine and sped off, leaving Unique standing there in the cold winter air wondering why.

$ $ $

A couple more days passed by and Unique and Bigg were still on the outs. Tired of being without him, she decided to go over his house and sleep there. Searching around the house for him she saw that he wasn't there so she took a shower, put on some pajamas and got into bed. Three hours later Bigg arrived home to find her lying in his bed watching *"Will & Grace"* as if nothing had happened.

"Hi, baby."

"What you doing here, Unique?"

"I came to see you and plus I wanted my ring back."

"Is that right?" he asked as he took off his shoes.

"I know you missed me." She smiled hoping he would give in. He didn't. "Look Bigg, I'm tired of playin' wit' you. You love me and I love you. All this unnecessary drama needs to stop."

"You caused all this by lying. As a matter of fact, since you're here, give me back my keys."

"Nigga please, I ain't giving you shit."

"You's a silly-ass broad."

"And you love it." She stared directly at him and smiled. "But for real though, what's going on with the case?" she asked, trying to change the subject.

"The Feds don't have a case. They couldn't find shit on them computers and they didn't find nothing in my office either so their so-called case against me is fucked."

"That's good, now are you coming to bed?"

"Since you won't leave I'm going downstairs to sleep on the couch," he said, grabbing his pillow and heading downstairs.

"Did you take your pills?"

"Why?"

"'Cause I wanna know!"

"Yeah! You happy now!" Smiling from ear to ear Unique hopped up out of the bed and followed him downstairs.

"You took them for real?"

Getting comfortable on the couch, he answered, "Yeah, now leave me alone." Bigg placed the covers over his head.

"What made you change your mind?"

"I talked to Carmella and she told me how worried you were. I'm sorry I scared you like that."

"It's OK, baby, I'm just glad you finally took them," she said, taking the covers off of his face and kissing his cheek.

"Take yo' ass upstairs. I'm still mad at you, we ain't cool," Bigg replied, pulling the covers back over his face. She hit him upside the head and ran back upstairs before he could catch her and hit her back. Turning the TV off, Unique smiled to herself. She didn't care whether he slept in the bed with her or not. She would take Bigg any way she could get him. As long as she was near him she would be all right.

$ $ $

Saturday February 5th, 2005, the night of the Cory Spinks - Zab Judah fight had finally arrived. Everybody and their mommas were out in the streets including Unique, Patience, Zoë and Chantell. The streets of downtown St. Louis were packed. All you saw were white tees and hair weaves. Girls were outside their cars dancing, trying to get attention from potential ballers and brothas already doing the damn thing.

Niggas were smoking weed and hollering at different females as they rode by looking fly. Every flavor from the ice cream truck was being represented. You had your Butter Pecan Ricans, fly colored Asians, French Vanilla mommies, Caramel Sundaes and even Chocolate Deluxe sistas were trying to get touched. Gangstas from every hood including Pine Lawn and Cochran to the East Side were out kicking it after the fight.

Everywhere you looked there were Benzes, Jaguars, Escalades, F-150s, and Hummers. You could just a smell a fight or a shoot out brewing in the air. The atmosphere was so thick with energy. If you were a dummy, or new to the game, you wouldn't know who had money or who was just stuntin' for the night, but Unique knew better. All you had to do was look a nigga from head to toe to tell if he had money.

There were a lot of stunters out that night and if you didn't know any better you probably would've gotten caught up in all the glitz and glamour of it all. Brothas were frontin' in rental cars. Females used their welfare checks to buy new outfits. Then there were the chicks that were stuntin' in their man's car like it was theirs just to upstage other females, but Unique was in a class all her own.

She could afford to buy herself nice things. The Mercedes G500 that she rode in was hers and was paid for by her. The Pirelli tires and Giovanna rims she also purchased herself. Bumping Ciara's *"Oh,"* she and the girls danced around in their seats to the beat. They got much attention from the opposite sex as they rode by but Unique's mind was on her boo, Bigg.

He was still mad at her and Unique couldn't stand the silent treatment that he was giving her. He had gone to the fight without her and that hurt her even more. Instead, he, Legend, NaSheed and Chris went together. She was sure that females were on his tip and trying to holla but Unique knew that she had nothing to worry about. Bigg loved her to death and when he saw the outfit she had on, he was sure to forgive her. That she was sure of.

Unique's red hair was pulled up into a sleek ponytail reaching all the way to the middle of her back. Black eye shadow adorned her almond-shaped eyes giving her eye a smokey effect, while bronzer highlighted her cheeks. A coat of nude M.A.C. lip gloss completed her facial look. On her body she rocked a fitted gray long-sleeve top with the back completely cut out, True Religion skinny jeans and black Givenchy heels.

Large silver hoop earrings, bangle bracelets and silver Isabella Fiore purse made up the rest of her outfit.

Not being out-done, Zoë sported a tweed Chanel blazer, cream spaghetti-strapped cami, tight fitting jeans and a pair of brown crocodile Celine heels. Her hair was perfectly styled in a short wispy style like Halle Berry and four-carat diamond earrings adorned her ears. The other girls were dressed and looked cute, too. Putting Ciara's "*Oh*" on repeat, they all bobbed their heads to the beat. Rapping Ludacris' verse, Unique raised her hands in the air and twirled her hips around in the seat as they sat stuck in traffic.

"Girl, this is my jam!" She snapped her fingers.

"*Oh! Oh!*" Zoë sang along. "Girl, what if we see Kiara tonight?"

"If we do I'm gon' beat that ass!"

"Unique?" Patience tapped her sister's shoulder.

"What?"

"Ain't that NaSheed over there?" She pointed toward the other side of the street.

"Yeah."

"You know Bigg and Legend ain't too far behind," Zoë added.

"Yup, there he is getting out of his truck," Chantell pointed out.

Staring at her man, Unique's heart began race just as fast as it did the first time they met. There he stood, leaning up against his truck, smoking a blunt with one hand in his pocket and looking sexy as hell. Black Giorgio Armani shades covered his eyes and he donned a red pinstriped LRG hat, white T-shirt, Diesel jeans and a pair of blue Timbs with red and white trim rested on his feet. His five-carat earring and Jacob the Jeweler diamond watch seemed to glisten underneath the night's sky.

Keisha Ervin

"I wonder if Legend is with him?" Zoë thought out loud.

"You know he is," Unique replied.

"Yo', Z, hook me up with Chris," Chantell chimed in.

"Girl please, you are too young."

"Ay, who is that all up in Bigg's face?" Patience asked.

"I don't know. Some chicken head obviously," Unique said with her lip curled up.

"Uh oh, it's about to be what?" Zoë sang.

"A girl fight!" Patience and Chantell sang, too.

"You damn right it is if that bitch ain't gone by the time I pull this car over."

Bogarting her way through traffic, Unique pulled over and parked. She checked her makeup and applied another coat of lip gloss before hopping out. Seeing Legend, Zoë quickly got out of the car. He was talking to a group of niggas. It looked like Cezar, Chris, NaSheed, Yayo and Bice. She walked up on him, mushed him in the back of his head and asked, "Why haven't I heard from you?"

Legend smiled. "What's up, boo?"

"Nigga, don't 'what's up boo' me." She pushed him in the chest while eying him up and down. Legend looked finer than ever. The man was most definitely out to prove something that night. He donned a green and yellow Girbaud jacket, green tee, LRG jeans and green and yellow Nike Dunks.

"What? What I do?"

"I haven't heard from you in almost two weeks. I got a problem with that."

"My bad, I was gon' get at you tonight, I swear."

"Yeah, whatever." She rolled her eyes.

"You look nice." Legend eyed her up and down.

"Thank you but I'm still mad at you." He wrapped his arms around her tight and kissed her neck.

"You gon' let me slide up in that tonight?"

Keisha Ervin

"Nope."

"Quit lying."

"I'm not," she lied, trying her best not to smile.

Across the street, Unique stepped out of her car and headed toward Bigg. She just knew that he was up to his old ways. Ready to bust his ass, she overheard Bigg and the girl's conversation as she walked toward them.

"What's good? You got a woman or what?" the girl asked.

"I'm engaged, sweetheart," Bigg replied, barely paying her attention.

"That ain't stopping nothing. We can still kick it."

"What don't you get? I got a girl. Take yo' skinny ass on across the street and holla at one of them niggas over there!"

Smiling to herself, Unique wondered how she could've ever doubted Bigg. With no fear in her heart, she pushed the girl to the side and grabbed Bigg by the face. No words were spoken as she passionately kissed his lips.

"Excuse you!" the girl said with an attitude.

"Nah sweetie, excuse you. This is *my* fiancé you're talkin' to." Unique flashed her ring.

"My bad."

"Yeah, yo' bad."

"Whatever, it ain't even that serious."

"Yeah, 'cause you ain't got him," Unique said as the girl walked away.

"What yo' hot ass doing down here?" Bigg asked, taking a pull from the blunt he just lit.

"I know you didn't think I was going to stay in the house."

"Nah, I knew you couldn't pass up the opportunity to buy a new outfit," he teased.

"You still mad at me?"

"What you think?"

"I don't know, you tell me."

Keisha Ervin

"I ain't mad no more. You hurt a nigga with that shit though."

"I'm sorry."

"The next time I tell you to do something, do it. You gon' be wife so we can't be lying to each other and shit. You gotta trust me as well as I gotta trust you. I don't be tellin' you stuff just to try and run your life. I'm only looking out for your best interest. I need you to believe in me, ma. Especially with these haters and open cases that I got coming up."

"I know baby, I'm sorry."

"Yeah, that's what yo' mouth say."

"I know, right." Unique laughed. "So, when did you and NaSheed start back talkin'?"

"That nigga called me a couple days after we got into it and apologized."

"Oh."

"Have you talked to Kiara?"

"Nope. I called her a couple of times but she ain't answering the phone. She knows what's up. When I see her it's like that for her ass."

"Look at you," Bigg laughed.

"I'm for real."

"I missed yo' big head ass though," he said, taking another pull from the blunt.

"I missed you, too," Unique said as she parted her lips for him to give her shotgun. She inhaled the smoke through her lungs and up through her nose, then exhaled the smoke and the stress that had been in her chest since Bigg left.

It's Better *14* That It Hurts

Zoë looked over to her right and couldn't help but smile. Legend lay right next to her in a peaceful sleep. She didn't know whether it was lust or love that drew her to him. It didn't matter though because whenever he called, she came running. He had her doing things that she thought she would never do in a million years. Zoë tried to fight her feelings but on the real she couldn't stop them if she wanted to.

The two still only saw each other when he wanted to fuck it seemed like, but no matter what, Legend continued to take care of her. The situation bothered her but Zoë figured that she would take him any way she could get him. Gazing over his face, she examined his low cut, mustache and sexy lips. Their relationship was strange; it was like they had some kind of power over each other.

After chilling downtown and catching breakfast with Unique, Bigg, Patience and the rest of the crew, Zoë and Legend headed back to his place. That morning consisted of nothing but hot sex and heavy moaning. They wore each other out exploring each other's bodies. Staring at the clock, she

Keisha Ervin

saw that it was mid-afternoon. She and Legend had slept most of the day away. Getting up out of the bed, she wrapped his sheet over her petite frame leaving Legend stark naked with no covers over him.

"Where you going?" he asked groggily before she exited the room.

"I got to go pee."

"Hurry back, my dick is hard."

"You are so nasty." She smiled in anticipation.

Zoë never peed so fast in her life. She couldn't get enough of Legend's good loving. When she reentered the room he was in the same position in which she left him — butt naked, with an erection the size of the Empire State Building. Legend's dick seemed to be pointing right in her direction. She even swore she heard it calling her name.

With a huge grin on her face, Zoë wasted no time getting down to business. There was no time for foreplay on her end. She was ready to get it on. Taking his dick into her hand she hungrily placed him in her mouth. Zoë's mouth was warm and moist — just how Legend liked it. Greedily she bobbed her head up and down while massaging his chest and balls with her soft, small hands. Legend was in absolute heaven. The sight of Zoë sucking his dick was more than he could handle. After a couple of minutes he was right where Zoë wanted him to be, hard as a rock. Pleased with her work, she slowly straddled him and eased his dick inside of her already wet pussy. It didn't take Zoë any time to build up a rhythm. She rode his dick like it was the last dick she would ever have.

Legend could only hold on for the ride. The visual of her perky brown breasts bouncing in the air had him going insane. Then suddenly his cell phone began to ring. Legend tried to ignore it but it was one of his special rings. Smacking Zoë on the ass, he instructed that she slow down a bit.

"Hello?" he answered out of breath.

"Where you at?"

"Why?"

"'Cause, I need to talk to you," the female voice on the other line said.

"At home."

"Well, I need to see you."

"Can it wait? I'm a little busy right now."

"No, it can't," the woman shot with an attitude.

"A'ight where?" Legend asked through a clenched jaw. Zoë was tightening her coochie muscles while riding him. She knew that he loved when she did that.

"Meet me in the food court at The Galleria; I have Cicely with me."

"A'ight give me an hour," Legend said hanging up. "You wanna play, huh?" he asked, flipping Zoë over.

Grabbing her waist, he began to hit it from the back. Zoë was cumming in a matter of seconds. Legend was hitting her with the death stroke again.

"Mmm ... yes ... just like that!" she moaned, cumming all over his dick. Grinning, Legend pulled out his dick and slapped her on the ass.

"Who was that on the phone?"

"My partna. He wants me to come over and look at his truck. He said the engine won't start."

"Oh," Zoë said, disappointed. "I thought we were going to spend the day together?"

"We will but it'll have to be later." Legend could see that she was upset so he walked over to her. Tilting her head up, he made her look at him. "What's with the sad face?"

"It's nothing. I'm cool."

"You sure?"

"Yeah."

"A'ight, hurry up and get dressed then while I hop in the shower."

Sitting there feeling used and stupid, Zoë hurried and got her clothes on. Once she was dressed she sat and watched as Legend got dressed. As Tupac's song *"No More Pain"* was bumping out of his surround sound speakers, Legend was rapping along. Just watching him walk around the room with his dick swinging back and forth made her nipples harden. If it weren't for his looks and the sex, Zoë knew that she would have been left him alone.

The more she thought about it though, the more Zoë knew that wasn't true. The pit of her stomach told her that she was much more than being in like with him — she loved Legend. No matter how hard she tried play it off, or deny what she was feeling, she knew that he had her hook, line and sinker. How he felt about her, though, was another question. She wanted desperately to ask him if he loved her but the fear of hearing the wrong answer caused her not to ask.

"You ready?" he asked, now fully dressed.

"Yeah," she sighed.

"What's wrong wit' you?"

"Nothing." She was clearly upset. Not wanting to press the subject, Legend locked the door behind them and headed to the car. Ten minutes later they were in front of Zoë's apartment building.

"So, when is the next time I'm going to see you?"

"After I get done helping dude wit' his tire, I'm gon' call you."

"I thought you said it was his engine?" Zoë said, catching him in a lie.

"You know what I mean," Legend laughed, playing it off.

"Yeah, OK, whatever," Zoë said, shaking her head as she got out.

Keisha Ervin

"Yo', what's your problem?"

"Nothing. Gon' and do what you got to do. I'll holla at you whenever." Getting frustrated with Zoë's attitude, Legend got out as well and met her in front of the car.

"I don't want to leave you like this."

"Why not? You do any other time," she said as tears began to sting her eyes.

"Yo', I know you ain't crying? What the fuck are you crying for?"

"It's nothing," she lied, swallowing the lump in her throat.

"I'm trying to understand you. What's with the attitude of all of a sudden? I thought you were OK with our situation. You knew I didn't want a relationship."

"It's nothing Legend, I'm cool."

"Look, after I get done fuckin' wit' dude I'm gon' holla at you, a'ight?"

"A'ight, whatever." She shrugged her shoulders, tired of playing games with him.

"I'm for real," he assured, looking her in the eyes while holding her face with his hands.

"I said a'ight."

As he kissed her on the forehead, Zoë closed her eyes and let the tears that had been dying to be released fall. Watching as he pulled off, she inhaled deeply and willed herself not to cry anymore. Zoë wasn't even in her apartment five minutes before her phone started ringing. Placing her purse down she hurried to answer it before the caller hung up. It was Unique.

"Hello?"

"You're just now getting home?"

"Yes, Momma Unique, anything else you want to know?"

"Nah, Miss Freak-a-Leak, do yo' thang girl," Unique teased.

"An-y-way," Zoë laughed.

Keisha Ervin

"But look, I didn't call to get all up in yo' business. I called to see if you would ride to the mall with me so I can find some silver heels to go with this ivory dress I got for Bigg's surprise party."

"Damn, I forgot about Bigg's party. I just got home, Nique, can't we go tomorrow?"

"Come on girl, please? I'll even buy you those black Dior logo sandals you've been wanting."

"Say no more, I'll be ready in thirty minutes."

An hour later the girls were on the highway, heading toward the mall.

"So how's Bigg doing?"

"He's doing a lot better since he started taking his pills," Unique replied while concentrating on the road.

"What's going on with the raid on his office?"

"His lawyers told him that the only thing he could do is sit tight. They don't have any evidence of wrong doing so he should be cool, but my fingers are still crossed."

"Everything is going to be fine."

"I hope so. Anyway, don't try and act like I didn't hear you sounding all sad earlier. What was up with that?"

"Girl, this whole Legend thing got me straight trippin'."

"What's the deal?"

"It's like I know he likes me but we never spend any time with each other. He only comes by when he wants some. He never calls when says he will. Like the other day, he called me and was like get dressed, I'm scooping you up. So of course, I got all excited. Girl, I waited for over three hours and that nigga never showed up but yet and still my dumb ass can't get enough of him."

"You're not dumb, you just in love with a man, Z."

"Shit, if this is what love feels like then I don't want no parts of it."

"Have you talked to him?"

"No."

"See, that's your problem. How is he supposed to know how you feel if you won't even tell him? You can't keep your feelings bottled up when it comes to shit like this, Z. Let that nigga know that it ain't cool to just come by to get some ass. Tell him that you want a commitment and if he can't handle it, then tell him to step."

"I guess." She shrugged her shoulders. "I'm just stuck between what I want and what I know is right. I want things to be right between us but something's telling me that it's not. Can you believe that I have actually cried over this nigga?"

"Shit, that's how it is sometimes."

"But Nique, I know better. I know this nigga ain't doing nothing but running game on me. I can't even concentrate on school. Fuckin' with this nigga got me going crazy for real."

"True story?"

"True story." Zoë nodded her in agreement.

"If he got you wound up like that then you need to talk to him, Z, because if you don't you just gon' keep on stressing over it."

"I guess you're right."

"You know I am. Now come on, let's go do some damage."

"Don't be rushing me," Zoë laughed as she jumped down from Unique's Lexus truck.

Five minutes later, the girls were walking into Nordstrom, Unique's favorite store. Walking over to the Dior section, Unique and Zoë were greeted by a sales attendant.

"Hello, I'm Farah. All of our tank tops are 20 percent off and if you need any help just let me know."

"Thank you. I do have a question," Zoë said, distracting the sales lady.

Roaming throughout the store, Unique kept a close eye on

Zoë and the sales lady at all times. With an all-black Gucci bag in hand, she walked around the store racking up merchandise. It was just her luck that the overhead music was turned up louder than normal. The music concealed the sound of her popping censors off the clothes.

"Hi, I'm Janette. Is there anything I can help you with?" the other sales lady asked, tapping Unique on the shoulder and scaring her half to death.

"No … no thank you. I'm fine," Unique stuttered as she turned around and gave off a fake smile.

"Well, let me know if you change your mind. I'll be over at the counter." The sales lady looked Unique up and down suspiciously.

"I'll do that."

As she looked down into her bag, she noticed that she had already stolen close to a thousand dollars worth of designer merchandise but Unique couldn't leave quite yet. She had to nab Zoë's Dior heels. Suddenly they appeared right before her eyes. Nonchalantly, Unique strutted over to the shoe section.

With a slight glimmer of nervousness she searched the ceiling for cameras. Seeing none she eyed the nosey sales attendant. Just as she hoped, her back was turned. Right then was the perfect opportunity, so at that moment, Unique snatched the shoes off the rack. *I know I'm bad! I'm bad! You know it*, Unique sang in her head. Deciding that she should purchase something before someone got suspicious, she grabbed a pair of trousers and switched the tag from three-hundred and fifty dollars to fifty.

"You ready?" Zoë whispered.

"Yeah, take my bag while I go pay for these pants." Walking over to the counter, Unique held her head up high as if she had done nothing wrong. "I'll take these, please."

"OK," Janette replied, pulling out the scanner. "Fifty dollars? I could have sworn these were three hundred and fifty dollars."

"If they're three hundred and fifty dollars then I don't want them," Unique said, scrunching up her face.

"Where did you get these from?"

"I got them from over there on the sale rack." Unique pointed to the left.

"They couldn't have been on the sale rack because we just got these pants in a few weeks ago."

"Look, I ain't got time for this. Either you gon' sell them to me for fifty dollars or you're not going to sell them to me at all!" Unique shouted.

"Is there a problem here?" Farah, the other sales lady, questioned.

"Yes there is. She's telling me that these pants aren't fifty dollars after I just picked them up from over there on the sale rack! Now, I came here to shop, not argue over some stupid-ass pants!"

"Ma'am, I'm sorry. Janette, have you forgotten that the customer is always right? If she says that she got them from off the sale rack then she did." Arching her eyebrow and tooting up her lip, Unique gave the girl the "now what" look.

"I think she owes me an apology." Unique smirked.

"Sorry," Janette spat.

"Thank you." After being rung up, Unique grabbed her bag, smiled and walked out of the store proud that she had wiggled herself out of another sticky situation.

"Remind me to give you back that book *Mina's Joint*," Unique said to Zoë as she caught up to her but Zoë couldn't hear her.

Her eyes were fixated on Legend and an unknown woman and a child, walking out of the mall together. Legend was carrying a little girl who looked to be about four with caramel skin just like his. The woman he was walking with almost tripped and fell but Legend reached his hand out to prevent her from falling. They laughed and smiled at one another. Feeling her heart drop out of her chest, Zoë closed her eyes and wished that it was all bad dream. Reopening her eyes she still saw what looked like Legend and his woman. Sensing that something was wrong, Unique stopped, too.

"What's the matter? Why you stop?"

Zoë wanted desperately to talk but she couldn't. All she could do was stare at Legend and cry. "What's wrong?" Unique asked, becoming worried. Looking in the same direction as Zoë, she saw her cousin's worst nightmare come true.

"Ah uh," Unique shook her head. "Don't you let another tear fall from your eyes, you hear me," Unique instructed forcefully. Nodding her head and wiping her eyes, Zoë agreed.

"How does my face look?" she sniffled.

Unique took Zoë's face in her hands and looked directly in her eyes and said, "Beautiful." Pulling her shoulders back and holding her head up high, Zoë prepared herself for a confrontation. Legend never even saw her coming, he was so involved in conversation.

"What's up, Legend? I thought you were helping your friend?!" Zoë yelled, coming across the parking lot. Hearing Zoë's voice caused Legend to almost shit on himself but he played it cool.

"I did, I mean I was," he stuttered as he kept on walking.

"Hold up! Don't walk away from me! I know you hear me talkin' to you!" she yelled, grabbing his arm.

"Look, can we talk about this later?"

"Nigga is you crazy? We're going to talk about this right now!"

"Zoë, what the fuck is your problem?" the woman with Legend snapped.

"Hold up! How the fuck do you know me?"

"Oh please, don't nobody know you!" The woman waved her off.

"Bitch, you just said my name! How the fuck do you know me?"

"Anyway, I ain't got time for this Legend, you betta get your lil' friend!"

"I'ma talk to you later, a'ight ?" he said, facing her.

"You got to be fuckin' kidding me?"

"Look, I said I was gon' talk to you later! Quit sweatin' me!"

Slap!!!! Slap!!!

"Nigga don't you ever … in your life … try to play me!" Zoë yelled, ready to slap Legend again.

"Ah uh, Z, come on! Fuck him. He ain't shit," Unique said, grabbing her arm and pulling her away.

$ $ $

Later that night, Zoë sat on her couch with a box of tissues crying her eyes out. All the lights in the house were out, the fireplace was burning and Destiny's Child's *"Is She the Reason"* was stuck on repeat. With her knees curled up to her chest, she tried to push the thought of Legend and the other woman out of her mind. But visions of them, hand in hand, continued to play repeatedly in her mind like a home movie.

So she's the reason I never see him, she thought. His girl was the reason he didn't come through and see her on a regular basis. She was the reason he didn't call every day. She was the reason he had to get up and go home as soon as they finished having sex. His woman and his daughter were the reason for everything. Shaking her head, Zoë reached for another tissue just as someone began beating on her door. It was

Keisha Ervin

Legend.

"What the fuck do you want?!"

"Man, you better open this muthafuckin' door!"

"I ain't got nothing to say to you."

"Come on, ma, open up the door," he whispered, placing his forehead on the door.

"Nigga, I ain't opening up shit! Go home to your family! I'm sure your daughter needs you!"

"Look, I'm tryin' my best not to clown wit' you but in a minute you gon' make me bust yo' ass."

"Nigga, fuck you!"

"Don't make me kick this muthafucka in!" he yelled, kicking the door with his foot.

"Huh! What the fuck is it? We don't have shit to talk about!" She sighed, swinging the door open.

"You gon' let me explain?"

"Explain what? That you played me?"

"I didn't know how to tell you."

"It was simple, all you had to do was say, 'I got girl!' How hard would that have been?"

"It was too late and I had already started catching feelings for you. I couldn't hurt you like that."

"Well, guess what nigga, you did! You should have told me so I could've had a choice in this!"

"Hold up, we're not together so why you trippin'?"

"I know we're not together! That has never been the issue! You should've let me know that you were seeing someone else!"

"I should have! I fucked up! What more can I say?"

"There ain't nothing you can say! You played me! If you had a woman then that was all you had to say! You didn't have to lie and you didn't have to keep it a secret! You could've been a man and let me know! Hell, I'm grown! We still could've

Keisha Ervin

kicked it! I could've handled it! Do you know how that made me feel, seeing you with her?"

"I'm sorry, you're right, I should've told you," he said, sincerely caressing her cheek.

"Don't touch me!" She pushed his hand away. "I can't believe you tried to play me! Nigga, do you not know who the fuck I am? You better be more careful! Take your wack-ass apology and step 'cause I ain't even tryin' to hear it!"

"If that's what you want then—"

"If that's what I want?! Nigga you got a woman and a child! What am I supposed to do, keep on fuckin' you and be your bitch on the side? I don't think so! I straight up got feelings for you!"

"Got feelings for me?"

"Yeah nigga, I love you."

"I got feelings for you, too, but this is my situation."

"Do you love me?"

"Come on, ma, why you gotta go there?"

"Do you love me or not?!" she pressed.

"I don't know."

"Huh … it's cool, boo. It was fun while it lasted. Now get the fuck out!"

"Are you not hearing me when I say that I got feelings for you? Why can't that be enough?"

"'Cause I deserve more," she yelled. "You are the first man that I have ever caught feelings for! I got enough on my plate with school and these streets than to be worried about you! I want more for myself than a fuck, Legend! I deserve to have a man that I come home to at night! I deserve to have somebody who is going to be there for me when I need him! Not somebody who I can only call when I want to cum!"

"Well since you don't want to listen to shit I gotta say, I'm up."

"Bye nigga!" Zoë slammed the door behind him. *Fuck him*, she thought. *It's better to hurt then to live a lie.*

$ $ $

Lying on her side curled up underneath the sheets, Zoë stared out the window as snow fell from the sky. The fireplace in her bedroom heated and lit up the entire room as she held her cordless phone in hand. Playing Russian Roulette for the eleventh time that day, she attempted to call Legend. Six digits into the number, once again, she hung up.

Zoë had made the conscious decision that she would rather play stupid than be without Legend. Never before had she craved the attention of a man. Nights and days passed by where she wished he would call and say, "Hey you," like he used to. She tried numerous techniques to get over him like sleeping the day away, but that didn't work because she would only dream of him. Talking to her friends only caused her to talk about him and the things they used to do.

Listening to the radio never worked because some sad love song would be playing. It was like the universe was commanding her to run back into Legend's arms but running back to him would hurt her more in the long run. Unbeknownst to Zoë, Legend was in his car driving, thinking of her as well. Driving down I-170 he replayed the fight they had over and over again in his mind.

He could see it like it just went down, her yelling and screaming. The words *get out* still rang in his ears. He vividly could still see the tears that ran down her face as he left. Legend remembered how he was about to explode with anger as he walked out, leaving her alone. He knew that he was wrong for doing Zoë the way he did.

Nothing in his life seemed to be the same without her. She

Keisha Ervin

honestly made his life better but the truth was, they couldn't be together. Legend should have been upfront with Zoë about his situation but fear always kept him from telling her the truth. Legend was slacking and he knew it. The whole ordeal should have never gone down. He wished that he could take it all back but in life there was no rewind.

If Legend could have his way, the day before would be today and he would take everything he said back. He should have stayed with her instead of dipping out like a punk. Instead of fighting, they should have been making love until the sun went down. Tired of wishing, Legend parked his car and got out.

Hearing a faint knock at the door, Zoë jumped up wondering if she was hearing things. She sat as still as she could and listened for the sound again. Hearing it again, she eased out of bed and headed to the door. She knew who it was without asking. Without hesitation, Zoë unlocked the door and opened it.

No words spoken between the two, Legend closed the door behind him and took her into his arms. He carried her back into the bedroom and gently laid Zoë down and gazed into her eyes. He couldn't make her any promises of a happily-ever-after or that they would be together but he needed to see her. The sound of fire crackling behind them as he turned down the bed distracted the voices that were in Zoë's head. Her conscience kept on telling her to kick him out but she couldn't.

Zoë knew that she was betraying herself by sleeping with Legend, so selfishly she let him back into her heart one more time. She didn't want to hear any promises or lies; she only wanted to feel the touch of his skin pressed up against hers. There in the dark, she placed her mind, body, soul and heart into Legend's hands. Holding one another closely, they lay

Keisha Ervin

face to face exchanging breaths and wondering if they were making the right decision.

Fuck it, she thought. Zoë closed her eyes, parted her lips and pretended that Legend was all hers. She told herself that she would deal with the repercussions of her decision in the morning. Invading her mouth with his, Legend felt Zoë's body melt into his arms. He softly kissed her neck while lying on top of her.

The cream satin camisole and short set that she wore was gently removed from her body as kisses were planted on her wanting breasts. Completely naked, not only physically but emotionally, Zoë took Legend's lips and kissed him deeply. Excited by the smell of his cologne, she guided him into her. She tried not to make eye contact with him as he rocked slowly inside of her.

All thoughts were lost when she looked him in the eye. The feelings she had for this man made her feel insane. Zoë never knew that another human being could have so much control over a person. To be with Legend, she would give up everything. Everything she wanted Legend had. From his appearance, to the way he dressed and the swagger in his walk. Financially he was straight and the fact that he was smart never hurt, but it still remained that he had a woman at home. Not wanting to think any more, she wrapped her legs around his back and pulled him closer.

"I missed you, ma," he whispered into her ear as he grinded in and out of her slowly.

"I missed you, too, baby," she moaned as tears ran down the sides of her face.

Legend held her thighs in both of his hands while he rotated his hips, working his dick around. Hitting all four corners, he licked and sucked her hard nipples. He pumped roughly, showing Zoë exactly what his deepstroke could do.

Feeling like she was on top of the world, Zoë called out for God.

"You like that?"

"Yes!" she screamed, scratching his back.

"Shit girl, what the fuck you doing to me?" he yelled, cumming.

"Legend!" Zoë screamed, cumming, too. Gripping her waist he pumped until he couldn't hold it any longer. Not wanting to cum inside of her, he quickly pulled out and came on the sheets. Panting heavily and still reveling from the tingling sensation in between her legs, Zoë lay there staring at the ceiling, wondering if she had made the right choice.

Keisha Ervin

KARMA

"Where are we going?"

"I told you that I wanted to get a drink at the WS before we went out to dinner," Unique said while checking her make-up in the mirror.

"You had me pull out my Bentley GT for this?"

"Bigg, stop complaining. You know you love when you get to drive this car."

"I can't believe you got me all dressed up in this hot-ass suit just to go to the WS! Niggas gon' be looking at me like I'm crazy!"

"No they won't. You look handsome."

"You can drink at the restaurant! I don't feel like being around a bunch of hard heads tonight! Let's just go to the restaurant," he whined like a child.

Just as Unique was about to check him, the sight of seeing Bigg in a suit took over. She had to admit that the man looked good in just about anything he wore. Gazing over at him she admired Bigg's all-black Hugo Boss tailor-made suit. His black satin tie, fresh cut and all-black Scooby Doos made his cycle complete. She was decked out in a satin ivory Ralph Lauren halter gown with a plunging neckline. Unique's hair was pulled to the back, swept into a side bun. Neil Lane chandelier diamond earrings adorned her ears while silver diamond-encrusted Gucci heels adorned her feet.

"Just 'cause it's your birthday doesn't mean that you get to act like a spoiled brat! Quit bitchin' and come on!" Unique rolled her eyes, grabbing her ivory mink stole.

"I better get some head tonight for this shit!" Bigg replied as he helped her out the car.

"Shut up, boy." She grinned.

Holding his hand, she led him through the revolving doors of the building as all of their friends and family screamed, "Surprise!" In front of Bigg stood everyone he was close to. From the staff at his record label to hustlers on the block, everybody was there to show love. The entire crowd was dressed in either winter white or black.

The ladies wore their finest gowns while the men donned their flyest suits. Around the room were hundreds upon hundreds of black and white balloons. Vases filled with white calla lilies were on each table. The lights were dimmed, music was bumping, go-go dancers danced on black podiums and the smell of fresh seafood and champagne filled the air. Kissing him on the cheek, Unique whispered, "Happy 28th birthday, baby."

"I can't believe you did this." He smiled, a little embarrassed.

"You're my baby and I love you. You deserve everything good that comes to you." Hugging her tight, Bigg patted Unique's butt and kissed her lips.

"Happy birthday, nigga!" Chris gave Bigg a pound and a hug.

"Thanks."

"Quit hugging that nigga so tight. You know he's getting old. You might break something!" NaSheed joked.

"This nigga," Bigg laughed.

"We got yo' ass, didn't we?" Legend confirmed.

"Yeah, ya'll got me."

"Happy birthday, Bigg!" Zoë exclaimed, giving him a hug. She was dressed in a long, white, beaded, spaghetti-strapped Monique Lhuillier gown.

"Ya'll here together?" Bigg questioned, being nosey.

"Nah." Zoë shook her head.

"It's a long story man," Legend added, feeling uncomfortable.

"Come on Z, let's go get a drink," Unique said, taking Zoë's hand and leading her away from an uncomfortable situation.

"Happy birthday, Bigg," Patience gushed, running over to Bigg.

"Baby sis, you look beautiful," Bigg replied, taking in her off-white, spaghetti-strapped Tracy Reese baby doll dress and silver open-toed Jimmy Choo stiletto heels.

"Thank you." She blushed.

"What's going on wit' you and Zoë?" Bigg turned his attention back to Legend, not missing a thing.

"Unique didn't tell you?"

"Tell me what?"

"They caught me wit' my BM and my daughter in the mall the other day."

"I ain't even know you had a daughter."

"I don't get to see her that much," Legend lied. "But enough about me. It's your birthday — let's celebrate."

"Damn, Nique went all out," Bigg said, examining the room but making a mental note of Legend's unexpected news of a child.

"Right, she got ice sculptures, balloons, flowers and candles everywhere," Cezar chimed in.

"You ain't seen that big-ass picture she got up of you yet, have you?" NaSheed asked.

"Nah."

"Come on, let me show it to you." At the bar, Zoë and Unique sat watching their men. Zoë couldn't take her eyes off of Legend. She had been eyeing him all night. Their night of passion still had her reeling.

"Girl, if you don't quit staring at that nigga I'm gon' hurt you," Unique warned.

"I can't help it."

"Look, evidently the bitch don't mean that much to him. 'Cause if she did, she would've been here tonight."

"I guess." Zoë sighed.

"Nah, fuck that 'I guess' shit! Bitch, what happened to the old Zoë? The old Zoë wouldn't have gave a fuck about another bitch! If you want his ass you better move that hoe to the side and claim what's yours!"

"You're right."

"I know I am but look, I gotta go get ready for Bigg's surprise."

"I can't believe you're actually going through wit' it." Zoë laughed.

"Girl please, Bigg knows whose pussy this is, he ain't gon' trip."

"Hold up, I'm coming wit' you."

"Can I get my grown man on for a second?" Bigg posed, holding a Lino Cuban cigar in one hand and a bottle of Cristal in the other while Jay-Z's *"Excuse Me Miss"* played in the background.

"Man, this my joint right here!" Chris bobbed his head as he watched the go-go dancers twirl their bodies like snakes.

"Where Nique go?" Bigg questioned, looking around for her.

"I don't know." Cezar shrugged his arms.

"Happy birthday, Bigg!" Queen Isis Jones greeted him with a warm smile.

"What's up, ma? Thanks for coming."

"You know I wouldn't have missed your birthday party for the world."

"Mind if I take a picture of you two for the *St. Louis American?*" Bill Beene, the entertainment editor, asked.

"Nah man, ain't no thing," Bigg said, holding Queen Isis Jones by the waist and smiling.

"On three. One, two, three." *Snap.* "Thanks Bigg, I appreciate it."

"No problem, any time."

"Excuse me, can I have everyone's attention?" Patience spoke into a microphone. "On behalf of me and my sister, Unique, we want to thank each of you for coming out and celebrating my big brother's birthday with us. We hope that you all enjoy yourself. There is plenty of food and champagne for everyone but before you get your grub on, we would like for Bigg to cut the cake. Bigg, will you please come to the front." Shaking his head, Bigg walked to the front of the room where a chair was awaiting him.

"Happy birthday to you! Happy birthday to you!" While everyone sang to Bigg, one of the go-go dancers wheeled out a white life-sized cake. *"Happy birthday dear Bigg! Happy birthday to you!"* The next thing Bigg knew, the cake's lids lifted open and Unique sprang out. Shocked, he doubled over in laughter as everyone applauded. Climbing out of the cake, Unique kissed Bigg on the lips and backed him into his chair.

"One, Two, Three, let's go
Lil' momma show me how you move it
Go head put your back into it."

Keisha Ervin

Popping her coochie, she and the go-go dancers went into the dance routine that had been choreographed especially for Unique. Clad in a trucker hat, black bustier, black booty shorts, fishnets stockings, go-go boots and a whip, Unique did her thing. Winding her hips and dropping it like it was hot, she danced around Bigg. Throwing nothing but twenties at her, Bigg smiled and smacked her on the ass.

Unique backed it up on him and grinded her hips slowly as the crowd clapped and cheered. Holding her waist, Bigg tried to kiss her neck but Unique slapped his hands away. She stood back up and went back into the routine with the go-go dancers. By the end of the song, Bigg's pockets were empty and Unique had over two thousand dollars in her hat.

"'Come here." Jumping into his arms, Unique hugged her man around the neck.

"Surprise!" She laughed.

"That was hot, ma."

"Thank you, baby, I was so nervous."

"Can I get that show again tonight?"

"Yep, but next time I'll be naked." She grinned while nibbling on his ear.

"Where did you get dressed at?" he asked, putting her down.

"I got us a suite for the weekend."

"Oh, you really doing it big?"

"A bitch don't wanna brag but you know how I do."

"Yo', shorty, that was hot!" NaSheed exclaimed.

"Right, I wish a chick would do something like that for me," Chris added.

"One day fellas, one day, but baby, let me go get changed."

"A'ight, hurry back," Bigg said, smacking her on the ass as she left.

"Ay, while Unique is getting dressed we can go upstairs to

my room and get blazed," NaSheed suggested.

"You ain't said nothing but a word, dog." Five minutes later the guys were in NaSheed's suite getting high. Loosening his tie, Bigg stared out the window and thanked God for allowing him to reach another birthday.

"You gon' hit this or what?" NaSheed asked, interrupting his thoughts.

"Yeah," Bigg answered, leaving the window. Walking into the bedroom, he saw that NaSheed had pulled out a DVD. "Yo', what's that? Mommy got a fat ass."

"Some lil' porn video I copped off the street yesterday."

"Put it in," Chris said as he rolled up another blunt.

"I'll be right back. I gotta go take a piss." Bigg excused himself from the room.

"Man, this gon' be some bullshit! This some old home-made in the kitchen porn! Screen all fuzzy, you can barely see them muthafuckas!" Chris yelled, disappointed.

"Negro please! He got ole girl in the doggystyle and every-thing!" Legend argued.

"Mouth full of balls!" NaSheed joked.

"Ahh, ahh, ooh that feels good!"

"Fuck that, you see ole girl ass!" Cezar grinned.

"He fuckin' the shit out lil' momma!" Legend added.

"GODDAMN LOOK AT THAT ASS!" Bigg yelled as he reen-tered the room.

"I don't hear you, you feel that?" the guy on the tape asked as he roughly pumped in and out of the girl's ass.

"Yes, yes, fuck me daddy!" the girl shrieked, sounding as if she wanted to cry. Ignoring her cries, the guy then took her legs and put them above her head so that the camera could showcase her vagina.

"Ooooh, look at that shit! Mommy got a fat-ass clit!" NaSheed shouted.

"Yo' dog, I would fuck her until I couldn't fuck no more!" Bigg stated, taking a pull from the blunt.

"Look at this nigga talkin' shit knowing his ass on lock down."

"Fuck all that! I would risk getting my ass kicked to hit that," Bigg countered, holding his dick.

"Fuck fucking the pussy. What about eating the pussy!" NaSheed suggested.

"This ole pussy eatin'-ass nigga," Cezar laughed.

"Do you see her titties though, dog? Them muthafuckas look all soft and pretty and shit," Legend pointed out.

"Right," Bigg replied as the camera panned to the guy's face. "Ay, wait a minute. Ain't that that nigga Tone, Unique used to mess wit'?"

"Yeah, that's that nigga," Chris answered.

"That's a nasty muthafucka! I know that lanky nigga from anywhere!" Bigg yelled and for a split moment his mind wondered if Tone had done the same thing to Unique.

"Yo', look at shorty face," Legend said, pointing to the screen.

"Yo' ... wait ... slow up on mommy's face," Bigg ordered.

"Fuck her face, go back to the bitch pussy!" NaSheed joked.

"Nah, nah, for real, ole girl look familiar! I seen her somewhere before! Slow that down." Grabbing the remote, NaSheed slowed it down then zoomed in on the girl's face.

"You like my dick in yo' ass?" Tone growled.

"Yes daddy yes, fuck me!" the young girl shrilled in pain.

Realizing who it was on the tape, Bigg yelled, "Oh my God! That's baby sis on the fuckin' screen!" Pacing and back forth, he held his head down and tried to get the image out of his mind.

"Goddamn! I ain't know Patience was doing it like that. I

Keisha Ervin

need to holla at mommy," NaSheed said, astonished.

"Nigga, turn that shit off before I shoot that muthafucka off!" Bigg shouted.

"Hold up dog. I got this room on my girl credit card, chill!"

"I don't give a fuck! Turn that muthafucka off!" Bigg barked. Running over to the screen, Chris pressed stop on the DVD player. "Where did you get that shit from?" he questioned NaSheed.

"I got it from Sammy off the street when I went to get some bootleg DVDs. Everybody got one."

"You ain't know that was Patience on there?"

"Nah, nigga, you saw the cover! The only thing on there was her ass!" NaSheed lied. He had seen the DVD beforehand. He knew that if Bigg saw it he would go crazy and kill Tone, and if Bigg killed Tone, he would go to jail. With Bigg in jail, NaSheed could get off scott free and go into the witness protection program as planned.

"Why would Patience fuck Tone?" Cezar asked, still stunned.

"I don't know but the tape had to have been made a couple of years ago because her hair was shorter," Bigg explained.

"What you think Unique gon' do when she find out?" Legend questioned.

"I don't know but can't none of ya'll tell her."

"You gon' tell her?" Chris asked.

"Yeah, but not tonight. I don't want to spoil her night. FUCK!" Bigg screamed while kicking a chair over. "This shit is gon' kill her when she find out!"

"Calm down, man!"

"Fuck that calm down shit! Didn't I tell you my girl rented this muthafucka! You breaking chairs ain't gon' solve nothing! Am I my brother's keeper?!" NaSheed yelled.

Keisha Ervin

"Yeah," Bigg answered.

"A'ight then! We gon' handle this shit but don't be trashing my muthafuckin' room!"

"I just want to know what kind of sick muthafucka fucks a 14-year-old girl?"

"Damn, she was 14 on that tape?" Legend asked, repulsed.

"Yeah!"

"Don't even worry about it, dog. It's a done deal. The boy is dead." Chris cocked his gun in the air, showing that he wasn't playing games.

"You're right. I gotta calm down though before Unique suspects something. Let me go splash some cold water on my face, man."

After splashing some water on his face, Bigg retied his tie, took a deep breath and headed downstairs. He found Unique on the dance floor with Zoë and Patience dancing the night away. A grin was plastered on her face and for a split second she almost seemed angelic. Unique had changed into a winter white Versace blazer with no bra underneath and a pair of crop pants with heels.

Waving at Bigg, she signaled for him to come over and join them. He shook his head no, smiled and continued to watch her dance to her favorite song, JLo's *"Get Right."* Looking at her made Bigg want to break down and cry. She was his everything and in a year she would be his wife. He couldn't imagine how the news of Patience and Tone would affect her. For the life of him, Bigg couldn't figure out why Patience would fuck Tone. Let alone let him catch it on tape. Until he told Unique, and they sat down and talked to Patience, he wouldn't know.

"All the ladies put yo' hands up! Put yo' hands up!" DJ Elite yelled as Destiny's Child's *"Soldier"* came on.

"Ah shit!" Bigg could see Unique yell as she shook her ass

to the beat. *"Know how to flip that money three ways ...*
Always riding big on the freeway... With that Midwest slang
that us country girls we like ... Low cut Caesar with the deep
waves ... So quick to make me his fiancée," she sang as she
winked her eye at him. Seeing Unique look so happy, Bigg did-
n't know if he could hurt her by telling her about Patience.
But he knew that she needed to know. Telling Unique was the
only way that they could help Patience.

"Yo', Bigg. I'm sorry about Patience. I know how this must
be tearing you up," Legend stated.

"The situation is fucked up, man. That's my gal sister on
that tape. Who knows how many niggas have seen that shit?"

"I know, I ain't even think about that part."

"I have."

"You weren't really serious about killing Tone, were you?"

"Hell yeah, I was serious! I'm gon' put two in that nigga —
one for Unique and one for me!"

"Well look dog, I'm up, happy birthday."

"A'ight Legend." Bigg hugged him.

"Why you ain't come out there with me?" Unique asked,
walking over to him.

"I'm a little tired that's all," Bigg lied as he gazed into
Unique's almond-shaped eyes, holding her close.

"What's wrong?"

"Nothing, I'm good, you a'ight?"

"Of course I'm cool, whenever you're around I'm good."
She kissed his nose.

"I love you, you know that, right?"

"Yes, and I love you, too."

$ $ $

After a weekend filled with nothing but lovemaking at the

WS, Unique lay across her bed reading the latest issue of *XXL* magazine. An article on Bigg, Chris and NaSheed was in the "Show & Prove" section. Grinning from ear to ear, she knew that Bigg's company was going to surpass everyone's expectations. Home alone and feeling nauseated, Unique glanced at the clock and wondered where Bigg had run off to. He had been in and out the house all day. Patience was gone, too. She had gone skating from 5 to 9 at Saints with Chantell.

Hearing Bigg enter through the front door, Unique called out for him. She had known that something had been bothering him but he refused to tell her what the problem was. Unique had decided that enough was enough. She told herself that by the end of the day she would know the truth.

Easing off the bed, she held her stomach and waddled into dining room. Unique's stomach was hurting. When she entered the living room she noticed that Bigg was on his cell phone. Holding up his finger, he instructed her to wait a minute before speaking. Shortly after he hung up the phone, he stared at her and sighed.

"Did you get me a 7-Up and some crackers?"

"Nah baby, I forgot. I had to do something else."

"You know I've been in the house all day sick and shit! You could've stopped and got me something from Walgreens, Bigg. Quit being so inconsiderate!"

"I'm sorry but come here," he said with outreached arms. "I need to talk to you." Taking a seat at the dining room table, she sat face to face with him.

"What you want? I wanna go back and lay down." Unique was now aggravated.

"For the past two days I have been wondering how I was going to tell you this. But there just ain't no right way to say it."

"What the fuck is going on, Bigg?! You don't want to

marry me no more? Is that it?!"

"Unique, that ain't even it, calm the fuck down!"

"Well, what the fuck is it then? I don't feel good! Why you bothering me?"

"Yo', chill! I got something to show you." As Bigg walked across the room to the entertainment system, she rolled her eyes.

"I don't feel like watching no damn DVD!" Unique spat as she picked up the DVD cover. "What the fuck is this shit? *Dime Hoes*! Nigga is you crazy?"

"Just watch the muthafuckin' DVD and shut up!" Bigg ordered, becoming impatient. Rolling her eyes once more, Unique got up and sat on the couch as the DVD began to play.

"Nigga, do I look horny to you? I don't wanna see this shit!"

"Unique, shut up and watch the fuckin' TV!" Seeing Tone's face, Unique became even more annoyed.

"Why you got me watching this bullshit? So what, Tone's a porn star, and?"

"Keep looking." Looking closely as the camera panned around to the girl's face, Unique sat stunned at what she saw.

"What the fuck is this shit?!"

"I didn't know how to tell you, ma."

"Tell me what? That you like watching lil' girls fuck grown-ass men?"

"Fuck nah! I didn't know how to tell you that your sister was fuckin' Tone!"

"Got me watching this ole sick-ass bullshit! What the fuck is wrong wit' you?!"

"I ain't the one on the muthafuckin' screen fucking yo' sister so calm the fuck down!"

"Why is my sister on a porn tape fuckin' Tone, Bigg? Why?!"

Keisha Ervin

"I want to know the same thing."

"This some ole bullshit," Unique cried, slumping down on the couch.

"I'm sorry, baby," Bigg whispered, consoling her.

"Why would he do this to me?"

"'Cause he's a sick fuck, that's why!"

"How am I going to explain this to mommy when I go see her?! I was supposed to protect Patience!"

"You did the best you could do, ma. Don't go beating yourself up over this shit."

"You don't understand, Bigg. My momma blamed me for everything that was wrong with her life! I thought by raising Patience for her that I could somehow make things right between me and her!"

"You can't blame your mother's mental illness on yourself. You ain't have nothing to do with that."

"I know." Unique continued to cry.

"Patience fucked Tone 'cause she wanted to."

"Uh uh, something ain't right about this shit! Patience would never fuck him off GP!"

"Whatever the reason is, I'm gon' handle it. Where is baby sis now?"

"She's gone skating with Chantell." Unique sniffed and wiped the snot from her nose.

"I told you I ain't want her hanging around that fast-ass girl! She's probably the one that put her up to doing the shit!"

"Well damn, Bigg, I'm sorry! It's already clear that I don't know what the fuck I'm doing! So go ahead, yell!"

"Yo', my bad, I'm just as torn up about this as you are. Patience is like a sister to me for real, you know that."

"I know. I just gotta go sleep. I can't deal with this shit right now," Unique said, getting up and heading to the bedroom.

Keisha Ervin

"You ain't going nowhere by yourself. I told you I'ma hold you down. Let me be there for you," Bigg said, holding her hand.

He picked her up and carried Unique into their bedroom and laid her down. Lying down beside her, he held her securely in his arms as he watched as she drifted off to sleep. A few minutes later, he kissed her on the forehead and left.

An hour later, Unique awoke drenched in sweat. She had had a nightmare about her sister being raped by Tone. Reaching for Bigg, she noticed that he wasn't there. Hoping that it was all a bad dream, she returned to the living room. She pressed play on the DVD she watched the horrid visual all over again.

"Unique, I'm home!" Patience yelled, coming through the door. Not able to turn the DVD off in time, Patience caught her sister watching the porn tape.

"Where you get that from?" Patience asked, trembling with fear. Without any words, Unique hopped up off the floor and charged toward her. Hitting her sister as hard as she could, Unique beat her sister until she lay curled up in a ball on the floor.

"How could you do this to me?!"

"Unique, I'm so sorry! Don't be mad at me! He made me do it!" She pulled her up by the hair and slammed her sister into the wall, slapping her face.

"I have broke my neck trying to take care of you and this is how you do me?!" Unique yelled into her sister's face. "What the fuck were you thinking, Patience?!"

"He said no one would ever know!" Patience began to cry.

"What?!"

"I'm sorry!" Patience sobbed uncontrollably.

"Why! Why did you do it?!"

"I'm sorry!"

Keisha Ervin

"Tell me what happened, Patience!" Unique yelled, shaking her.

"He told me that he loved me and that since he took care of us that was what I was supposed to do."

"What?!"

"Tone said that if I didn't sleep … with him that he would put us out and that we wouldn't have anywhere to live. He said … he said that he wouldn't pay for mommy to go … to the clinic no more and he that … if I ever told you he would kill you and mommy and I believed him."

"Patience, why didn't you tell me?" Unique cried as well, holding her sister.

"'Cause he was gon' kill you. Who would've taken care of me then?"

"You should've told me. I would've helped you. I would do anything for you."

"I'm sorry."

As more and more tears fell, Unique became angrier. Having heard enough, she headed back into the bedroom and pulled out a pair of jogging pants and Timbs. She unlocked her safe and pulled out her .380.

"Unique, what are you doing?" Patience asked, fearing the worst.

"Don't go nowhere, you hear me! Stay here. I'll be back!"

"Don't go over there, Unique! What if something happens to you?" Patience cried hysterically.

"You heard what I said, Patience. Just do as I ask, OK?" Unique cried. Nodding her head, Patience agreed as she watched Unique grab her car keys and coat, storming out of the house on a mission to kill.

Keisha Ervin

Intent 2 Kill

16

Playing the tape back as he sat in Federal Agent Lansing's office, Legend couldn't help but feel bad. He was about to turn over evidence of Bigg saying that he would kill Tone to the District Attorney's office. Little did Bigg know that Legend had on a wire the night of his party. He knew all about the DVD of Patience and Tone. Once NaSheed got word that the DVD was floating around, he brought it in and showed it to Federal Agent Lansing.

Lansing couldn't have been happier. They finally had something that they could use to make Bigg snap. The whole thing was set up perfectly. NaSheed would show the DVD and Legend would catch Bigg's reaction on tape. Just as expected, Bigg exploded and threatened to kill Tone. The only thing left to do was wait until Tone came up dead or missing.

"You're here early," NaSheed said as he entered the room. Ignoring him, Legend continued to sit deep in thought. "Oh, so you not talkin' to a nigga now?"

"Shut the fuck up, NaSheed!"

"A'ight nigga, damn." NaSheed put his hands in the air as

a sign of surrendering.

"You really don't care that you're sending your best friend to jail, do you?"

"When it comes to my freedom? No. I don't give a fuck if it was momma. I would send her ass to jail, too."

"You ain't shit."

"And neither are you."

Grabbing him by the collar, Legend whispered, "If I didn't give a fuck about losing my job I swear to God I would fuck you up right now."

"Boys, what is this?" Federal Agent Lansing questioned.

"It's nothing," Legend said, letting go of NaSheed and pushing him back into his chair.

"If he keeps this up I'm going have to file charges against the police for harassment," NaSheed scoffed, fixing his shirt.

"So what did you get?" Federal Agent Lansing asked.

"We got that nigga on tape saying that he was going to kill Tone just like I said he would."

"Good, let me hear it." Legend pressed play on the tape recorder and played back his entire conversation with Bigg. "NaSheed, you are a fucking genius. You might not be going to jail after all."

"Ay, what can I say." NaSheed grinned.

"Can I go now?" Legend asked, upset by the whole situation.

"Yeah, that's all for now. I'll call you when we have something else."

"A'ight."

"Ay, Legend, it's just a job. Don't take it so hard," NaSheed said, trying his hardest to get under Legend's skin.

"Nigga, fuck you." Legend slammed the door behind him.

"Legend!" his partner of three years called out.

"What's up, Tori?"

"I just wanted to say sorry again for the other day."

"It's cool."

"No it's not." She pulled him to the side. "I know how much you like Zoë. My mind just went blank when she approached us. I didn't mean to say her name, though. I will say that you're dead wrong for getting in so deep with these people, but I understand."

"I don't think you do. I think I might really love this girl."

"Damn, it's like that?"

"Yeah, but it's fucked up 'cause I know it can't work out."

"I don't know what to say, man."

"Me either. I don't know what I'm going to do. On the real, sometimes I wish that I never took this case."

$ $ $

The clock read 9:55 as Zoë sat at her desk studying for a sociology test, listening to Faith Evans' *"Catching Feelings."* She tried her best not to think about Legend but found it very hard not to. It seemed like every time she tried not to think about him, her mind would drift off to some moment they shared together. Whether it was their first kiss or their first date she could vividly remember them all.

"I'm not going to call him. But what could one phone call do? It's not going to hurt anything," she said out loud. Not able to take it anymore, she picked up her phone and dialed his number. Zoë let it ring four times before hanging up. Feeling stupid for even calling him, she got up to get a drink of water. *He's probably with his baby momma*, she thought.

Ring… Ring … Ring

Zoë was halfway to the kitchen when she heard the phone ring. She turned around and quickly made a mad dash for the telephone.

"Hello?" Zoë answered, almost out of breath.

"You just call me?"

"Yeah, I was just calling to see what you were doing," she lied, knowing fully well that she just wanted to hear the sound of his voice.

"I ain't doing shit. What you doing?"

"Nothing ... I was kinda hoping I could see you tonight."

"I wish I could but I ain't gon' be able to do it tonight. My day has been all fucked up."

"What happened?"

"I don't even want to talk about it." Unsure of what to say or do they both sat quiet for a minute.

"Well ... I didn't want to bother you so ... I'll let you go."

"A'ight. I'm gon' holla at you later," Legend said, needing to clear his head. Hanging up and feeling even dumber, Zoë vowed to never dial Legends' number again.

$ $ $

Knock!!! Knock!!!

"Who is it?"

"It's me."

"And to what do I owe this surprise?" Tone asked, opening the door.

"I need to talk to you." Unique pushed past him. Searching around the house, she made sure that no one else was there.

"Well hi to you too, Unique."

"I saw the video, you sick bastard!"

"What video?" Tone played stupid.

"Now you wanna play stupid. The video of you fuckin' my sister you stupid bastard!"

"Oh, that video." He grinned while taking a seat on the couch.

Keisha Ervin

"How could you do that to her, Tone? She looked up to you!"

"Patience is not as innocent as she seems. Trust me. She wanted it."

"What?! My sister wouldn't fuck you off GP! I know you threatened her!"

"Who the fuck you think you talkin' to? You better calm the fuck down! So what I fucked her? What you gon' do, tell yo' bitch-ass boyfriend?!" Unique didn't answer. "That's what I thought! Fuck you and that nigga!"

"I hate you! I wish I never met you!"

"Bitch, I took care of you! I took you and yo' lil' pissy-ass sister in! If it wasn't for me, you wouldn't have shit! Yo' crazy-ass momma didn't even want you! You thought I gave a fuck about you crying to me all those nights about yo' mother? I didn't give a fuck! You need to be thanking me for all the shit I did for you!"

"Fuck you!" Unique yelled, pulling out her .380 and aiming it at his head.

"What you gon' do with that Unique, kill me? You ain't no killer. I taught you a lot of things but I ain't teach you to be a killer. Put the gun away, you're making a fool out of yourself." Tone picked up the Sunday paper and continued reading as if Unique weren't there.

"You're right, you didn't teach to me to be a killer, Bigg did."

Pow!! Pow!!

Unique pulled the trigger and fired at Tone twice but missed. He charged toward her and tackled her to the floor, causing Unique to drop the gun. With all of her might she hit Tone as hard as she could. Unique tried her best to get him up off of her but Tone was too strong. He grabbed her hair and hit her square in the face, causing Unique to lose her vision for a

Keisha Ervin

minute.

Even more enraged, Unique kicked and scratched until she was finally able to break loose. Seeing that he was about to grab the gun, Unique kicked Tone hard, causing him to fall back and hit his head on the edge of the wooden coffee table. Shocked by her actions, she sat wondering if he would get back up. Seeing that he didn't, Unique got back on her feet and gathered what little strength she had and headed over to Tone. He was out cold and blood was trickling from the back of his head. Unique leaned to check and see if he still had a pulse. Feeling one, she stood back up, grabbed her purse and headed out of the door, never looking back.

$ $ $

"Unique! Unique! Where the fuck she at?" Bigg said to himself just as he was about to dial Unique's cell phone number. Looking up, he saw her car pulling into the driveway.

"Where have you been?" he questioned as she walked through the door.

"I went to see Tone," she spoke calmly.

"What the fuck?! I told you that I was going to handle it! You hard-headed!"

"I know but I had to talk to him. Where is Patience?"

"I don't know. She wasn't here when I came in, and talk to him for what?"

"He threatened Patience into having sex with him, Bigg. He told her that he was going to put us out and that if she ever told me he was going to kill me and mother."

"Did he admit to it?"

"Not in so many words but I know he said that shit."

"Please tell me you didn't do anything stupid, Unique." Avoiding his eyes, Unique didn't say a thing. "Baby, tell me you didn't?"

"I'm sorry, Bigg. It had to be done but I didn't kill him. He was still alive when I left. "

"What happened?"

"I tried to shoot him but I missed. We ended up getting into a little tussle. While we were fighting I kicked him and he fell back and hit his head on the coffee table."

"A'ight, I'm gon' handle this."

"I'm sorry, Bigg, I just couldn't let him get away with doing that to my sister," Unique cried.

"I know, baby, I know. Did you touch anything?"

"No."

"Where is the gun?"

"Right here," Unique said, going into her purse but not finding it. "Fuck!"

"What?!"

"I left the gun at Tone's house."

"Did anybody see you go in?"

"No. I don't think so."

"A'ight, well look, you stay here. Go take a shower and burn those clothes in the fireplace, OK?"

"All right."

"I'll be back in a minute." Getting in his black Chevy Caprice, Bigg called NaSheed. He let the phone ring ten times before he hanging up. Calling his cell phone again two more times, NaSheed finally picked up.

"Hello?" he answered out of breath.

"Damn nigga, what the fuck were you doing?!"

"Nothing. What's up, man?"

"I need you to meet me downtown in front of Tone's crib in about twenty minutes."

"A'ight, where that nigga stay?" After giving NaSheed directions, they both pulled up to Tone's house at the same time.

"What's up?" NaSheed said as he hopped into Bigg's car.

"I got a situation. Unique tried to kill Tone tonight."

"What?!" NaSheed said surprised.

"Yeah, she went ballistic when she saw the video."

"Damn, yo' chick really is 'bout it, 'bout it."

"Hah, hah funny, but look we gotta go up in this nigga's crib."

"For what?"

"Unique and him got into a fight, he fell back and hit his head, she got nervous and ran out but she forgot to get her gun. She did say that he was out cold when she left though."

"Damn."

"I swear to God if that nigga still alive when we walk up in here I'm gon' kill him myself," Bigg said, cocking his gun.

"A'ight nigga, calm down. Come on," NaSheed said, hopping out of the car and making sure the coast was clear. With his shirt covering his hand, Bigg checked the lock and saw that the door was still open. Walking in together, they both saw that Tone had more than a head wound. He not only had a head wound but was shot point blank in the head and in the heart.

"I thought they just got into a fight?"

"I thought so, too. Unique said she didn't kill him."

"Well somebody shot that nigga."

"Damn, it's cold than a muthafucka up in here. What that nigga got the air on, full blast?" NaSheed said. Spotting Unique's gun on the floor, Bigg picked it up without covering up his hand.

"Here, I need you to get rid of this for me." Bigg handed the gun to NaSheed, forgetting to wipe his fingerprints off of it.

"A'ight, I got you." NaSheed took the gun, holding it with

Keisha Ervin

his shirt covering his hand.

"Don't fuck this up, man."

"Am I my brother's keeper?"

"Yeah, nigga, just don't fuck up like I said."

"I won't, I got you," NaSheed replied as they left back out. With his shirt covering his hand, Bigg wiped his fingerprints off the doorknob. After giving each other a pound and a hug, NaSheed watched as Bigg pulled off with a sly smile on his face. He had all the evidence he needed to put Bigg away and to save his own ass.

$ $ $

It was the crack of dawn, the house was quiet and everyone was asleep. The sun had just begun peeking through the clouds and the bedroom was still a color of gray. Unique and Bigg lay face to face as his lips lightly touched her forehead, holding her tight. It had taken her hours to finally fall asleep.

Memories of Tone's eyes staring at her as he lay lifeless awoke her every time she drifted off to sleep. Finally after three attempts at sleep she was able to go without waking up. Little did Unique know that her worst nightmare was about to come true. Nobody knew what was happening outside the front door of the loft.

Federal Agent Lansing, Legend and a squad of policemen stood on the opposite side of the door ready to tear the door down. The warrants had just been handed off to Federal Agent Lansing and the cue to proceed was given. Holding a battering ram in hand, two officers pounded on the door causing it to break immediately. Startled by the sound, Unique jumped up, wondering if she had just heard what she thought she heard.

"Bigg!" she called out but it was too late. Their bed was

Keisha Ervin

already surrounded with officers.

"Kaylin McClain, you are under arrest for the murder of Antonio Robertson. You have the right to remain silent. Anything you say can and will be held against you..." Federal Agent Lansing said with pleasure as two officers yanked Bigg out of bed and threw him on the floor.

"Get the fuck off me!" Bigg barked, trying his best to get away as the officers tried to handcuff him.

"Let him go!" Unique screamed.

"Resisting arrest ... I'll add that to your list of charges as well." Federal Agent Lansing smirked.

"Fuck you, white boy!" Bigg spat.

"No, fuck you," Federal Agent Lansing said, grabbing a hold of Bigg's neck as he talked. "'Cause when I get done with you, your black ass will never see the light of day again."

"Get off of him!"

"Unique, be cool. Don't say nothing," Bigg spoke calmly, still dressed in a white tee, Girbaud jeans and Timbs from the day before. He could barely look at Unique as he was hand-cuffed. It was like her whole world was tumbling down around her. Bigg was her everything and he knew it. A part of him wanted to break down with her but Bigg had to keep it gangsta. He could never let the cops see him sweat.

"No, don't take him! He didn't do anything, I did it!"

"Shut up, Unique!" Bigg ordered as he was led out the room.

"Unique, what's going on?" Patience asked as she walked into the room.

"They're taking him away like they took mommy away!"

"I'll be back home in no time, ma, I promise."

"No, I won't let them take you! Please just listen. He did-n't do anything! I did!"

"Ma'am, calm down," one of the officers spoke, trying to

grab her hand.

"Shut the fuck up! Don't touch me!" Unique shouted as she followed Bigg.

"Ma, you ain't got on no clothes. Let Patience take you back into the room," Bigg pleaded. Unique only had a bra and lace boy shorts on.

"No! Bigg, I can't leave you!" Furniture was flying everywhere as the police ransacked her loft. Locking eyes with her, Bigg saw the pain and frustration that was written all over Unique's face. "Bigg, don't go," she cried. Seeing Legend standing in their living room, Unique thanked God. "Legend, make them stop. They're taking Bigg away!"

"I can't," he said looking away. Noticing that his jacket read *FBI*, Unique's heart dropped.

"OH HELL NO!" she screamed, punching him in the face.

"Handcuff her now! She's going in too for assaulting a police officer!" Federal Agent Lansing ordered.

"On my momma, if anyone of ya'll touch my girl, you're dead!" Bigg seethed with anger.

"Threatening a police officer? I'll add that to the list of charges that I have on you." Federal Agent Lansing smiled.

Restraining her with his arms, Legend said, "I'm sorry." Harking up as much spit as she could, Unique spit in Legend's face.

"Fuck you, you heartless bastard!"

"Let my sister go!" Patience yelled. As an officer began to cuff Unique, Legend stopped him.

"It's cool, don't cuff her. I deserve it."

"Get the fuck off of me, pig!"

"Take her in the room, Patience!" Bigg yelled again.

"Don't touch me, Patience!" Unique warned. Not knowing what to do, Patience stood still.

"Baby listen, just call my lawyer. He'll take care of everything."

"I can't let them take you, Bigg," Unique cried.

"Unique, just trust me."

Frozen stiff, Unique stood in the middle of the floor as the police escorted Bigg out of the apartment. Turning around once more, Bigg mouthed the words *I love you*. At that moment every aspect of their relationship replayed in her mind. From the moment they met at Club Plush to when he proposed to her on their bed. Wrapping a sheet over her sister, Patience tried her best to console Unique.

But Unique was inconsolable; without Bigg her life didn't have a purpose. She walked over to the window and peeled the curtain back as they placed Bigg into the squad car. As if he could feel her watching him, Bigg looked up and winked at her. Unable to speak or move, a waterfall of tears ran down her face as they pulled away, leaving Unique once again all alone.

Keisha Ervin

17
Puzzle Pieces

"He was a muthafuckin' cop *and* had a girl? That nigga really played me," Zoë said, still in disbelief.

"He played all of us, Z. Who knows how much information he got on Bigg."

"I'm glad I didn't tell his punk ass about us stealing cars. Shit, we might be locked up, too."

"I just gotta get my baby out of there."

"Everything's going to be fine, I promise you."

"I just thought of something. What if they send him to the psychiatric ward instead of to a regular cell?" Unique paced the room, becoming more worried.

"Don't even let your mind go there, Nique. You got enough shit to worry about."

"You're right, you're right, everything's going to be fine," Unique reasoned with herself.

"They just fuckin' wit' him, they ain't got no real evidence. Besides, neither one of you killed Tone."

"Exactly, the real killer is still out there. We need to find out who did it."

"Right, but look at this shit!" Unique picked up her torn couch cushion. "Look at my muthafuckin' house! How am I going to clean up all this shit?!"

"Don't worry about it, Nique. I'll have a cleaning crew come over here to clean up for you. What you need to do is pack as much shit as you can and get the fuck up out of here."

"You know what, they probably had a search warrant for Bigg's crib, too. I know his shit is fucked up."

"I'll have the cleaning crew go over there, too, but until this shit gets cleared up you and Patience are coming to stay with me."

"Where is Patience?"

"She's in her room packing."

"Girl, what would I do without you?"

"I don't know but you can quit wit' all that mushy shit and go pack up," Zoë joked.

Ring ... Ring ...

"That might be Bigg." Unique rushed over to the phone. "Hello?"

"What's good, shorty?"

"You, I've been worried sick. What they say?"

"They said that they found the gun a couple of blocks from Tone's house with my fingerprints on it. They also got me on tape saying that I was going to kill that nigga."

"Oh my God, this is all my fault."

"Fuck all that. Don't you realize that nigga NaSheed set me up!"

"What?!"

"Come to find out that nigga been working with cops. Apparently he sold fifteen keys of coke to an undercover cop. Instead of him serving time they told him that if he could give them me that he would get off scott free."

"How you find that out?"

"Legend told me."

"You actually talkin' to that pussy-ass nigga?"

"I'm using him just like he used me. That's the rules of the game; that's how it goes."

"Just be careful, baby."

"I will but look, they not gon' give me bail."

"What? Why not?"

"I'm a murder suspect, Nique, they ain't letting my ass back out on the streets."

"How are we going to get you out when we don't even know who killed Tone?"

"I don't know but I'm gon' think of something. I gotta go to court tonight at 7."

"Damn, that only gives me enough time to wash my ass and jump on the highway."

"Yeah, but look, I gotta go. My time is up."

"OK." Unique's voice cracked as she tried not to cry.

"No tears, OK."

"I got you, I'm a soldier." She laughed, playing it off.

"I love you."

"I love you, too."

$ $ $

Unique walked into the St. Louis City Circuit Court with her hair pulled back in a ponytail and her head held up high. As she walked into the building, news reporters stuck microphones into her face while the paparazzi flashed photos. Dressed in a peach floral top, white full skirt, Manolo Blahnik sandals and peach Marc Jacobs Guinevere tote bag, Unique breezed past them all like a pro. With Zoë by her side, she felt as if she could do anything.

As they entered the courtroom, another court case was in

session so they sat down and waited until Bigg's case began. Ten minutes later, Bigg was escorted out in an orange jumpsuit and handcuffs with shackles around his feet. Unique couldn't stand to see her man chained up like a common criminal — if anything it should've have been her. Looking over to her left she saw a Federal Agent approaching the prosecution's table. Federal Agent Lansing had decided to prosecute for the state personally.

He informed the judge that besides being charged with first degree murder, Bigg was also being investigated for drug-trafficking, money laundering and a series of assaults. Leaning over and whispering to his lawyer, Bigg seemed to be upset by the news.

"Your Honor, the state is asking that bail be revoked," Federal Agent Lansing requested as he returned to his seat.

"Motion denied. Bail will be set at one million dollars cash and all assets of Kaylin McClain will be frozen until further notice."

"But Your Honor," Paul, Bigg's lawyer, tried to speak.

"Next case please," the judge said, banging on the gavel.

"What the fuck just happened?" Unique yelled at Paul.

"I honestly don't know."

"I don't know is not good enough! This is my fiancé's life we're dealing with here!"

"Unique, calm down!" Bigg shouted.

"I will not calm down!"

"You're not making the situation any better by yelling, Unique."

"How am I going to bail you out if I can't get to any of your money?"

"An appeal will be on Judge Sheffield's desk by the morning, I promise."

"It better be, as much money as I'm paying you!"

Keisha Ervin

"Baby girl, just keep your head up. Everything's going to be a'ight." Bigg gave his fiancée a half smile. Seeing her man trying to be so strong made her defense weaken and tears come to her eyes.

"I'm sorry," she apologized, trying to fight back tears.

"Me and Paul will think of something!" Bigg shouted as he was led out of the courtroom.

"Come on, Nique, let's go home." Zoë held her hand.

"I can't leave him, he needs me!" Unique snatched her hand away.

"Bigg is gonna be all right."

"No he's not, because I'm not all right without him!"

"Come on, Nique, you're making a scene," Zoë said as people began to stare at them.

"I don't give a fuck! Fuck these people! They can all kiss my ass," Unique spat as she stormed out of the courtroom with Zoë hot on her tail.

"Hold up girl, you know I got on heels!" Zoë yelled after her. Not paying attention and in a mad rush to get out of the courthouse, Unique bumped head-first into NaSheed.

"What the fuck do you want?!"

"I came to see you." He smirked and rubbed his chin.

"What you need to see me for? I ain't got nothing to say to you," Unique spat with her arms folded across her chest.

"Come on, Unique. You can quit bullshittin' now. Bigg's not here. You and I both know that there's this chemistry between us." He stroked her hair.

"Negro please. I don't think so." Unique smacked his hand away.

"Eww, what are you doing here?" Zoë asked, finally catching up.

"I came to check on my girl."

"Oh, so I'm your girl now?"

Keisha Ervin

"Yeah, that's if you want to be."

"Unique, you better check this nigga before I do," Zoë snapped.

"How you gon' come at your man's girl like that? I thought Bigg was your best friend?" Unique questioned.

"First rule." NaSheed came closer and whispered into her ear. "There is no such thing as friends in this game, ma."

"You know what, NaSheed? You're right."

"Pause. He's what?" Zoë questioned, perplexed.

"He's right, Z, there is no love in this game. I'm glad you made me see that, NaSheed." Unique smiled coyly.

"I'm glad I could, too, but check it. Here's my number. Call me when you need a shoulder to lean on." He smirked and walked away.

"I will."

"Bitch is you crazy? He's the one who put your man behind bars and you sittin' up here macking wit' his ass? Bigg is going to kill you when he finds out. You know that, right?"

"Trust me, Bigg will get over it." Unique smirked, fanning herself with the card.

$ $ $

"Hey Unique, I haven't seen you in a while." Nurse Sandy smiled.

"I know, things have been a little hectic. I'm sure you've heard about Bigg in the news."

"Yes I have and I have kept you and Kaylin in my prayers ever since."

"Thanks, Sandy, so how has she been?"

"She's been OK; we had a tough time with her last week. I think she might've sensed that something is wrong."

"It's my fault. I've been so busy dealing with Bigg that I

Keisha Ervin

haven't had enough time to come see her."

"Don't go beating yourself up. Just go on in there and see her."

Smiling, Unique did as she was told. Nurse Sandy had been a godsend to her mother over the years. In front of the cold, steel door she peeked through the window at her mother. Syleena was still in the same spot as she was the last time Unique came to visit. Sitting in a wooden rocking chair, she swayed back and forth with a blank stare on her face.

"Mommy, it's me," Unique said, slowly entering the sunless room. "How you been? I missed you ... so you're not talking to me today, huh? That's cool, I understand. I haven't been here that much lately." Placing her purse down, Unique walked over to her mother and began stroking her hair. "Your hair is pretty; Nurse Sandy did a good job on your ponytail. Patience is still getting straight A's in school. For some reason, I haven't been feeling that well but I'll be all right. You look so pretty today, Momma. I see you got on your new pink robe that I bought you for Valentine's Day ... Come on Momma, talk to me. I need to hear your voice right now."

Standing beside her mother, Unique waited for her to make some kind of sound or movement but she made none. "OK, since you're not going to talk, I'll do all the talking. I got something I need to tell you, ma ... you're not gon' like it though," Unique said, sitting on the floor by her mother's feet with her head rested in her lap.

"First off, Momma, the doctors say that you're real sick. I didn't know how to tell you this, but you got brain cancer, Momma. The doctors are doing all they can to help you though." Unique gazed up into her mother's eyes. Seeing no sign of a reaction she continued on. "I haven't even told Patience. She wouldn't be able to handle it if she knew. Speaking of Patience, I let you down, Mommy. I was so busy trying to make sure that Patience and I had a roof over our heads that I neglected to protect her," she sobbed.

"You remember that guy Tone I was seeing? Well ... he did something really terrible to Patience. I don't know how we're going to get past this. I was so stupid, Ma, because I trusted him. Then there's Bigg, he's locked up for something he didn't even do and I don't know how I'm going to get him out. Everything's fucked up and it's my entire fault." Staring up at her mother, she immediately became angry. "Why don't you say something? Goddamnit, Momma, talk to me! I'm getting sick of this shit! When are you going to be there for me?! I need you, Momma. Talk to me please!" Unique cried freely for the first time all week.

"Let's have a tea party, Nique. You still got that tea set I bought you?"

"Momma, you know it's me?"

"Go get the tea set, Nique, I wanna play."

"Momma, you remember that?"

"Of course I do, Nique."

"Good, so you remember me," Unique said happily.

"You're my child. Why wouldn't I remember you? Now go and get your tea set. I want some tea."

"I'm sorry, Momma. I don't have the tea set anymore."

"It's OK, Sweet Pea. I love you anyway, Diana," Syleena spoke, caressing Unique's cheek.

"Momma, my name is Unique."

Suddenly out of nowhere, Syleena began to spaz out. "Get away from me!" she yelled, pushing Unique off of her. She jumped up and stood in the corner of the room with her hands shielding her face.

"HELP, GET HER AWAY HER FROM ME! WHAT IS SHE DOING HERE AGAIN?! SANDY!"

"Momma, it's OK. It's me, Unique," she pleaded.

Keisha Ervin

"I DON'T KNOW YOU! GET AWAY FROM ME! I THOUGHT I GOT RID OF YOU! GET OUT OF MY HEAD! YOU MAKE ME SICK! QUIT CONTROLLING MY MIND! " Syleena shouted while hitting herself in the head repeatedly.

"I'm not trying to control your mind, Momma."

"YES YOU ARE! YOU'RE THE SAME ONE THAT CONTROLLED MY MIND A LONG TIME AGO! I'M SICK OF YOU! I WANT YOU GONE! YOU'RE NOT GOING TO GET ME THIS TIME, YOU'RE NOT! I WON'T LET YOU!"

"It's OK, Syleena. I'm here," Nurse Sandy gently spoke. "I'm sorry, Unique, but you're going to have to go."

"OK." She nodded and left the room. Gazing through the window, she watched as Nurse Sandy and two orderlies strapped her mother down to the bed. Sandy gently rubbed Syleena's head as she used a syringe to sedate her. The scene wasn't anything new to Unique; most of their visits ended this way. It was just that this time she needed her mother the most and once again she wasn't there for her.

$ $ $

"How did it go when you went to see Aunt Syleena?" Zoë asked as she and Unique stood in their lanes at the shooting range.

"She remembered me for a second but then she started trippin' again, thinking I'm trying to control her mind and shit." Unique aimed her .380 at the target in front of her. With one eye open and the other one closed, she pulled the trigger without hesitation, emptying the whole clip. Stepping back and pulling the goggles from over her eyes, she smiled at a job well down. Every last shot had landed in either the head or the heart.

"I don't know why Bigg gave your ass a gun." Zoë shook

Keisha Ervin

her head, laughing.

"Don't hate."

"Whatever; watch this," Zoë said, doing the same thing.

"I don't know why I gave yo' ass a gun," Unique joked.

"Girl, I still can't get over the fact that Legend is a cop."

"Have you talked to him?"

"Nope, I haven't talked to him since the night all that shit went down."

"Fuck that nigga. He's dead in my eyes."

"How can you say fuck Legend when you just accepted NaSheed's number the other day?"

"Zoë." Unique turned to look at her.

"Zoë my ass. Yo' ass is trippin'. I don't know what kind of shit you on but you done lost your mind. Here I was thinking that you was all in love with Bigg but I guess I was wrong. You sure I don't need to check you into Malcolm Bliss with your momma?"

"Don't play with me. Stop being so simple minded. There is a bigger picture to all of this. You know I always have a plan."

"If you say so, but anyway, what you got to tell me?"

"It looks like I only have one way to get Bigg out of jail and out the country."

"And what's that?"

"Time to start back robbing niggas for they whips. I already have two hundred thousand left in my safe so all I have to do is rob eight hundred thousand dollars worth of cars."

"Damn, Nique, that's gon' be damn near impossible to do in such a short time."

"I know it is but I gotta make it happen. If you don't want to help me that's cool, I'll understand."

"Don't make me slap you in yo' face. You're my cousin, my blood, I'm gon' always be there for you."

Keisha Ervin

"A'ight then it's set but, oh, one more thing, we need Kiara and Kay Kay to make it happen."

"Are you sure?"

"Yeah. I can't stand Kiara's ass for what she did but without her I'm not gon' be able to make this shit happen. I can be woman enough to set aside my feelings for Bigg's sake."

"*OK* … if you say so."

"Trust me, I got this," Unique said, turning and shooting at the target again.

"*Ooh I think they like me…I think, I think they like me,*" Unique's cell phone rang. "Speak of the devil. What it do?"

"What's up, Nique? This Kay Kay."

"What's up?" Unique replied, putting her cell phone on speaker so that Zoë could hear as well.

"Ay, I heard about Bigg. That shit is fucked up."

"Yeah, it is. I'm real torn up about it."

"Ump, yeah, right," Zoë whispered, rolling her eyes.

"Was that Zoë?" Kay Kay asked.

"Yeah, that was her. Don't pay her no mind."

"The reason I called is because I got your message."

"Oh you did."

"Yeah, girl, everything you said was true. Too much shit is going down right now and we're cousins, we shouldn't be fighting. There shouldn't be no beefs between us so I suggest we all get together for lunch tomorrow and squash this shit."

With one eyebrow raised, Unique contemplated Kay Kay's offer. She did, in fact, miss her cousins. Kiara and Kay Kay were like her sisters. She couldn't live the rest of her life without them. Even though Kiara had done some fucked up shit, they still were blood no matter what.

"A'ight, where?"

Keisha Ervin

Anything 4 Love

A year had gone by since all four girls sat in a room together, let alone shared a meal together. Kiara and Kay Kay waited patiently on the deck of Landry's Seafood Restaurant and Bar with bated breath. Both of their pockets had been suffering severely since Unique and Zoë left the business. When Kay Kay told Kiara about the meeting, Kiara couldn't believe her ears. Unique had put any and all ill feelings for Kiara aside for the sake of Bigg. She wanted to let bygones be bygones. They would all meet and have an adult conversation like the adults they were.

"What's taking them so long?" Kiara asked, rubbing her nose while situating her glasses on her face.

"I don't know but you need to get yourself together," Kay Kay spat, irritated by her presence.

"Don't start, Kay Kay!"

"Whatever." Kay Kay shook her head in disgust. "There they go now."

"About time." Kiara rolled her eyes.

"What's up, cousin?" Unique hugged Kay Kay.

Keisha Ervin

"Hey girl. What's up, Zoë?"

"Shit, cute shoes."

"Thank you. I got them from Petit Peton when I went to New York a month ago."

"Can we get this thing started?" Kiara asked, clearly needing a fix.

"Well hi to you, too, Kiara," Unique snapped.

"My bad. What's up, Nique?" She stood up trying to hug her. Hating the touch of Kiara's skin against hers, Unique stood still not hugging her back.

"OK, that's enough." Unique pushed her away.

"Zoë."

"Hi Kiara," she spoke dryly.

"Is there anything I can get you ladies?" the waitress asked.

"No thank you," Zoë replied.

"I'll have a Sprite, please," Unique requested.

"OK, coming right up."

"Now that we're all here, what's been going on with everybody besides the usual?" Kay Kay questioned.

"Well, shit, you already know about Bigg," Unique started.

"Nah, all I know is that he got locked up for killing Tone. What made him do it?"

"I don't know, I guess he was jealous."

"What?" Zoë asked, confused yet again.

"Come on, Z. You ain't gotta front no more. You knew that Tone and I was still fuckin' around."

Kiara grabbed her ice water and sat up at full attention. "So you and Tone was fuckin' around for real?" she asked.

"I mean, yeah. That is what you told Bigg, right?" Unique questioned with her head tilted to the side, awaiting her answer.

"Giiirl, I was just fuckin' wit' Bigg that night. He took it the wrong way."

"Uhmm hmm, I just bet, but anyway, Kay Kay, what's been up with you?"

"Nothing. Tryin' to get this paper, that's all. Things been real slow since you and Z left."

"For real?" Unique said as she sipped on her drink.

"On the real though, Nique, I'm feelin' like you. I'm getting sick of this whole thing. I think I'm about to be out the game, too."

"Excuse me?" Kiara snapped.

"You heard me. This shit ain't making us no money no more so we might as well get out while we're ahead. Besides, I'm the one taking care of your daughter. I need to be able to provide her with some kind of stability."

"Fuck stability. We need to get this money!"

"I mean really, do you ever think about Arissa?"

"This is not about Arissa, this is about me!"

"Still the same ole Kiara, all about self," Unique snickered.

"What the fuck is that supposed to mean?"

"Be easy, ma. I'm just making a statement. Kay Kay, I feel you when you say you want out, but me and Zoë want back in. I already told ya'll about Bigg. Well, what I didn't tell you is that all of his assets are frozen and his bail is set at a million dollars. All I have is two hundred grand left so I need eight hundred to get Bigg out on bail—"

"No you don't," Zoë interrupted.

"What you talkin' about?" Unique was caught off guard.

"I have a hundred g's sitting around collecting dust. You can have it."

"Are you serious?"

"Yeah."

"Nique, I can give you fifty grand," Kay Kay added.

"I can't take ya'll's money."

"Yes you can, and you will. Once this whole thing is over we gon' get our money back, plus some."

"Thank you, so now all I need is six fifty." They all looked at Kiara and wondered when she was going to chip in. Seeing that she wasn't, they resumed the conversation.

"That shouldn't be that hard to get. I already have a job lined up that will bring us in enough money for you and us but it's in St. Louis."

"Ah uh, we can't do that! I'm already hot, police already watching me like hawk! Ah uh, no no."

"Nique, we don't have no other choice," Zoë complained. Breathing in and out, Unique wondered how things had come to this. Zoë was right, they had no other choice, they had to do the job.

"A'ight, where?"

"Out in St. Charles."

"Who are we gonna work with?"

"This guy named Anthony who I'm seeing. He has a crew of lil' locs that have been helping him steal cars. What they do is steal cars and then ship them overseas. A lot of people overseas are willing to pay double for the cars, more than what we do here in the states. He needs for us to steal two cars for him and he needs for us to help load the cars onto the freight containers on the 26th."

"What kind of cars are they and when are we going to get 'em?" Kiara asked.

"One's an Aston Martin Vanquish and the other is a Ferrari F30 Spider and I was thinking later on this week," Kay Kay answered.

"Sounds good to me. Come on, Z, let's go. I gotta go pick up Patience from school." Unique stood up, preparing to leave. "Oh, but before I forget, this is for lying on me, bitch!"

Whap! Whap! Unique punched Kiara in the face twice,

causing her to fall backward out of her chair and for her nose to bleed. With nothing but determination on her face, Unique strutted around the table and grabbed Kiara by the hair. While holding her head back she drew her hand back and punched her dead in the mouth.

"And if I ever catch you lying on me again I'm gon' beat ya ass worse than that!" Standing up straight, Unique dusted her clothes off and grabbed her purse and shades before security came. Walking out of the restaurant with a smile on her face, Unique felt better then she had in weeks.

"Damn Nique, you ain't have to fuck her up like that. She probably won't help us now." Zoë was concerned.

"Fuck Kiara! She'll do anything to feed her habit!"

$ $ $

"*What makes you think that I'm gonna wait forever ... When we both know that you're never gonna leave her ... What makes you think that I don't want a man I can call my own ... What makes you think that I don't want a family ... What makes you think that I wanna be unhappy,*" Zoë sang as she made up her bed, thinking of Legend.

"Girl, how many times are you going to play that song?" Unique asked with her face twisted up.

"Until I believe it."

"I'm sorry, Z. I've been so preoccupied with Bigg that I haven't even been there for you." Unique plopped down on the bed Zoë had just made. "You sounded good though."

"Thank you, it's just that I want to know why. Like was I a part of the plan or did I just happen? I need to know if what I felt was genuine or was it all based on a lie. I mean, before Legend came along, everything in my life was a sure thing, but with him I always felt confused. I just need to know the truth so I can finally move on."

"I don't know, Z. If I was you I wouldn't fuck with his snake ass but that's just me. You had a relationship with this man so I guess if you need answers, call him."

"I can't talk to him. I might snap and kill him."

"Even though I don't want you to have any contact with his slimy ass, you need to find out the truth for yourself."

"OK. Give me a minute by myself so I can call him."

"A'ight, let me go get this big head girl up and ready for school." Sitting on the side of her bed, Zoë bit into her bottom lip, inhaled deeply and dialed his number.

"Agent Johnson speaking," Legend answered, not expecting it to be Zoë.

"Did I catch you at a bad time?" Zoë asked, caught off guard by the way he answered the phone. Hearing the sound of her voice, Legend leaned back into his chair, closed his eyes and pictured her face.

"Nah, you cool. How you been?"

"OK. I called because I needed to talk to you about something."

"I've wanted to talk to you, too, but I was afraid of how you might react to seeing me so I laid low."

"Well can you meet in like an half an hour at Forest Park by the waterfall?"

"Yeah, I'll be there."

Forty five minutes later, Zoë arrived. Sitting there for a second, she watched as Legend paced back and forth. Almost a month had passed since they last saw one another. *For him to be a Federal Agent, he sure looks like a thug*, she thought. Nothing had changed in his appearance. He had on a NY Mets baseball cap, a white tall tee, LRG jeans and peanut butter Timbs. She could tell that his hair had been freshly cut by the way his hat was cocked to the left. Zoë hated that the sight of

Keisha Ervin

him still caused her breath to shorten and her nipples to harden. She tapped him on the shoulder, getting his attention.

"What's up?" he spoke, not sure whether he should hug her or shake her hand.

"Nothing," she spoke, unsure of what to do, too.

"You look nice." He eyed her short black hair, sky blue chevron striped Juicy jogging suit and sky blue and yellow All Star Chuck Taylors.

"Thanks."

"You want to sit right here?" Legend asked, pointing to a bench in front of them.

"Yeah, that's cool."

"I've been thinking about you a lot lately."

"Really, me too."

"Look, Z, I know that I have a lot of explaining to do but before I do I just wanted to tell you that I love you, too. I just couldn't tell you that night because I was already getting in way over my head when it came to Bigg's case. I wasn't supposed to get attached and I did, not only to Bigg, but to you, too. I didn't know that I would meet you and grow to have feelings for you. You caught me off guard for real and I didn't know what to do."

"I just … wish that you would have never let it get this far. I mean, did you ever think about how I would feel when I found out the truth?"

"Believe it or not, I thought about it every day. I was brought in to do a job. Bringing in criminals is what I do. My job was to bring Bigg down and I did that. I know it might sound fucked up but that's my job. I will say, though, the day you walked into that studio, my whole agenda flipped."

"So, was the part about you having a girlfriend and daughter even true?"

"Nah, the girl you saw me with was my partner, Tori. That

was her daughter I was holding. We were meeting up because she wanted to talk to me about a case she was working on."

"Oh my God, so I went through all those nights of crying my eyes out for nothing?" she asked, heated.

"I'm sorry, ma."

"I can't believe this shit." She shook her head in disbelief.

"You wanted to know the truth so I'm giving it to you. I love you and I'm sorry for how everything went down."

"Do you know that you locked up an innocent man? Bigg didn't kill Tone. Somebody else did!"

"We have his fingerprints on the murder weapon, Zoë."

"I shouldn't even be telling you this but since you say you care about me so much, maybe you'll do the right thing. Nique saw the tape of Patience and Tone. She went over there. She fired twice at him but missed. They got into a fight and he hit his head on the table — that's how he got the wound on the back of his head. Unique checked his pulse before she left and he was still alive. Nique got scared and left but she forgot her gun so Bigg and NaSheed had to go back and get it before the police found Tone's body. Bigg gave the gun to NaSheed without any gloves on and then I guess NaSheed snitched and told the police where the murder weapon was since he was working with ya'll."

"So, during the time Unique was gone and Bigg came back, somebody else had the opportunity to finish what Unique started," Legend said out loud, putting the pieces together. "About how much time you think passed after Unique left and Bigg arrived at Tone's house?"

"I don't know, maybe thirty minutes to an hour."

"I knew something wasn't right!" Legend snapped, standing up and pacing again.

"What?"

"We had until April to bring Bigg in. If I didn't arrest him by then I was going to be off the case and on traffic duty. My boss Federal Agent Lansing told NaSheed that if he didn't come up with some incriminating evidence against Bigg that he was going to go to jail for ten years for selling drugs to an undercover cop."

"So, he lied on Bigg just so he could get off."

"Yep."

"Bitch-ass niggas!"

"Plus, Lansing had two coroners perform autopsies on Tone."

"Why?"

"I don't know, but I'm going to find out. You gotta help me find out who killed Tone."

"I can't help you."

"Why not?"

"'Cause I don't trust you."

"If I wanted to lock you up I could. I know all about ya'll's lil' ring of car thieves."

"How you know about that?"

"I'm a cop, what do you expect?"

"So, you knew about that the whole time we were together?"

"Yep."

"And you were never going to bring us in on that?"

"Nah, I told you ... I love you." He grabbed her hand and took her into his arms.

"I hate you," Zoë cried, burying her face in his chest.

"I know, I know," Legend said, kissing her on the forehead.

$ $ $

Unique couldn't contain her excitement as she walked through the cold steel doors. She was finally going to see Bigg

Keisha Ervin

after being away from him for two weeks. Talking on the phone just wasn't enough. Unique needed to see, touch and feel her man. As she stood in the middle of the room, she searched the crowded visiting hall for him.

Unique spotted him seated in the back of the room and smiled. Even though he had only been in jail a few weeks, Bigg was already starting to show signs of stress. His hair and beard were in desperate need of a clipping and lining. The orange jumpsuit did not compliment his muscular arms and long legs but all in all, Bigg was still the finest man she had ever seen.

For the first time in two weeks, Bigg smiled once he saw Unique. He missed seeing his boo. His light brown eyes seemed to gleam as soon as he laid eyes on her. Unique was his everything. Living without her for the past two weeks had been like hell on earth but Bigg knew he had to stay strong for her. He knew if Unique saw him break down that she would break down, too.

"Baby," Unique's voice cracked as she tried to speak.

"What's up, shorty?" Bigg took her into his arms and held her tight. "I miss you, ma," he whispered into her ear.

"I miss you, too."

"That's enough, McClain," one of the guards yelled from across the room. Mean mugging him, Bigg held Unique's hand and sat across from her at the table.

"How you been? Ain't nobody been fuckin' wit' you, have they?" she asked.

"Nah, these niggas in here know how I get down."

"Oh, just making sure. I didn't want to have to pull out my .380," Unique joked.

"Look at yo' ass."

"Have they been giving you your medication?"

"Yeah, I'm good." Staring at Unique for a minute, Bigg

Keisha Ervin

noticed a difference in her appearance. "Is it just me or have you gotten thicker since the last time I saw you?" he questioned, not missing a beat.

"You know, I just came off my period. I always look thicker after I come off."

"Oh, I thought—" He paused.

"Thought what?"

"Nothing," he said as he eyed her closely, paying careful attention to her midsection.

"I do have something I need to talk to you about."

"What is it?"

"After your hearing, when I was leaving out, I ran into NaSheed."

"What?!" Bigg yelled, enraged.

"See, that's why I didn't tell you this over the phone. 'Cause I knew you were going to flip out."

"You damn right I was gonna flip out! What the fuck that nigga say to you?"

"Can you calm down please before one of these guards come and get yo' crazy ass and take you up outta here?" Taking a couple of deep breaths, Bigg calmed himself down before speaking again.

"OK, I'm calm. What he say?" Giving him a quick look, Unique made sure he was really calm before she spoke.

"Baby, he came on to me."

"Hold up, pause. He came on to you?"

"Yes! That crazy muthafucka was tryin' to holla at me! Can you believe that shit?"

"Yo', I put that on everything I love that nigga is dead."

"Fuck NaSheed. We can handle him later. What we need to concentrate on is getting you out of jail."

"You're right, boo. It's just that this shit be getting to me sometimes. Dude was supposed to be my boy. I was just get-

Keisha Ervin

ting my life back together and now I'm back at the very place I swore I would never be again."

"I know baby, I know," Unique cooed while stroking Bigg's cheek. "But check it, I've figured out a way to get you out of here."

"How?"

"I got a job set up."

"What kind of job?"

"Me and the girls are gonna steal these cars—"

"Uh uh, ain't no way hell I'm gon' let you do that," Bigg interrupted. "The police already watchin' you like a hawk."

"That's what I was saying, but Bigg, this is the only way I'm gonna be able to get you out."

"You heard what I said, Nique. I'm not gon' risk you getting locked the fuck up too. It's a done deal. Let me and Paul handle this."

"But Bigg—"

"But Bigg nothing, now promise me you gon' listen to your man."

"I promise," Unique lied.

"You know I love you, right?"

"Yeah, I know."

"You miss me?" he asked, taking her hand into his.

"The question is, do you miss me?"

"Hell yeah. I can't wait to get out of here. These last two weeks have been hell. I don't know how much more I can take, ma."

"Everything's gonna be all right, I promise."

"I hope so."

"Do you remember when we first met how I tried to play all hard to get and shit?"

"Yeah, I remember. I knew yo' ass was full of shit." Bigg laughed wholeheartedly.

"But you never gave up. Why is that? I was such a bitch to you."

"Because you were different from any other chick I ever met. You was tough and all but I knew that a soft side lurked somewhere inside your hard ass. Plus the way you made a nigga laugh I had to get you ... and when I saw that ass pass I had to hit ya." Bigg grinned, quoting lyrics from Eightball & MJG.

"Shut up, Bigg." Unique giggled.

"But I promise, shorty, me and Paul gon' think of something. There gotta be away outta this mess."

"I hope so, baby. I really do."

19
Ride or Die

The 26th was fast approaching and Unique couldn't wait. She was all too ready to get the shit done and over with. As she lay on the couch with a pillow tucked in her arms, she stared up at the ceiling. The sound of Raheem DeVaughn's song *"You"* was playing softly in the background as she sat and thought. A lot had been on Unique's mind lately. Not only was she dealing with Bigg's situation, but now she also had to deal with the unexpected news of a baby. Yes, Unique was pregnant. After her visit with Bigg, she started to notice how her appetite increased and how suddenly she was always tired.

Even though she had all the signs of being pregnant, Unique still ignored it. She chalked it up to just being stressed out. But once the morning sickness kicked in, she knew something was up. That very same morning while Patience was at school, she took a pregnancy test. After a three-minute waiting period the results came back positive.

Unique didn't know what she was going to do. On one hand she was elated to be having Bigg's baby but then on the other hand there was the possibility of having to raise their child alone. Unique didn't know anything about kids. Before Bigg, she never even considered having any. Now she was faced with the possibility of raising her first child alone. Just when she thought things couldn't get any worse, Nurse Sandy phoned to inform that her mother's condition was getting worse by the day. The news couldn't have hit Unique at a more inopportune time. She swore if one more thing happened she was going to lose her mind.

"Hey Nique," Patience spoke, coming through the front door.

"What's up, baby sis? How was school today?"

"Fine," Patience sighed, dropping her book bag to the floor. Lifting Unique's legs up, she sat down and placed them onto her lap. "What's wrong wit' you? Why you lookin' all sad?"

"Momma's nurse called and said she's getting sicker."

"For real?"

"Yeah, I don't know what to do."

"Everything's gonna be all right, Nique. Just pray on it. That's all you can do."

"I'm so sick of people telling me everything's gonna be all right! Shit, ain't nothing ever been right! I swear if it ain't one thing it's another and I'm sick of it!" Not knowing what to say, Patience sat quiet. She knew her sister needed to vent.

"But anyway, we need to talk," Unique continued after taking a couple of quick breaths.

"Talk about what?"

"This whole Tone situation."

"What about it? We already talked."

"I don't call me beatin' your ass talkin' about it, Patience."

"Well, I don't want to talk about it, Unique," Patience said, trying to get up.

"Girl, you better sit your ass down!" Unique demanded.

Keisha Ervin

Rolling her eyes, Patience plopped back down and folded her arms across her chest. "Now like I was saying, what Tone did to you was real fucked up. I still can't get over that shit but what fucks me up the most is that you didn't think you could tell me what was going on?"

"How many times do I have to tell you that the nigga said he would kill you and Mommy if I told you!" Patience shot, becoming defensive.

"You know I would've believed you if you would've told me, right?"

"Yeah, Unique, I was just scared."

"Now when was all this happening?"

"He would only mess with me when you weren't at home or when you were out of town."

"Wait a minute. That day I came back from Los Angeles something happened, didn't it, because when I walked in the house Tone's pants were unzipped."

"Yeah."

"Hell naw, I can't believe I didn't peep that."

"Believe me, I tried to tell you, I just couldn't bring myself to say it out loud. Tone made me feel ... so ... so ... dirty and nasty." Patience began to cry.

"It's all right, baby, I'm sorry." Unique sprang up and consoled her sister.

"I feel like I'm losing my mind, Nique! I can't sleep at night! I wake up in cold sweats from having nightmares."

"After all this shit with Bigg is done with, I promise we're going to get you some help."

"Help?!"

"Yes, honey, you need to go counseling."

"What I need to go to counseling for? I don't need to talk to no shrink!" Patience snapped, offended.

"Yes you do, Patience. You just said yourself that the shit

is getting to you. Look at me." Taking Patience's face into her hand, Unique forced Patience to look at her. Staring deep into her sister's eyes, Unique said, "Tone … raped … you. No matter what he told you, you didn't deserve that. He's the sick one, not you. Now we're going to counseling and I'm not taking no for answer. We're going to get past this shit and we're going to do it as a family."

$ $ $

April 26th, 2005 — the morning of the heist. It was 1 o'clock and Unique stood nestled in her favorite blanket staring out into the sky. Thoughts of Bigg and all the things they had gone through since being together filled her mind. Their relationship had been a whirlwind. Lies, jealousy, the cops and even murder all tried to consume them but somehow they were making it through.

Unique wasn't giving up. She was willing to get her man back at any and all costs. It just worried her at times that maybe this would be their fate — Bigg being in jail for life and Unique raising their child alone. Frustrated with the entire situation, she tried her best to not to think about Bigg, only to focus her eyes on a picture of them together at his 28th birthday party.

They had had such a good time that night. He was her everything and there wasn't anything in the world that she wouldn't do for him. There was no one else for Unique. She was convinced that God made Bigg especially for her. Pulling her shirt up over her stomach, she imagined what would one day become a perfect, round, protruding belly. Unique still hadn't told Bigg that she was pregnant. She couldn't bear to tell him that he was gonna be a father while he was still locked up in jail.

Keisha Ervin

"OK baby, mommy has to take care of some business tonight so can you please chill out until I get done?" Unique looked down and spoke to her belly. She was referring to the non-stop morning sickness she had been experiencing.

After rubbing her stomach and daydreaming, she folded up her blanket and headed into the bathroom to shower and dress. Thirty minutes later and fully-clothed in an all-black scull cap, hoodie, jeans and Timbs, Unique grabbed her car keys and left the house. A little nervousness began to settle in the pit of her stomach as she took the elevator down to the main floor but Unique shook if off. Wasn't nothing or nobody gonna stop her. Taking a deep breath, she calmed herself down and walked around the building to the parking lot.

Except for the street light on the opposite side of the street, it was pitch black outside. Summer was fast approaching so the sounds of crickets and birds chirping filled her ears. Thinking of Bigg and their baby again, Unique smiled slightly to herself. She couldn't wait to be wrapped up in his arms again. Listening closely to her surroundings, just as she was about to place her key in the lock, Unique heard footsteps creep up behind her. She reached for her gun and quickly turned around. Realizing it was Legend, she took a deep breath and put her gun away.

"Damn, Legend, you almost got yo' ass killed! What the fuck you doing creeping up behind me and shit?"

"You need to chill. I came to talk to you."

"Talk to me about what?"

"I know what you, Zoë, Kay Kay and Kiara are up to."

"I don't know what you talkin' about so if you ain't here to arrest me, I would advise you to get the fuck outta my face," Unique spat, dead serious.

"Yo', all that cursing ain't even necessary, ma. I'm tryin' to help you out!"

"Let me tell you something, *Mr. Police Officer*, there ain't shit you can do for me besides get my man outta jail! But, oh, wait a minute, I forgot you're the one who put him there in the first place!" Unique said, pointing her finger in his face in place of the gun.

"Shorty, look, I understand that you're upset but we ain't got time for that right now. I know Bigg didn't kill Tone."

"Whoopty fuckin' doo! We all know that! Instead of going off what that lying-ass muthafucka NaSheed told you, you would've known that, too!"

"Look, this my last time telling you. I ain't got time to be arguing wit' you. Either you gon' listen or not."

After looking at him like he was crazy, for a brief moment Unique contemplated what Legend had said. Deciding she should at least hear what he had to say, she rolled her eyes and let out a loud grunt while folding her arms underneath her breasts.

"All right, I'm listening. What you got to say?"

"I have evidence that will get Bigg out of jail by morning."

"Get the fuck outta here." Unique twisted her lips to the side as if to say he was lying.

"I'm telling you, I'm serious. I have solid evidence that Bigg didn't kill Tone. I'm going to turn it over to Paul first thing this morning."

"So, let me guess. This is the part where I'm just supposed to believe you and we all live happily ever after. Well let me tell you something, if that's what you think then you got me and life all fucked up! 'Cause I don't trust you! Never have, never will!"

"Well fuck it then! Do you, sweetheart! I don't give a fuck! I'm tryin' to help yo' ass out! But let me tell you something, if you and your girls go through with this little plan ya'll got going on, all ya'll gon' go to jail. As a matter of fact, I'ma per-

Keisha Ervin

sonally lock every last one of ya'll up. Now it's up to you. What you wanna do?"

Contemplating her choices, Unique stood clueless. On one hand a part of her was telling her to trust Legend but then experience was screaming *SNAKE*. Going with her gut instincts, she sighed and prayed to God that she was making the right decision.

"So what's this so-called solid evidence you got?" she asked, putting her keys back in her pocket.

$ $ $

As Unique stood back and watched the bailiff unlock the cuffs on Bigg's wrist, she said a silent prayer to God thanking him for allowing her to follow her first mind. Turns out, Legend was telling the truth. He had come up with solid evidence that would get Bigg out of jail. After doing some major investigating and questioning, he learned that besides Unique, Bigg and NaSheed visiting Tone's house that fateful night, another person had visited as well.

An unidentified caramel-colored woman reaching five feet ten in height entered Tone's place of residence at around 10:15 that evening, approximately fifteen minutes after Unique existed. An elderly woman from the block informed Legend of this. She had been peeking out her window the entire time but was too afraid to contact the police. The lady also stated that she was absolutely sure that Bigg and NaSheed did not enter Tone's house until a little after 10:45.

With that bit of knowledge in hand, Legend then went to talk to the coroner who had performed the first autopsy on Tone. His name was Joe Black. Joe confirmed that Tone was officially considered brain dead at around 10:17 that night. Meaning that there was no way Bigg could have killed Tone.

Besides that, the coroner also stated that rigor mortis had already started to set in because of the temperature in the room. Whoever the woman was who killed Tone turned the air conditioner all the way down to speed up the process. She must have been trying to make it look like the person who was there before her, Unique, was the killer but instead ended up screwing her own self over.

Joe also told Legend that he had informed Federal Agent Lansing of this. He said that once Federal Agent Lansing learned that Bigg wasn't the killer he became infuriated. Federal Agent Lansing said that he refused to look like a fool and took Joe off the case. He warned Joe that if he ever told anyone the truth about the autopsy report, Joe would wind up on the very same cold steel table he worked on. Soaking up the information being fed to him, Legend sat in shock. He couldn't believe the lengths Federal Agent Lansing had gone to convict Bigg. It took him a while but after doing some much needed persuading and arm twisting, Legend got Joe to turn over the real autopsy report.

That morning in front of Judge Sheffield, the prosecuting attorney, Federal Agent Lansing, Unique, Zoë, Legend and God, Bigg's attorney Paul presented the newly-found evidence to the court. Judge Sheffield was appalled to say the least. Not only was Bigg acquitted of all charges but Federal Agent Lansing was charged with perjury and withholding evidence. An APB was put out for NaSheed's arrest as well. The only thing Unique could do was cry tears of joy. Running over to Bigg, she wrapped her arms around his neck and hugged him tight. Letting a tear slip, Bigg hugged her back just as tight. For the first time in almost two months he was able to hold her. It felt good. Bigg couldn't have been happier.

"Congratulations, Bigg," Zoë exclaimed, giving him a hug, too.

Keisha Ervin

"Thanks, Z." He grinned. Turning back to the love of his life, Bigg took Unique back into his arms and said, "I love you, ma."

"I love you, too." She grinned as she wiped her eyes.

"Now when is my baby due?" he questioned with a smile.

"What?"

"You heard me. When is my baby due?"

"December 31st."

"I knew yo' ass was pregnant. Why you ain't tell me?"

"I'm sorry, baby, I wanted to but I just couldn't tell you while all this shit was going on."

"It's cool, ma, I understand."

"Ooh, baby, I can't wait to get you home." Unique grinned, kissing his lips softly.

"I know, me too, but first let me go holla at Paul for a second."

"OK," Unique replied, hating to let him go.

"Girl, I know you're happy." Zoë happily gave Unique a hug.

"I sure am. I got my man back. Now hopefully we can get on with our life without any more drama creeping up."

"Right, but I still can't get over the fact that Federal Agent Lansing was withholding all that evidence. He must have had some kind of a grudge against Bigg."

"I guess so."

"Come on, let's get out of here," Bigg said as he wrapped his arms around Unique's waist.

"Thank God! I'm hungry as hell," she stated, rubbing her stomach.

"Shit you, me too. A nigga hungry than a muthafucka. I'm ready to fuck up some food."

"Still the same Bigg," Zoë laughed.

"Ay, Zoë, you ready?' Legend asked, interrupting their

Keisha Ervin

repartee.

"Yeah. Bigg, once again welcome home. And you Miss Thang, I will be calling later," Zoë said, giving them both another hug goodbye.

"A'ight girl, talk to you later."

"Ay, Legend," Bigg called after him as he and Zoë walked away.

"What's up?"

"Thanks."

"No problem." He smiled slightly.

"You ready to get up out of here, lil' momma?"

"Yes," Unique replied gleefully.

As they walked out of the courthouse hand in hand, Bigg was swarmed with news reporters and cameras. News had already traveled that he was acquitted of all charges.

"Mr. McClain, how does it feel to be vindicated?" one of the reporters asked.

"It feels good. Now that this is over I can finally get on with my life and live peacefully with my fiancée and child. Now if you'll excuse me, me and my girl have some catching up to do."

"But Mr. McClain!" the news reporters continued to shout.

But Bigg wasn't trying to hear them. Smiling, he and Unique descended down the long flight of steps together looking like the young couple in love they were. Flashbulbs and microphones were steadily placed in Bigg's face but he didn't care. He was a free man. The day couldn't have gotten any better. Not a cloud was in the sky. The sun was out and shining brighter than ever before. For once, life was good for Kaylin McClain.

Then out of nowhere a shot of nervousness ran through his veins. He didn't know what it was, but something wasn't right. Searching the crowd he looked for any odd or peculiar faces. Not spotting anyone suspicious, he continued to walk with Unique only a few steps behind him when he noticed Kiara standing before him, holding a gun.

Bigg could barely recognize her. She looked like a full-fledged basehead now. Her hair was nappy and matted together and she looked as if she hadn't slept in days. Kiara was no longer the thick five-foot-ten chick she used to be. Her shapely frame was now very thin and emaciated. Crazed with anger, tears streamed down her face as she held the gun in front of her.

For a minute Bigg thought the gun was aimed at him but it wasn't. It was aimed at Unique. Unique was so happy that she didn't even notice Kiara standing there. A smile a mile wide was plastered on her face as she rubbed her stomach and followed Bigg. Not strapped with a gun himself, Bigg didn't know what to do. With no time to spare, he quickly turned and reached for Unique's hand.

"Baby, watch out!" he yelled.

Jolted by the sound of his booming voice, Unique looked in the same direction as Bigg and spotted Kiara standing with the gun but didn't move. She was frozen stiff. Not a muscle in her body could move. A deafening silence seemed to fill her ears as everyone, including Legend and Zoë, ran and ducked for cover. Not thinking he would need his gun that day, Legend left it in the car. People flew past Unique in search of cover but she wasn't coherent to any of that. At that moment, her entire life seemed to flash in front of her eyes.

Memories of her mother being sent away, meeting and making love to Bigg for the first time and the news of her pregnancy all filled her mind. Staring into Kiara's eyes she mouth the word *why* as the first shot was fired. Not willing to let it go down like that, Bigg was determined to protect Unique and their unborn child at all costs, including his life, as the bullet charged from Kiara's gun.

"BIGG, NO!" Kiara screamed as he got in the way.

Fully charged with adrenaline, he grabbed Unique and shielded her with his body. Four more shots riddled the air, all hitting Bigg in the back.

"Bigg!" Unique screeched in sheer agony as her body fell to the hard cement ground.

For a minute, time stood still as everyone including Unique wondered if the worst was over. It seemed like it had all been a dream. A little dazed from the fall, she shook her head in an attempt to regain consciousness. Once reality set in that she was on the ground underneath the man of her dreams, Unique screamed out for help.

"SOMEBODY HELP ME!" she screamed at the top of her lungs as she tried to free her one hundred thirty pound frame from under Bigg's one hundred eighty. Without hesitation, Legend and Zoë ran over to help. Gently, Legend pulled Bigg's limp, bloody body from off of hers. Paralyzed from the shock of her actions, Kiara stood still clicking the gun, praying for more bullets to come out. Once she realized that there was no more ammunition left, words of venom began to spew from her mouth.

"NO!!!! He wasn't supposed to die! It was supposed to be you! You ruined everything, you stupid bitch! I hate you! I hate you!" she screamed as the officers quickly restrained her.

Ignoring her comments, Unique concentrated all of her energy on helping Bigg. There he was, the man she was set to marry, covered in blood. Bigg's lifeless body lay in her arms begging to be rescued and resuscitated. Unique couldn't believe her eyes. This all had to be a bad dream.

"Baby, get up! Get up, it's me, Unique! Please don't die! Please don't leave me!" Unique cried hysterically as blood gushed from Bigg's nose and mouth. Blood was all over

Keisha Ervin

Unique's hands and clothes as his body violently shook. "Don't you do this to me, Bigg! You can't leave me! You better not die!"

"Unique, don't move him," Legend warned.

"Shut the fuck up, Legend! I'm not letting him go! I will never let him go! He needs me!"

With all of his might, Bigg fought his hardest to hold on. He could see Unique crying out to him, begging for him to live. This made him fight even more, but after a while his strength began to dwindle. Bigg's breathing was fading by the second and his heart rate was decreasing rapidly. Slowly, without notice, his eyes began to close.

"No, Bigg, no! Don't you do it!!! You better not die on me! You promised you would never leave me! You promised!! Will somebody help me please?!"

"Unique, the ambulance is almost here. I can hear them down the street," Zoë assured, stroking her arm.

"OK, OK, thank you, God. I knew you wouldn't let me down. Everything is gonna be OK." Unique closed her eyes and rocked back and forth as she held Bigg in her arms. She didn't even realize that she had smeared his blood all over her face. Smiling, she opened her eyes and said, "See, baby, I told you everything was gonna be fine." Sniffling, Unique looked down at Bigg to only find that his breathing had stopped and his eyes were closed shut.

"Bigg … Bigg … no, baby!" She shook his body profusely in hopes of waking him up. "Bigg, wake up! Baby, don't do this to me! I need you!" Seeing that he wasn't waking up, Unique lost her mind. "NO! NO, BIGG! NO! YOU PROMISED! YOU PROMISED! YOU PROMISED! AHHH!!! WHY!!!! YOU SAID YOU WOULD NEVER LEAVE ME! WHAT ABOUT THE BABY?! I CAN'T DO THIS WITHOUT YOU! BABY, I NEED YOU! COME BACK! SOMEBODY HEEEELP ME!!!!"

Keisha Ervin

20
A New Day

A year and a half later, Unique sat silently staring at the headstone before her, praying that it was all a dream. Ever since she was a little girl she feared this loss but with family and friends around her, she knew she would make it through. Life hadn't been the same since the courthouse shooting. A week after the shooting the funeral took place. Unique could barely walk that day. She cried so much. Only a few people attended the funeral. Family and loved ones were the only people invited.

Zoë took care of all the arrangements. With Unique being in the state she was, she couldn't handle the heavy load. Everyone at the funeral took the loss hard. None harder than Unique, though. She cried so much that she became sick. At the burial she fainted twice. Unique was so weak that afterward she had to be admitted to the hospital. The doctors told her she was suffering from dehydration.

Unique hadn't eaten or slept in days. The doctor told her if she didn't pull herself together quickly, that in a matter of days she would lose her baby. At that point, Unique could have cared less. She didn't know whether she was coming or going. Her whole life had been torn to shreds. If it weren't for Zoë and Patience's constant nagging, she would have never eaten or slept again. Once she was released from the hospital, Unique headed right back to the place she felt most at home, Lake Charles Cemetery.

Everyone around her thought she had lost her mind. Every day from then on she would spend all of her time at the gravesite talking to the headstone. There wasn't any other place in the world she would have rather been. Unique absolutely hated going home.

Night after night she would wake in a cold sweat from dreaming of the shooting. That day still haunted her. After being arrested, Kiara confessed to killing Tone. The last Unique heard, she was trying to plead insanity. With schizophrenia running in their family, Kiara had a good chance of getting off, but everyone knew it was her jealousy toward Unique that drove her to do it. The police never found NaSheed. Shortly after Bigg's first hearing, he fled the country. No one had heard from or seen him since, except for Unique.

Constantly she wondered how her life had gotten so out of hand. All Unique ever wanted was to provide herself and her sister with a better life. Nobody was supposed to die or get hurt. Now here she was the most hurt of them all.

Halfway into her pregnancy, Unique had enough. She was tired of wondering why and feeling sorry for herself. There would be no more of her being sad and miserable. From then on she decided she would devote all of her time to getting her life together and raising her baby. Just as predicted, on December 31st, Unique welcomed a healthy baby girl into the world. She was named Zion. As late winter began to show signs of spring, sitting in the graveyard, Unique held her beautiful baby girl in her arms and introduced her to the spirit before her.

"I know it's been a while since I visited, but I wanted you to meet somebody. Her name is Zion. I had her on New Year's Eve just like the doctors said. She looks just like you. She has your eyes and everything. Every time I look at her, I think of you," Unique said as tears began to fall from her eyes.

"We miss you so much. It's been hard living without you but I know that you are in a better place. I know this might sound crazy, but sometimes at night I think I see you. It's almost like I can feel you there with us. Wherever you are I know you're watching out for us. It's real hard living without you but I know in time everything will be OK."

"Unique."

"Huh?" she whispered as she wiped her eyes and turned around.

"We're going to miss our flight. We need to go."

"OK, here I come." Sitting for a second, Unique tried her hardest to find the strength to say goodbye once again. "We'll be back to see you soon, I promise. I love you and I promise to take real good care of our girl." Wiping one last tear from eye, she leaned forward and kissed the headstone, wishing the spirit goodbye.

$ $ $

The sun beamed from the sky as Unique stood in the cockpit of a forty-three foot sailing boat. Dressed scantily in a long platinum blonde wig, two piece yellow bikini and sarong, she guided the boat with absolute precision. Not one bump or wave was felt as the boat glided across the Mediterranean Sea. For the past three weeks, Unique had been living the high life in Saint Tropez, France.

Keisha Ervin

All of her life she heard of different celebrities and socialites who had visited the city and now finally she was there. Removing her Fendi shades from her eyes, Unique glanced upon the clear blue sea. The view was absolutely breathtaking. Seagulls and other birds filled the sky. With all the turmoil Unique had been through in the past year and a half, she found something so fascinating to be rare so she soaked every minute of the feeling up.

"Baby, you OK?" a voice said from behind.

"Of course, I'm with you." She smiled as she turned around to greet her guest.

"You weren't thinking about Bigg, were you?"

"No. I haven't thought about him in months."

"Good, 'cause for a minute there I thought you were still hung up on that nigga," NaSheed said, approaching with his arms wide open.

Leaving the wheel, Unique grinned and walked into his welcoming arms. While she was pregnant, NaSheed reached out to her, expressing his condolences. At first, Unique was caught off guard by the call but after the initial shock of it all wore off, the conversation began to flow.

"You know I heard what happened and I just wanted to let you know that if there's anything you need, I'm here for you," he told her.

"Thanks. I really need someone to lean on right now." Unique sniffed.

"I told you I would be there for you when you need me."

"I know, it's just been hard."

"Well, I don't want to hold you. A nigga just wanted you to know I'm here if you need me."

"OK," Unique replied, hanging up.

And from then on, the two talked every day. NaSheed was so overcome with grief, because truly, Bigg was his boy. Over and over he apologized for all the hell he put them through. He said that back then, he took the sucker's way out and that if he could do things all over again he would do things differently.

He wouldn't have lied on Bigg and set him up. He said he would've been truthful about his situation and handled it like a man. Unique had to do a lot of soul searching, but she eventually forgave him. Every time she and NaSheed talked, their conversations lasted for hours. Unique would sometimes find herself up until the crack of dawn smiling and laughing at his silly jokes. NaSheed made her feel comfortable. She liked it. For the first time since her loss, Unique was able to open up.

One night while talking, NaSheed began to express his feelings for Unique. He said that from the moment he saw her at Plush, he caught feelings. He told her that it should've been his baby instead of Bigg's that she was carrying. At first, Unique didn't know how to take his revelations, but after a while his come ons became a welcomed gesture. It was time to move on. As much as NaSheed and Unique talked, you would've thought that he would have felt comfortable enough to tell her where he was hiding out but he wasn't.

No matter how many times she pressed the subject, he wouldn't give in. Unique had to continuously tell him that the past was in the past and that today was a new day. She had no hard feelings toward NaSheed. When she forgave him she meant it and eventually he believed her. Then finally after hours and months of talking on the telephone, Unique wore him down. NaSheed gave in and told her his whereabouts.

He was in St. Tropez, France. NaSheed was head over heels in love with Unique. He wanted nothing more than to build a future with her as his wife and to be a father to her baby. NaSheed promised Unique the sun, moon and everything else underneath the stars if she would consider moving to France with him. Deciding that she needed a change, Unique agreed to come visit him on the condition that they take things slow.

"How many times do I have to tell you that Bigg is in the past? You are my future. There's nobody else I want besides you."

"Now that's what a nigga wanna hear." He playfully slapped her on the ass. "You're with me now. I don't want you thinking about that nigga no more."

"Trust me, I wasn't. You want something to drink? I feel a toast coming on."

"Yeah, do that shit baby," NaSheed replied as he took over steering.

With the robotics of a Stepford wife, Unique sauntered over to the bar and poured them both a glass of champagne. Looking over her shoulder, she gazed at NaSheed who was staring at her and winked her eye. Once his head was turned, Unique quietly placed her hand into the cup of her bikini top and pulled out two Rohypnol pills. Quickly she dropped both pills into his glass and stirred them around with her finger. The pills dissolved in a matter of seconds. Smiling at a job well done, Unique rejoined NaSheed at the wheel.

"Here you go, baby," she said, handing him his drink.

"So what you wanna toast to?"

"Uhmm let me see ... let's toast to ... starting anew and repaying old debts."

"Sounds good to me." NaSheed nodded as they clinked glasses. A hint of redemption danced in Unique's eyes as she watched him down the entire glass of champagne.

"That hit the spot. You mind getting me another?"

"No baby, sure thing." Unique smirked as she took his glass. Before she even returned with his second drink, the drug began to kick in. NaSheed was leaning over the wheel clutching his stomach, moaning.

Keisha Ervin

"Baby, what's wrong?" Unique cooed.

"I don't feel good. I think I might have food poisoning."

"Wow, that's odd. I don't a feel a thing."

"Yo', I feel like I'ma pass out. Help me over to the couch."

"Sure thing, sweetie."

Taking her precious time, Unique walked over to NaSheed. She was in no rush to help him. For months she had been picturing this day. Unique was going to enjoy every last minute of it. As the effect of the pills took over, NaSheed began to catch on to the fact he had been set up.

"You drugged me!"

"What was that, baby?"

"You heard me, bitch! You drugged me! You fuckin' put something in my drink!" NaSheed spat as saliva dripped from his bottom lip.

"Damn right I did, you stupid fuck!" Unique snapped.

"I swear to God I'ma kill you! I'm bury you right alongside that punk-ass nigga of yours!"

"See, that's where your plan is fucked up." Unique forcefully grabbed NaSheed's face as he dropped to the floor.

"What you talkin' about?!"

"Bigg ... isn't ... dead," she whispered as another boat pulled up alongside theirs. "Baby, tell this nigga you ain't dead!" she yelled.

"You know this nigga always has been hard of hearing," Bigg quipped as he joined their boat. Donned in army fatigues and tennis shoes, he looked better than ever. When he walked there was a slight limp in his stride, but Bigg was still the shit. "I don't think you stuttered. Did you stutter, baby?"

"No, I don't think I did." Unique shook her head.

"This shit ain't real! They said you was dead! There was a funeral and everything!" NaSheed screamed, scooting back in horror as his worst nightmare came true.

"Sorry, sweetie, that funeral was for my mother," Unique spat, bursting his bubble. A couple days after the courthouse shooting, Syleena succumbed to brain cancer.

"NaSheed, NaSheed, NaSheed ... I know you didn't think you was gonna cross me and get away with it? I trusted you, man. You were supposed to be my boy. That's fucked up how you did me but it's cool cause payback is a muthafucka," Bigg confirmed, pulling out a chrome infrared Glock.

"Come on Bigg, man, we boys! We supposed to be brothers! It ain't gotta go down like this, man!" NaSheed pleaded.

"Nigga, fuck you! You ain't my muthafuckin' brother! Ever since I've known you, you been out for self! Well guess what, nigga, I ain't dead but you for damn sure getting ready to be!"

"Come on, Bigg! We been friends for years! We can talk about this!"

"Nigga, what the fuck I just say? We ain't got shit to talk about!"

"So it's like that?! It's like that, Bigg?! Well fuck you then, nigga! You gon' shoot me, shoot me!"

"A'ight if that's how you want it."

POW!! POW!!

Total silence filled the air as Unique and Bigg looked upon NaSheed's lifeless body. Two bullets had been placed in his head. A steady stream of blood oozed from the back of NaSheed's head as his eyes stayed transfixed on Bigg.

"You a'ight?" Bigg asked Unique.

"Yeah, I'm fine. You?"

"Better than ever." He smiled, taking her into his arms.

Letting her go, Bigg told Unique to gather the rest of her things so they could burn out.

"Yo' Legend, come help me get rid of this nigga."

"A'ight," Legend said as he turned their boat's engine off and joined Bigg.

Keisha Ervin

"You got the body bag and weights?"

"Yeah, right here." Legend pointed to a big black duffle bag.

Bigg placed his hands underneath NaSheed's arms while Legend grabbed his feet, lifting him up. Gently they placed his body in the all-black body bag. Once that was done, they began filling the bag with weights and heavy stones. After zipping the bag up and wrapping it with a metal chain, Bigg and Legend used all the strength they had to pull NaSheed's body over to the side of the boat and dump him over. They watched closely as the body sank to the bottom of the sea. A sense of accomplishment rushed over Bigg as he realized that vengeance was finally his. With no time to waste, he and Legend took turns changing their clothes. Bigg wasn't taking any chances of getting caught.

"Oh, I forgot the gasoline," Legend remembered after he finished dressing. Once he got back to the boat, Bigg was already wiping down the steering wheel and everything else they touched. Tilting the gas can over, Legend doused the entire boat with gasoline.

"Baby, you ready?" Unique asked with her hand covering up her nose, already changed and ready to go.

"Yeah, let's get outta here," Bigg said, taking one last look to make sure everything was cool.

Leaving their old clothes behind, Bigg helped Unique exit the boat and onto theirs. Legend was right behind them. Legend and Bigg then took off their shoes and threw them aboard, too. Taking one last look, Bigg dug into his right pocket and pulled out a matchbook. He dug into his back pocket and pulled out an already rolled blunt. He struck the match, placed the blunt in his mouth and lit it.

Bigg took a long pull off the weed-filled blunt and inhaled deeply. A smile crept onto his face as he threw the still-lit

Keisha Ervin

match aboard NaSheed's boat and watched it ignite immediately. Taking his cue, Legend revved up the engine and headed back to shore. Zoë, Patience, Kay Kay, Chris and even newborn Zion were all there to greet them. Since the shooting, Zoë and Legend had been inseparable. They were living together and he no longer worked as a cop. Legend quit the force and began working with Bigg. He was now a silent partner in Bigg Entertainment.

Even though he was no longer part of a duo, Chris' rap career skyrocketed. His first solo CD, *"I Gotta Get Mine,"* went triple platinum and even produced three hit singles. He and Kay Kay were even dating. After Kiara was arrested, Kay Kay filed papers to become Arissa's legal guardian. Once the court reviewed her petition, they had no problem granting her guardianship.

Just as promised, Unique and Patience attended counseling sessions. They discussed everything from their mother's mental problems to her death, to Patience being molested. The sessions lasted five months but the girls got through it and became closer than ever. Bigg was in the hospital for almost a month after the shooting.

He wasn't even able to attend Syleena's funeral but Unique didn't care. Her main was concern was his health and getting better. Thankfully for Bigg, none of the bullets hit his spine but he had lost a lot of blood. The doctors had to give him two blood transfusions.

Bigg felt like he was losing his mind while he was stuck in the small hospital room. He hated hospitals. They reminded him of the mental clinic his mother put him in as a child. The only thing he wanted was to go home. After a month, he was able to. Now he and Unique were back together, happier than ever. Bigg was taking his medication, Bigg Entertainment was producing hit after hit, Zion was healthy, Patience was recovering from her trauma and Syleena's soul was finally at peace. And now that NaSheed was finally taken care of, Unique could rest and live happily ever after with the man she loved more than life itself.

The sun was now setting and clouds of orange and pink hues filled the sky. Hopping off the boat, Bigg turned and reached for Unique's hand, helping her down. Looking into his eyes she smiled and saw forever. At first she didn't need a man for anything but now the man that stood before her was her very reason for living.

"You love me?" she asked.

"More than you know. You love me?"

"You know I got you. I'ma always hold you down."

ORDER FORM
Triple Crown Publications
PO Box 6888
Columbus, OH 43205

NAME	
ADDRESS	
CITY	
STATE	
ZIP	

	TITLES	PRICE
	Dime Piece	$15.00
	Gangsta	$15.00
	Let That Be The Reason	$15.00
	A Hustler's Wife	$15.00
	The Game	$15.00
	Black	$15.00
	Dollar Bill	$15.00
	A Project Chick	$15.00
	Road Dawgz	$15.00
	Blinded	$15.00
	Diva	$15.00
	Sheisty	$15.00
	Grimey	$15.00
	Me & My Boyfriend	$15.00
	Larceny	$15.00
	Rage Times Fury	$15.00
	A Hood Legend	$15.00
	Flipside of the Game	$15.00
	Menage'A Way	$15.00

SHIPPING/HANDLING
1-3 books $5.00
4-9 books $9.00
$1.95 for each add'l book
TOTAL $_____

FORMS OF ACCEPTED PAYMENTS:
Postage Stamps, Institutional Checks & Money
Orders. All mail-in orders take 5-7 Business days
to be delivered

ORDER FORM

Triple Crown Publications
PO Box 6888
Columbus, OH 43205

NAME	
ADDRESS	
CITY	
STATE	
ZIP	

TITLES	PRICE
Still Sheisty	$15.00
Chyna Black	$15.00
Game Over	$15.00
Cash Money	$15.00
Crackhead	$15.00
For the Strength of You	$15.00
Down Chick	$15.00
Dirty South	$15.00
Cream	$15.00
Hoodwinked	$15.00
Bitch	$15.00
Stacy	$15.00
Life	$15.00
Keisha	$15.00
Mina's Joint	$15.00
How to Succeed in the Publishing Game	$20.00
Love & Loyalty	$15.00
Whore	$15.00
A Hustler's Son	$15.00

SHIPPING/HANDLING
1-3 books $5.00
4-9 books $9.00
$1.95 for each add'l book

TOTAL $_____

FORMS OF ACCEPTED PAYMENTS:
Postage Stamps, Institutional Checks & Money Orders, All mail in orders take 5-7 Business days to be delivered

ORDER FORM

Triple Crown Publications
PO Box 6888
Columbus, OH 43205

NAME	
ADDRESS	
CITY	
STATE	
ZIP	

	TITLES	PRICE
	Chances	$15.00
	Contagious	$15.00
	Hold U Down	$15.00
	Black and Ugly	$15.00
	In Cahootz	$15.00
	Dirty Red *Hardcover**	$20.00
	Dangerous	$15.00
	Street Love	$15.00
	Sunshine & Rain	$15.00
	Bitch Reloaded	$15.00
	Dirty Red *Paperback**	$15.00
	Mistress of the Game	$15.00
	Queen	$15.00
	The Set Up	$15.00
	Torn	$15.00
	Stained Cotton	$15.00
	Grindin' *Hardcover ONLY**	$10.00
	Amongst Thieves	$15.00
	Cut Throat	$15.00

SHIPPING/HANDLING
1-3 books $5.00
4-9 books $9.00
$1.95 for each add'l book

TOTAL $_____

FORMS OF ACCEPTED PAYMENTS:
Postage Stamps, Institutional Checks & Money
Orders, All mail in orders take 5-7 Business
days to be delivered

ORDER FORM

Triple Crown Publications
PO Box 6888
Columbus, OH 43205

NAME	
ADDRESS	
CITY	
STATE	
ZIP	

TITLES	PRICE
The Hood Rats	$15.00
Betrayed	$15.00
The Pink Palace	$15.00
The Bitch is Back	$15.00
Escape from the Madness	$15.00
Still Dirty *Hardcover**	$20.00
As Cold As Ice	$15.00

SHIPPING/HANDLING
1-3 books $5.00
4-9 books $9.00
$1.95 for each add'l book

TOTAL $_____

FORMS OF ACCEPTED PAYMENTS:
Postage Stamps, Institutional Checks & Money
Orders, All mail in orders take 5-7 Business
days to be delivered